"That kiss was a mistake. I don't feel that way about you anymore." Okay, maybe she could deny it, but she could tell by the look in Knox's eyes that he didn't believe her.

"In any case, anything like that between us would be foolish, and it would only complicate things. We aren't going there again, Knox, and now I think it's time we say good night."

She breathed a sigh of relief when he nodded and turned to walk to the front door. Her legs were still shaky as she accompanied him.

"I'm sorry about my little breakdown," Allison said.

He turned to face her, and before she could read his intentions he grabbed her and once again planted a kiss on her lips.

It was short and searing and when he released her his eyes sparkled with a knowing glint. "The next time you try to tell me you don't feel that way about me anymore, say it like you really mean it," he said, and then he was gone into the night.

* * *

**The Coltons of Shadow Creek:
Only family can keep you safe...**

* * *

If you're on Twitter, tell us what you think of Harlequin Romantic Suspense!
#harlequinromsuspense

Dear Reader,

Welcome to Shadow Creek, a small town in Texas and home to Livia Colton, a killer on the run.

I can't get enough of the Colton family! This book introduces a whole new branch as tortured and heroic as the rest.

Knox Colton's mother's escape from prison throws his world into a tailspin. He returns to Shadow Creek to find out that he fathered a son nine years before, a fact that stirs his anger against his old lover.

For Allison Rafferty, the woman he left behind, Knox's presence back in town, back in her life, evokes memories of both love and heartache.

However, when their son is kidnapped, the two of them must come together and support each other as they go through the darkest days of their lives. Will their love for each other be the shining beacon that gets them through the ordeal?

I hope you all enjoy this first installment of The Coltons of Shadow Creek and find Knox and Allison's love unforgettable!

Happy reading,

Carla Cassidy

COLTON'S
SECRET SON

Carla Cassidy

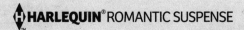
HARLEQUIN® ROMANTIC SUSPENSE

Special thanks and acknowledgment are given to
Carla Cassidy for her contribution to
The Coltons of Shadow Creek miniseries.

ISBN-13: 978-0-373-40201-4

Colton's Secret Son

Recycling programs
for this product may
not exist in your area.

Copyright © 2017 by Harlequin Books S.A.

HARLEQUIN®
www.Harlequin.com

Printed in U.S.A.

Carla Cassidy is an award-winning, *New York Times* bestselling author who has written more than 120 novels for Harlequin. In 1995, she won Best Silhouette Romance from *RT Book Reviews* for *Anything for Danny*. In 1998, she won a Career Achievement Award for Best Innovative Series from *RT Book Reviews*. Carla believes the only thing better than curling up with a good book to read is sitting down at the computer with a good story to write.

Chapter 1

Shadow Creek, Texas, held nothing but broken dreams, betrayal and heartache for Knox Colton. He had thought he'd never return to the small town where he'd grown up, but here he was again after a ten-year absence.

Forced to take a sabbatical from his job as a Texas Ranger, embarrassed and humiliated by his mother's crimes, he'd really had no other place to go.

He now clenched his fingers around the steering wheel as a whisper of heated anger burned in the pit of his stomach. Nothing like being a Texas Ranger and having one of the FBI's most wanted as a mother.

Livia Colton had created plenty of chaos and damage in his childhood, and now she was affecting her grown children's lives once again.

He rolled down his window to allow in the sweet-scented early March air and drew in a deep breath. The last thing he wanted to do was to carry his simmering anger into the peaceful sanctuary his younger sister called home.

His anger eased at thoughts of his youngest sister, Jade. Despite the nine years difference in their ages, he'd always been particularly close to her.

A smile curved his lips as he turned into Hill Country Farm, Jade's home. Ahead of him was her house, but around the house were her passions. Vegetable gardens were just beginning to awaken with what would be summer bounty. Stables and a riding arena were on the right, and a barn with chickens, goats and pigs was on the left.

The house itself was small, but exuded a sense of stability and welcome. Pots of purple pansies sat on the porch, dipping and waving their heads in the light spring breeze.

Before he'd stopped his car, Jade stepped out on the porch, a wide smile of greeting on her pretty face. He parked and got out of the car and she raced toward him, her dark brown ponytail bouncing as her sweet laughter filled the air.

She jumped into his arms and he picked her up and spun her around. His cowboy hat flew off his head before he deposited her back on the ground and gave her a firm kiss on the forehead.

"Oh, Knox, I've missed you so much," she said.

"And I've missed you," he replied as he picked up his hat and plopped it back on his head. "You look terrific, Jade."

She stepped back from him and eyed him. "You don't look half-bad yourself, big brother." She gave him a playful punch in the stomach. "At least you haven't gone to seed in your old age."

"Hey, I'm only thirty-three. I'm still in my prime," he retorted.

She linked her arm with his. "Come on inside. I've got the coffee on and I made a batch of homemade cinnamon rolls."

"Hmm, nothing better on a Saturday morning than cinnamon rolls and time with you," he replied.

Minutes later the two siblings sat across from each other at the round oak table in the kitchen that smelled of spices and sunshine. Yellow curtains fluttered at the open windows as the sweet scent of new grass and budding flowers drifted in.

"So, how's Ranger life?" Jade asked as she set a small plate with a cinnamon roll the size of the palm of his hand before him.

"It was great until two weeks ago." He frowned down into his coffee cup and then looked up and met his sister's gaze. "And then day before yesterday I was told rather forcefully that a sabbatical might be a good idea right now."

Jade's brown eyes darkened. "Because of Mother's escape from prison." Knox gave a curt nod of his head. "How long are you on sabbatical for?"

"An undetermined amount of time," he replied. "I have become somewhat of an embarrassment with a mother who plotted and succeeded with an elaborate escape from Red Peak Maximum Security Prison. I was told to lie low until she was no longer a hot news item and was caught." The burn of anger was back in his stomach.

"I can't believe she managed to pay off so many guards and got into the infirmary and through two more security checks before cutting a hole in the floor and slithering down into the sewer system."

"A new sewer system that she somehow arranged to be built," he added drily. "And you've probably heard that in the construction site she was picked up by a white van outside the prison walls."

"And the van had no plates or distinguishing marks when it was found abandoned near the Mexican border," Jade added. "I watch the news, too."

What had been kept out of the news was that there had been blood found on the side of the van, blood that hadn't belonged to Livia Colton, but Knox wasn't telling that to Jade or anyone else. Knox had been told this by his boss before the upper brass cut him out of the information chain.

The information was being intentionally held back by the authorities. Someone had been at the scene at the Mexican border with Livia and that someone had apparently been hurt. Knox had a feeling the identity of that person was already known to somebody in law enforcement, but it was a piece of information that hadn't been told or leaked. By now, the blood left behind at the van would have been analyzed and he couldn't help but believe DNA had been matched to somebody.

"Then you know the latest is that she was spotted

in Mexico, and that's where I hope she stays until she burns in hell," Knox said forcefully.

Jade reached across the table and grabbed his hand with her much smaller one. "Knox, you need to release some of that anger. It knots up in your veins and makes me believe the Hulk could pop out of you at any time."

A wry grin curved his mouth. "Maybe what I need to keep the Hulk inside is a couple of bites of this magnificent cinnamon roll."

She flashed him a beautiful smile. "Dig in."

As he enjoyed not one, but two of the breakfast treats, Jade caught him up on her business. She ran a rehab center for off-track Thoroughbred horses, hoping to give them second careers as pleasure riding mounts or hunter-jumpers.

It was obvious she loved what she did; it shone from the happiness in her eyes, in the flush of her cheeks as she spoke about the horses. Knox had loved being a Texas Ranger, but his mother had stolen that from him, at least for now.

At least Jade seemed to be thriving, despite the fact that their mother had been in prison for drug charges and murder.

"So, where are you staying while you're in town?" Jade asked.

"I was going to see about staying in the apartment at Mac's, but Thorne insisted I bunk with him, so I'm at his place." Mac Mackenzie was the closest thing to a father figure that Knox knew; Thorne was his son with Livia, although all of Livia's children shared the Colton last name. Thorne had a ranch not too far away from

Jade's. "Wht's new with everyone else?" he asked, wondering about the rest of their Colton siblings.

Jade shrugged. "Nobody has heard anything from River lately, so we're all assuming he's still a marine and someplace overseas. Claudia is apparently living her dream in New York and Leonor is still in Austin."

"Or helping Mother stay hidden in Mexico."

"She wouldn't do that," Jade protested. Knox raised an eyebrow and Jade continued. "I know Leonor was the last to believe that Mother was guilty of all the charges against her, but she would never aid her in an escape."

Knox didn't reply. He wasn't sure what his sister might do to help their mother. She'd clung to her belief in Livia's innocence far longer than any of the other siblings and had been the only one who had visited Livia in prison.

"Why don't you take me outside and show me around," he said, suddenly tired of thoughts of their mother.

"I'd love to," she replied. He grabbed his hat from a nearby chair and together they walked out of Jade's door.

It was with great pride that she pointed out the vast gardens and the area that was a petting zoo where local schools often brought their classes to visit.

"I love it when the children come," Jade said. "And these animals love all the attention they get on those days."

They reached a pasture fence, beyond which were several of the horses she'd devoted her life to giving a second chance at a different kind of life.

He turned to look at her. "You're happy here." It was a statement, not a question.

She smiled. "I am." The smile faded away and her eyes darkened. "And I'll feel a lot happier when our mother is once again behind bars. I worry that she knows I helped put her there in the first place."

Knox pulled her into an embrace. "Don't worry, Jade. It would be stupid for her to show up here, and we both know that she isn't a stupid woman."

No, Livia definitely wasn't stupid. She was a cunning, manipulative sociopath who had seen her children only as tools to be used to gain her wealth and power. She trotted them out for photo ops when it served her purpose and then handed them off to a nanny and forgot about them until the next time they could be useful to her. And that had been the very least of her crimes.

"You're right," Jade replied as he released her. She stared out into the distance for a moment and then laughed. "You remember her lacy handkerchiefs?"

"How could I forget? She thought carrying one made her look all high society, and God forbid if she couldn't find a particular one in her drawer. She'd have all of us searching high and low for a pink- or lilac-colored hankie. But enough about her, let's go see your stables."

As they walked toward the stables, Jade told him about the racehorses that came to her, many of whom might otherwise have been headed to the glue factory, or sadly sold for meat.

"The first thing I have to do is make sure they're healthy," she explained. "And then they have to be socialized with both people and the rest of the herd."

They entered the stables and Knox immediately spied a young boy sweeping up. "Cody, come and meet my brother," Jade called out to him.

The boy set the broom aside and approached them with a friendly smile on his face. "This is my brother Knox," Jade said. She placed a hand on the boy's shoulder. "And this is Cody, the best nine-year-old helper and horse lover I've ever met."

"It's nice to meet you, sir." The boy stuck out a hand to shake.

Knox took the small hand and studied the boy's face. Bright blue eyes, oddly familiar, gazed up at him. Cody's light brown hair was neatly cut and his smile was broad enough to illuminate an entire room.

"It's nice to meet you, Cody, and you can call me Knox."

"Do you like horses, Knox?" the boy asked him.

"I love them," Knox replied.

"Knox is a Texas Ranger," Jade said.

"Wow." Cody's eyes widened. "That's awesome."

Those eyes...the shape and the bright blue color... what about them felt so familiar to Knox? "Thanks. So you sweep up around here?"

"I do whatever Miss Jade wants me to and then she lets me ride the horses," he replied.

"Sounds like a lot of responsibility," Knox replied.

Cody nodded. "I can handle it." He looked at the wristwatch he wore. "Now I need to finish up sweeping because my mom is going to be here any minute."

"And who is your mom?" Knox asked, wondering if he knew the woman.

"Her name is Allison Rafferty," Cody replied.

Allison Rafferty? Knox's brain exploded with a flash of sweet memories. Allison was the woman he'd once loved, the woman who had betrayed him and the one he'd never quite been able to forget.

He stared at Cody. Those eyes…no wonder they looked so familiar to Knox. Each morning when he looked into a mirror, he saw those same ones staring back at him.

Shock waves shuddered through him and he was vaguely aware of Jade telling Cody to go ahead outside and wait for his mother. The complicated memories he had of Allison disappeared beneath a veil of pure white anger.

Knox turned to his sister, his heart beating hard and fast. He felt gut-punched. Cody was nine years old and had his eyes. Almost ten years ago, he'd contacted Allison when he'd heard she'd had a baby that she'd insisted belonged to an old boyfriend. She had to have gotten pregnant by another man during the time they'd been dating. He'd been utterly destroyed by her cheating and that had been the end of any relationship he had with her.

She'd lied.

Knox knew with a gut instinct that Cody was his son. He stared at Jade. "Did you know?"

Jade didn't pretend not to know what he was talking about. "I've always suspected, but Allison has never said anything to me, and I haven't asked her."

A son. Emotion welled up to press tight against his chest. He had a son, and he'd already lost nine years because Allison had lied to him. He'd always known that she was just another woman who'd betrayed him, and this only confirmed it.

"I think I'll step outside and wait for Cody's mother to arrive," he said.

"Knox, you aren't going to do anything crazy, are you?" Jade asked worriedly.

He smiled grimly as an icy cold shell wrapped around his heart. "Don't worry. I'm not crazy." His fellow Rangers and several news agencies had nicknamed him Fort Knox because he was the unbreakable Ranger who had no heart. He was always in control of his emotions.

The sound of a car approaching from the distance tensed all of his muscles. He drew several deep, long breaths and then prepared himself to face the woman who had kept the secret of his son from him for nine long years.

Allison Rafferty couldn't help the smile that curved her lips as she saw Cody and Jade standing just outside the stables. The sight of her son always made her heart expand with pride and joy.

It was impossible to hold on to the worries of running the construction company when she was with her son. On Monday she was going to have to fire a man, never a pleasant thing, but in this case necessary. But for this afternoon and evening all she had to think about was making homemade pizza and watching a movie with the little man in her life.

She parked and turned off the car engine, then got

out of the car. At the same time a tall, broad-shouldered man wearing a black cowboy hat stepped out of the stables and into her view.

Knox.

Her breath hitched in her throat and she froze in her tracks. For a long moment her brain refused to function as she stared at him, and then a million questions fired off in her head.

Knox Colton… What on earth was he doing there? Oh, God, she didn't want him there. Why wasn't he in El Paso doing whatever he did as a Texas Ranger?

"Hello, Allison." His eyes beneath the rim of his hat were icy blue.

He knows.

The two dreadful words echoed in her head as her heart began to beat an unsteady rhythm. "Knox, what a surprise," she said and took several slow steps forward.

"It's been a day full of surprises," he replied with a pointed glance at Cody.

"Cody, why don't you come inside with me and let Knox and your mother visit for a few minutes," Jade said. "I think I've got some of those chocolate cookies that you like in the pantry."

Cody looked at Allison for permission and she nodded her head, still stunned by Knox's presence. She watched as Jade and Cody headed to the house and a million old memories fluttered through her mind.

Knox, dressed in a navy tuxedo to take her to the high school prom… Knox, naked and beautiful as he made love to her in the pool house at La Bonne Vie, his family home.

He had been her first love, her only love and the man she believed would be her forever love. They'd dated all through high school and after that whenever she could get back to Shadow Creek from the college she'd attended in Massachusetts.

They'd drifted apart during the last of those days, but when she'd had to quit college and return to Shadow Creek to take over her father's construction company, she and Knox had resumed their love affair. The memories of loving and being loved by him warmed her.

She watched until Jade and Cody disappeared into the house and then she turned her gaze back to Knox. Any warmth her memories had generated instantly cooled beneath the chill of his arctic gaze. She raised her chin and waited for him to speak, her heart beating even more frantically.

"You've kept him from me for nine years."

She wanted to protest. She wanted to reiterate the falsehood she'd told him years ago when she'd been pregnant and he'd called to see if the baby was his. But it was one thing to utter a lie over a phone line, quite another to stare into somebody's eyes and lie.

"You left town," she replied. He'd left her utterly brokenhearted and not knowing if she would ever have a future with him. That had been one of the reasons she'd lied to him, because he'd distanced himself from her, indicating that he didn't want to be with her anymore. There had also been the fact that she hadn't wanted her newborn son in any way associated with the Coltons, considering that Livia had just gone to jail for her heinous crimes.

"And then you had your new life with the Rangers. I didn't think you'd care," she said.

"You thought wrong. I had a right to know that he is my son, and he has a right to know that I'm his father." His words were short…clipped, and he took a step toward her.

Anger and fear leaped into her chest. "You haven't told him, have you?" How long had he been there with Cody today? What might he have already said to her son?

"I haven't told him anything yet." His tone was cold, dispassionate, and reminded her that his reputation was that of a heartless, emotionless man.

"Please don't tell him," she replied hurriedly. "What are you doing here in Shadow Creek? Last I heard, you were in El Paso protecting the border."

For the first time a flicker of something dark shadowed his eyes. "I decided it was time for a vacation, and don't try to change the subject. You've had nine years with Cody and now it's my turn to have time with him."

Everything inside of her stilled. Her heart stopped beating and her lungs quit drawing breath as she stared at him wordlessly. She'd always wondered in the back of her mind if this day would come, but over the years she'd convinced herself it wouldn't. But here it was and she was so ill-prepared for it.

"How long is your vacation?" she finally asked.

"I don't know yet." He shoved his hands in his jean pockets. "I have a right to spend time with him."

She didn't care what was right in this situation; all she cared about was the best interest of her son, and she didn't believe him spending any time with Knox was in Cody's best interest.

"We've done fine without you. I just don't think it's a good idea," she replied. "Especially now that your mother has escaped from jail."

His shoulders stiffened. "My mother has nothing to do with this. I have rights, Allison, and if I have to get a lawyer and fight for them, I will." The resolve in his eyes let her know he wasn't playing. He was dead serious.

"I don't want you to hurt him, Knox."

His jaw tightened. "That's the last thing I intend to do."

She sighed. "If you promise that you won't tell him you're his father until I think he's ready to hear it, and if the two of us can remain civil with each other, then I guess we can work something out so that you can spend some time with him."

Worry fluttered through her. She didn't want to do this, but Knox did have a right to get to know his son. The last thing she wanted was a custody battle. She had to do this right for Cody's sake.

"I promise." He pulled his hands from his pockets and took another step closer to her. "I don't want to screw up his life, Allison. I don't want to screw up your life." His eyes narrowed. "But you should have told me."

A flush of warmth filled her cheeks. "I did what I thought was best for everyone at the time."

"You thought wrong."

His anger was controlled, but she saw it in the tense

set of his broad shoulders, in the thin line of his lips and in the depths of his beautiful blue eyes. "When?"

Next year...the year after, or maybe when he turns eighteen, she wanted to reply. "Next week?"

"Not good enough," he replied.

She forced herself to breathe. "You can see him tomorrow after church. We're usually home around noon."

"Then I'll pick him up at twelve thirty."

A new panic leaped into her throat. "Pick him up? Where are you going to take him?"

"I thought I'd take him to Mac's ranch. I haven't had a chance to stop in there and say hello since I've been back in town." He crooked an eyebrow up. "If you're worried that I'll steal him away from you, then you need to relax. I wouldn't do that to him."

Relax? How could she when his very presence there had shaken her to her very soul? How could she relax when he apparently wanted to step into a parent role, even though he'd walked away from her...from their love so easily almost ten years before?

"Then we'll see you tomorrow." She was ready for this conversation to end. She needed to go home and process just how much he'd turned her world upside down.

"I'll send Cody out." He headed for the house.

Allison got back into the car and finally drew in a deep breath. She'd always felt half-breathless when around Knox. He was ten years older than he'd been the last time she'd seen him, but those years had only made him more attractive.

He was deeply tanned, which made the blue of his

eyes more intense. His light brown hair was clipped short, emphasizing his chiseled, handsome features.

Despite the shock of seeing him, in spite of the simmering anger that had marked their conversation, she had to admit that he still held some sort of sensual power over her.

She'd wanted to brush her fingers through his hair, feel the strength of his arms around her and taste his lips once again.

Foolish, foolish thoughts. She'd been devastated when he'd left her ten years ago. Ten years was a long time. She had no idea what kind of a man he'd really become, and the last thing she wanted was to allow Fort Knox back into her life in any capacity.

Jade's front door opened and Cody came running out. Allison drew another deep breath to steady her emotions. Whether she liked it or not, Knox was back in her life for now. She just prayed he wouldn't do anything to hurt Cody.

Chapter 2

Anger still ripped through Knox as he headed back to Thorne's ranch. The only thing that tempered it was the remaining shock of discovering he was a father.

Knox had never known his father. Livia had divorced Tad Whitman when Knox was only two and then she'd changed his last name to Colton and moved to Austin. He wasn't even sure if Tad Whitman was really his father. There had been rumors that Tad's father had gotten Livia pregnant.

After that there had been a succession of stepdaddies and new siblings, but never a real father figure in his life on a permanent basis other than Mac. Knox wanted better for Cody.

Maybe Cody already had a father figure in his life. The thought gave him pause. He hadn't asked if Allison was married and another man was raising Cody as his own.

She was certainly attractive enough to have caught some man's eyes. He hadn't been so consumed by his anger that he hadn't noticed she was even prettier now than she'd been when they'd been an item.

Her dark blond hair had been pulled back into a messy knot at the nape of her neck, emphasizing her high cheekbones and sensual mouth. The green blouse she'd had on had toyed with her hazel eyes, turning them more green than gold.

And nobody wore a pair of jeans like Allison. The denim hugged her long, slender legs and reminded him of how much he had loved those sleek legs tangled with his.

He tightened his hands on the steering wheel and embraced his anger. It was far easier to sustain that emotion than drift into ridiculous thoughts of his past relationship with Allison.

He'd spent far too many nights in the past thinking about her, missing her and wondering what might have been if they'd made different decisions so long ago. He'd also spent many of those nights hating her.

Almost ten years ago he'd called her to see if the baby she'd had was his. She'd told him it belonged to an old boyfriend and she'd gotten pregnant during the time after she and Knox had renewed their relationship. He'd hated her then for betraying his love.

He'd already been reeling because of his mother's arrest. He'd told Allison in the midst of that drama that he just needed some time and distance from her. He'd needed a couple of weeks to pull himself together and to make sure his siblings were doing okay. But with his younger sisters taken care of and the rest of the clan self-sufficient, Knox had left for Texas and gotten a job as a Ranger.

He'd never really intended to leave Allison forever, but it had taken him months to get his head back on straight after his mother's trial and all that dust had settled. Life with the Rangers had been all-consuming and just about the time he felt it was right to reach out to Allison again, he'd heard she'd had a baby.

The timing was right for the child to be his, but then she'd told him it wasn't and he'd been devastated. Her betrayal had been just another blow by a woman…one he couldn't get past.

But this betrayal cut even deeper. Dammit, she should have told him about Cody. He'd already missed so much of his life. Not only had he missed out on the wonder of his birth, but he'd also missed Cody's first step, his first word…so many firsts.

He took the turn into Thorne's ranch a little too fast and dust kicked up as the back tires of his sports car spun out. He quickly righted the car and pulled to a stop in front of the attractive ranch house.

"Hey, are you looking for a second job as a race-car driver?" Thorne shouted from the door of the barn as Knox got out of the car.

Knox waited as his half brother approached him. Thorne's dark skin gleamed in the sunshine and his smile eased some of the tension in Knox's gut, some… but not all.

Thorne's smile fell and he obviously felt the tension radiating from Knox. "What's up?"

"Have you ever seen Allison Rafferty's boy?"

"Sure, I've seen him around town with Allison. Why?"

"Have you ever noticed that he looks a lot like me?"

Thorne's light brown eyes narrowed slightly. "Why don't we go inside? This definitely feels like a sit-down talk."

Knox nodded. The two men didn't speak again until they were seated across from each other at the kitchen table. "I just found out that Allison's son is mine," Knox finally said.

Thorne's eyes widened in surprise. "I had no idea," he replied. "I remember there was some speculation and a little scandal when everyone realized she was pregnant, but I figured if the baby was yours you would be here with her."

Knox fisted his hands on top of the table. "She lied to me, Thorne. Almost ten years ago she told me her baby's father was an old boyfriend. She's kept him from me for all these years."

Thorne leaned back in his chair, his expression thoughtful. "Can you really blame her?"

Knox stared at Thorne in surprise. The last thing he'd expected was for his brother to defend Allison.

"Think about it," Thorne continued. "You had pulled away from her when Mother was arrested."

"I had to make sure all of you were going to be okay. I thought I was going to take physical custody of Jade and Claudia. I was more than a little out of my mind when I left, but I always figured I'd eventually wind up with Allison."

"Did you tell Allison that at the time?" Thorne asked.

Knox frowned. "No, I just told her I needed a little break from her." He hadn't wanted her to know how crazy he was at the time; he hadn't wanted her to see him as weak. And then he'd heard about the baby and it had been the light in a sea of darkness…until she'd told him the baby belonged to an ex.

"Knox, you were gone and the Colton name was being dragged through the mud because of Mother's arrest. The whole town had turned against us. Is it any wonder she didn't want to burden her child with anything Colton?"

Myriad emotions flooded Knox's head and he rubbed a hand in the center of his forehead where a headache had begun to pound. No, it wasn't any wonder Allison hadn't wanted that. At that time, Knox hadn't wanted to be a Colton, but she still shouldn't have lied to him when he'd asked her point-blank about the baby.

"Allison is well respected in Shadow Creek." Thorne leaned forward. "Now her reputation is stellar. She's known as a great single mother, a savvy business-woman, and is generous in charity work. She gained a lot of respect for nursing her sick father until he passed two years ago."

"She isn't married?"

Thorne shook his head. "From everything I hear she's totally devoted to raising her boy."

"Why are you telling me all this?" Knox asked.

"Because she has a good life here and I don't want

you to blow into town and screw things up for her before you leave once again and she has to pick up all the pieces."

"I have no intention of screwing anything up for her. I just want a relationship with my son," Knox replied firmly. "Thorne, you have a great relationship with your father. You don't know what it's like not to have one in your life, but I do and I want better for Cody."

"Don't be a father to him for as long as you're back in town and then forget about him when you return to Ranger life," Thorne advised.

"I don't want to be just a vacation father. I want to be in his life in a meaningful way until the day I die." Knox's heart swelled with love for the boy he had yet to really know.

Thorne grinned. "Then congratulations, it's a boy."

Knox laughed. "Thanks. I'm picking him up tomorrow and I thought I'd take him over to your father's place. I figured maybe we could throw a couple of lines into the pond and do a little fishing."

"You know Dad would love to see you," Thorne replied and stood. "I'm surprised Allison agreed to letting you take him."

"I threatened her with lawyers," Knox admitted.

"Whew, you must have been mad. And now I need to get back out to the barn. I've been cleaning tack all morning." Knox stood as well and on impulse gave his half brother a quick man hug.

"What was that for?" Thorne asked in surprise.

"For the hard talk and good advice."

"Anytime," Thorne replied and then he headed out the back door.

Knox sank back down at the table, his thoughts on his younger half brother. Knox had been five when Thorne had been born, but it hadn't taken him long to realize Thorne didn't look exactly like him. Instead, Thorne had the same dark skin and curly hair as their African-American ranch foreman, Joseph "Mac" Mackenzie.

Rumors had flown in the small town, and Livia, with her usual wicked machinations, had thrown her husband at the time under the bus. She'd transformed Wes Kingston, the father of her son River, from a dashing rancher to an abusive husband who eventually divorced her. Mac had stayed on as foreman at the ranch to be near his son. He'd even bought some of the land to ensure that he'd never be displaced.

Wes Kingston hadn't been the last of his mother's lovers or husbands, and each one had left her financially better off until she was one of the wealthiest people in the area.

Her last husband, Fabrizio Artero, had been a successful Argentine horse breeder. He'd been a decent stepfather and had doted on Jade until he'd been kicked in the head by a horse and died.

Knox got up and moved to the window to stare out at the pastures in the distance, his thoughts still consumed by the woman who had given birth to him.

Livia hadn't made it into the inner society circles in Austin, but here in Shadow Creek she'd ruled as queen. She'd built a much-needed hospital, had funded most of the 4-H program and had thrown elaborate barbecues that had been the talk of the town.

Nobody had known the depths of Livia's deceptions until she was arrested and indicted on charges of human and drug trafficking, among other crimes. Nobody had known that she'd been a ruthless general working for an organized crime group. She'd even been found guilty of murder.

She'd been under investigation by the FBI for years and they'd finally gained the evidence they needed to put her away forever. La Bonne Vie, the family's beautiful mansion, their land and all the livestock had been confiscated by the authorities. The place had remained vacant since then.

Knox could only hope the authorities would find Livia as quickly as possible and get her back behind bars where she deserved to spend the rest of her life. He hoped his mother didn't even know that he was back in Shadow Creek.

He turned away from the window and shoved thoughts of his mother out of his head. She wasn't his problem anymore, other than the fact that her latest escapades had screwed up his job for now.

He went down the hallway to the bedroom where he was staying and sat on the edge of the bed as thoughts of a different woman filled his mind.

Allison Rafferty.

His blood warmed as he thought of how the sun had sparked in her hair. For a moment he imagined he could smell the apple and spice scent she'd always worn, the fragrance that had once represented tangled sheets, sweet sighs and lovemaking.

She'd been in his blood for years. She'd been his first lover and he'd once thought they would be together forever. There had been other women during the times they'd been broken apart, but none had touched him like she had.

He jerked himself off the bed. He didn't want to sit around and think about Allison and what they had once shared. She wasn't the woman he'd once believed was good and pure. Hell, half the reason he'd left town in the first place was to shield her from any evil his mother might bring to her life.

She was nothing more to him than a woman who had lied, who had kept the secret of his son for far too long. He'd have to deal with her because of Cody, but he would never, ever forgive her.

The next day, Allison watched the spring sunshine flood through one of the beautiful stained glass windows of the First Methodist Church of Shadow Creek. Reverend Johnson stood at the pulpit and droned on with his sermon about turning the other cheek and forgiveness, but Allison was too busy praying to pay much attention to what he had to say.

In less than an hour Knox would pick up Cody and spend the day with him. She prayed that Knox would keep his promise and not tell Cody that he was his father. She hoped Knox was in this for the long term and she desperately prayed that he wouldn't break her son's heart.

She'd never prayed as hard as she did now, with Cody wiggling in impatience next to her and a wealth of anxiety pressing tight in her chest.

She should have told Knox no. She should have held her ground and not allowed him to spend any time with Cody. Now it was too late to go back on it because she'd already told Cody, who was excited about spending time with Knox.

Normally after church she and Cody lingered and visited with friends and neighbors, but today they hurried to the car immediately after the service was over.

"I can't wait for Knox to pick me up," Cody said as soon as she was on the road and headed home. "I've never been to Mr. Mackenzie's ranch before. What do you think we'll do there?"

"I don't know. But I'm sure whatever you do, you'll have fun," she replied. "And you know how nice Mr. Mackenzie is."

"Yeah, he's cool. Knox is really cool, too. Did you know he's a Texas Ranger?" Cody's voice held all the excitement of a boy anticipating a brand-new adventure.

"Yes, I knew that," Allison replied.

When they reached their two-story house just off Main Street, Cody was nearly out of the car before she had completely parked. He raced to the porch and danced in impatience as he waited for her to join him and unlock the front door.

"I've got to hurry. He'll be here in fifteen minutes," Cody exclaimed.

"Make sure you hang up your church clothes," Allison yelled after him as he scurried up the stairs to his bedroom.

In fifteen minutes, her entire life would change and she couldn't begin to guess if the changes would be good or bad. She tucked her keys back into her purse and then walked through the living room and into the kitchen.

No matter what she thought of Knox Colton, he would now be back in her life. Her biggest concern was that he would be around just long enough to completely capture Cody's heart and then he'd be gone once again.

He'd do to her son what he'd done to her. Even though ten years had passed, despite all the life that she had lived in that passage of time, she still remembered the anguish that had filled her heart when Knox had told her he needed time away from her. She'd been blinded by her hurt, and that's why she'd lied to him in the first place.

There was no question that Cody could use a male figure in his life. Since the death of Allison's father two years ago, there had been no masculine influences for him. She hadn't considered dating. Raising Cody and running the family business had been enough.

She sank down at the table and wondered what on earth she was going to do with herself during the time Cody was with Knox today. For a little more than nine years her life had revolved around her son. On most Sundays they spent the day together, playing games and watching movies and cooking his favorite foods for dinner. Sundays had always been special for them because it was the one day a week when she wasn't at work at the family construction business.

She didn't even know if he'd be back by dinner this evening, and he hadn't eaten any lunch. Should she make him a quick sandwich? She quickly dismissed the idea. Surely Knox knew that if he was picking Cody up right after church he would need some lunch.

She tried to shove her anxiety aside as Cody came into the kitchen. Church clothes had been replaced by a pair of jeans and his favorite blue-plaid flannel shirt.

"Looks like you're all ready to go," she said around the sudden lump in her throat.

He nodded and his eyes grew somber as he slid into the chair next to hers. "Will you be okay today without me?"

She looked at her son in surprise. "Buddy, I'll be just fine. I might spend the day doing some girlie stuff." A nine-year-old shouldn't have to worry about his mother spending a Sunday afternoon alone.

"Girlie stuff?" Cody looked at her curiously.

She nodded. "I might take a nice, long bubble bath and then paint my nails and watch a sappy movie."

"Sounds boring," Cody replied. "What color are you gonna paint your nails?"

"I was thinking maybe purple with green sparkles." She waited for it and she wasn't disappointed.

Cody laughed. The wonderful, boyish sound filled the kitchen and wove a path straight to Allison's heart. "You are not," he finally replied.

At that moment the doorbell rang.

"I'll get it," Cody said. He shot off his chair and

fight-or-flight adrenaline pulsed through Allison. She heard Cody's excited voice and then Knox's deeper one.

She took a couple gulps of air in an attempt to still her nerves. She didn't mind sharing Cody, she just wasn't sure she wanted to share him with Knox Colton. But she reminded herself that it didn't matter what she wanted anymore.

She was just starting to rise from her chair when the two walked into the kitchen. "Don't get up." Knox waved her back down.

"Cody hasn't had any lunch," she said, as if that was the most important information he needed to know. He needed to know that Cody hated green peppers and that he sometimes ran too fast for his own safety. Knox needed to know that Cody had a heart of gold and cared deeply about others.

There were so many things he needed to know, but her voice failed her in that moment. She'd always thought her kitchen was large and airy, but it seemed much smaller with Knox's presence.

He looked ridiculously handsome in a pair of tight jeans and a dark blue, long-sleeved polo shirt that hugged his lean stomach and emphasized his broad shoulders and muscular biceps. His black cowboy hat rode at a cocky angle on his head.

"Don't worry, I'll see that he gets lunch," he replied and ruffled his hand on top of Cody's head. Cody looked up at him with a big smile. "I planned on bringing him home sometime after dinner. Does that work for you?"

"I'd like him home by seven at the latest. He has school tomorrow. We should exchange cell phone numbers." She hoped Cody didn't feel the tension in the air. Although Knox's tone of voice was pleasant enough, his gaze was cold as ice as it lingered on her.

"That's a good idea," he agreed.

"And then we'll go, right, Knox?" Cody asked eagerly.

Knox laughed. Oh, Allison had forgotten the magic of his deep, wonderful laughter. "And then we'll go," he agreed.

For just a moment his gaze met Allison's and the icy cold had been replaced with a warmth that stole her breath away. It was there only a couple of seconds and then gone.

He averted his gaze to sweep the kitchen. "You've got a nice place here."

"Thank you," she replied. "I bought this house after Dad passed away." She'd been shocked to discover that her father had a substantial life insurance policy when he'd passed. It had been enough money to buy the house outright and had given her and her son some financial security.

"I'm sorry for your loss," he replied. "John was a good man."

"Thank you. He'd been sick for a long time." A hollow wind blew through her as she thought of her father.

"Grandpa Rafferty helped me build a birdhouse. It's hanging in a tree in our backyard," Cody said. "Maybe when we come home later you can see it and you can also see my room. But now shouldn't we get going?"

Knox grinned down at Cody. "Yeah, let's get going."

Allison got up to walk them to the door. "I'll see you this evening."

"See you later, Mom. And don't paint your fingernails purple and green," Cody replied.

With that they were gone, taking half of her heart with them. The house had never been as silent as it was then, with only the sound of her heart beating in her ears.

She returned to her chair in the kitchen and stared unseeing out the nearby window. Not for the first time in the past two years, she wished her father was still there.

John Rafferty had been a single parent after Allison's mother had died of cancer when her daughter had been five. He'd been both mother and father to her, and eventually good friend and mentor.

He could build a bookcase and braid her hair. He could renovate a kitchen and bake cupcakes for a school party. Unfortunately a heart attack had left him in a wheelchair and eventually his weakened, diseased heart had just stopped working.

Growing up, she'd spent much of her time with the smell of freshly cut wood as familiar as the sound of her own voice. After school and on the weekends, she spent time at the construction company her father owned, the same one she now owned and operated.

What a hypocrite she was, sitting there and missing her own father and at the same time half wishing Cody's had never shown up in town.

Cody deserved to know his dad. She could only hope

and pray that Knox took far better care of Cody's heart than he had of hers.

With the day stretching out in front of her, she moved from her chair at the table to the one at the small kitchen desk. She opened the laptop and powered it on.

Every couple of days, it was usual for her to check out *Everything's Blogger in Texas*, a wildly popular site that served up the gossip of the area. It was a guilty pleasure, just like watching the *Real Housewives* franchise once a week.

Today the cover story was of a Dallas socialite who had been arrested for drunk driving after leading the police on a dangerous chase.

The headline on the second lead story was Femme Fatale Still on the Loose. Allison clicked to read the article. It was a rehash of Livia Colton's escape from prison with nothing new added to the story since her disappearance.

A slight chill ran across her skin as she thought of Knox's mother. The last thing she had wanted was for Livia Colton to find out she had a grandchild. Allison had always known the woman was a hateful witch, but she hadn't known how truly dangerous she was until her arrest and subsequent trial. Fear of Livia Colton had been part of what had made her lie to Knox about Cody's paternity.

Was that why Knox was back here? Was it possible he was not really on a vacation at all, but rather was on duty here in case his mother showed up?

And if that was the case, then once his mother was

back behind bars, would he once again leave Shadow Creek to return to El Paso and not look back?

She had to believe that he intended to be more than a hit-and-miss father in Cody's life. She also had to believe he'd protect Cody at all costs. At the very least she had to give him the benefit of the doubt until he proved differently.

The hours of the day crept by achingly slowly. She took a long bubble bath and painted her nails a pearly pink and tried not to wonder about what Knox and Cody were doing. She dusted the living room and ran the vacuum cleaner in an effort to keep herself busy.

After that she headed back to the kitchen, made herself a salad for a late lunch and then whipped up some of Cody's favorite double chocolate chip cookies.

While they baked she sat at the table and found her brain working through a hundred questions in her mind. Was Knox married? Was Cody his only child or did he have a family in El Paso?

She should have asked him more questions yesterday at Jade's place, but the shock of seeing him, the horror of realizing he knew about Cody, had made her half-brain-dead.

She told herself that her curiosity had nothing to do with how the very sight of him had stirred old memories, of how the scent of him…a familiar clean, woodsy scent, had evoked a pool of heat inside her stomach.

The only reason why she was curious about his life was that she needed to know how Cody might fit into it. What would a custody agreement look like between them? Would she now be sending her son to stay for a month in the summer with Knox and a stepmother? Would she now have Christmases without her son? Or Easters? Or Thanksgivings?

And what about his mother, who was now on the run from the law? Dear God, she didn't even want to think about Livia getting anywhere near her son.

She needed to find out tonight exactly what Knox wanted. She had always kept a controlling hand on her life. She'd had to be in control to wear the many hats she wore.

At the moment, everything felt wildly out of control and she still had three hours before they'd be home. One thing was certain: she wasn't going to let Knox Colton leave her house tonight until he'd answered some important questions.

Chapter 3

It had been a day of wonder for Knox. If he had imagined the kind of son he would want, it would have been a boy just like Cody.

Cody was bright and curious and extremely well mannered. No matter what he thought of Allison, Knox had to give her credit for doing a stellar job in raising the boy.

Knox found Cody's laughter intoxicating. He even liked the way Cody's forehead crinkled just a bit when he was thinking hard. He was easygoing and a real pleasure to be around.

"I had so much fun today," Cody said as Knox pulled into Allison's driveway.

"Me, too," Knox agreed. "I'd like to spend more time with you. Would that be all right with you?"

"Sure, that would be cool as long as it's okay with my mom," Cody agreed.

"Oh, I think it will be fine with your mother," he replied.

They got out of the car and Knox placed a hand on Cody's shoulder as they approached the front door. His chest swelled on contact with the slender shoulder beneath his hand. His son. He just couldn't get over it.

He dropped his hand back to his side as Cody went through the front door. "Mom, we're home," he called out. He glanced back at Knox with one of his wide grins. "Hmm, she must have made cookies."

Knox followed Cody inside. The house smelled of baked chocolate and lemon polish. It smelled the way a home should.

She stepped from the kitchen and into the living room and for a moment Knox's breath caught in his throat. She looked exquisitely feminine, clad in a casual, soft pink maxi dress that hugged her slender curves on its way down to her ankles. The scoop neck exposed a delicate collarbone, and the color emphasized her warm, peachy complexion. Her hair was loose and fell to her shoulders in soft waves.

She looked even more beautiful when her face lit up and she leaned down to give Cody a hug. "I can tell by the look on your face that you had fun today," she said and then looked up at Knox.

He'd always told her that her eyes were the window to her emotions, that he could always tell what she was thinking, what she was feeling by gazing into them. But those hazel depths told him nothing now. They were shuttered against him and revealed nothing whatsoever.

"Mom, we went to Mac's house and he has pictures of Knox and his brother and sisters on the wall, and then we went fishing in the pond and I caught two big crappies and Mac fried them for dinner and…" Cody paused for breath.

She laughed. "Why don't we go into the kitchen and have some cookies and you can tell me all about it." Once again she looked at Knox. "I made a fresh pot of coffee just a few minutes ago."

"Cookies and fresh coffee? I'm in," he replied. He followed her and their son into the kitchen where he and Cody sat at the table. Allison got a platter of cookies, a glass of milk and two cups of coffee before she joined them.

"Now tell me all about the fish."

Knox leaned back in the chair and watched mother and son interact. She was so patient, and gave him her sole attention as he relayed the activities of the afternoon between bites of cookie.

"Sounds like you had a full day of fun," she said when Cody was finished telling her everything he'd experienced from the time Knox had picked him up until they'd walked through the door. "And now it's bath and bedtime." Cody had eaten two cookies, drank his milk and finished his stories.

"Before that, can Knox come up and see my room?" he asked.

"Okay, but only if it doesn't take too long. A growing boy needs his sleep," Allison replied.

Cody looked at Knox with a grin. "She always tells me that." He scrambled off his chair. "Come on, you'll like my room. I've got bunk beds and a horse collection."

"Then I'd definitely better take a look," Knox replied. He gazed at Allison. "Are you coming up, too?"

She shook her head with a small smile. "I'll just sit here and eat a cookie. Besides, I've seen his room before."

Knox followed Cody up the stairs and at the top the air smelled of apples and spices; the scent instantly tightened his gut with an unwelcome heat.

They passed one doorway and Knox glanced in. It had to be Allison's bedroom. A double bed was covered with a lavender-colored floral spread and white gauzy curtains danced in the evening breeze.

It was far too easy to imagine himself in that bed with her, her naked body in his arms and her eyes simmering a deep gold with sparkling green shards as he took possession of her. What was wrong with him? How was it possible to desire a woman he didn't even want to like?

Cody's room was definitely that of a horse lover. Navy curtains hung at the window with rearing stallions riding the lower borders. The bunk beds were covered with matching navy spreads and a bookcase held miniature figurines of horses in all kinds of poses. One shelf also held a row of books about horses. Glow-in-the-dark star stickers glistened on the ceiling above the top bunk.

"Isn't my room cool?" Cody asked as he sat on the edge of the bottom bunk.

"Totally," Knox replied. "Do you sleep on the bottom bunk or on the top?"

"On the top. Last year I slept on the bottom, but Mom finally let me move to the top and then we got the stars to put on the ceiling."

Knox smiled. "That's where I would sleep if I had bunk beds, and I like the stars, too."

The grin that Cody gave him shot straight through to Knox's heart. He wanted to claim this child. He wanted everyone in the town, everyone in the entire world to know that this bright, beautiful boy was his.

He wanted to grab Cody to his chest and hug him… protect him from any hurt that might ever come his way. Raw emotion ripped through him and he realized that the alien, rich feeling was a father's love for his child.

He cleared his throat. "You'd better get yourself into the bathtub before your mother comes up here and yells at us."

"Mom doesn't yell at me even when she's mad," Cody replied, but he got up off the bed. "Are we gonna hang out again?" His bright eyes gazed at Knox eagerly.

"Absolutely. I'm going to go downstairs right now and make some arrangements with your mother. And don't forget to wash behind your ears. I thought I saw a potato growing behind one of them this afternoon."

Knox went back down the stairs with Cody's giggles ringing in his ears. He hoped Allison wasn't going to give him a hard time about spending more time with Cody. He wanted more, he needed more.

"He's got a great room," he said as he reentered the

kitchen where she still remained at the table. "And he's a great kid, Allison. You've done a terrific job with him."

"Thanks. He's a good boy, but like all kids he occasionally does have his moments. Would you like another cup of coffee?" She looked slightly fragile with her shoulders curved as she leaned forward and wrapped her fingers around her cup.

"I'll get it." He picked up his mug from the table and carried it to the coffeemaker on the countertop. He poured the coffee and then returned to the chair across from her. "So, when can I get him again?"

"Next Sunday?" Her full bottom lip held the hint of a tremble.

Crap, she was making him feel like a big, bad monster attempting to tear her little baby boy from her loving arms. He shook his head. "No way, I'm not waiting an entire week to see him again."

"Are you married?" Her cheeks flushed and she quickly picked up her cup and took a sip.

"Why do you want to know?" He crooked up an eyebrow. "Are you interested in resuming where we left off while I'm back in town?"

Her back stiffened and her eyes flashed. "Don't be ridiculous. That's the last thing I want. I just need to know a few things about your personal life if we're going to work out a reasonable custody agreement."

At least he'd shaken her out of the soft vulnerability that had made him want to embrace her rather than fight for his rights.

"I'm not married and I don't have a significant other,"

he replied. "My life for the past ten years has been all about my work."

She gazed at him curiously. "Why are you really here in town? Are you on vacation, or are you actually working in case your mother shows up here?"

He leaned back in the chair and tamped down the resentment that threatened to rise up in his chest, a resentment that had nothing to do with Allison.

"Yeah, I'm here because of my mother, but not for the reason you think. None of the authorities really believes she'll show up here in Shadow Creek, but I was told to take a sabbatical because of my relationship to her. I'd become an embarrassment because of her prison escape."

Allison studied him for several long moments. "I'm sorry, Knox," she finally said. She was one of the few people outside of his siblings who knew the extent of Livia Colton's destructiveness. "Do I need to worry about her? I never wanted her to know about Cody."

"She shouldn't be a problem, considering I didn't even know Cody existed until yesterday," he replied drily. "What did people think when you started showing?"

"The gossipmongers went crazy for a couple of months. I heard everything from I got pregnant after a one-night stand to the father being one of the men who worked for my dad." She looked down and then raised her gaze to meet his. "Your name popped up as a potential candidate, but when you didn't come back to town that particular rumor died."

He didn't want to think about her being alone and

pregnant and the subject of scandal and gossip. "Now, about Cody."

She sighed and reached up and grabbed a strand of her hair and worried it between two fingers, a habit he remembered her having whenever she was stressed. "He gets out of school every day at three thirty and walks home from the bus stop." She dropped her hair and frowned. "I guess you could pick him up here every Tuesday and Thursday afternoon and then have him back by bedtime."

"That will work. And what about the weekends? I can still have him on Sundays?" What he'd really like would be to have Cody every single day. He'd like to wake up in the mornings and fix him breakfast, see him off to school and then spend the evenings with him and tuck him into bed.

"I work on most Saturdays and Cody usually spends time out at Jade's or comes in with me to the office. Maybe instead of Sunday you could take him on Saturdays while I'm working."

He could tell by the hollowness in her eyes, by the slight thinning of her lips, she wasn't happy, but he couldn't help that. She wouldn't be in this position if she hadn't lied to him in the first place.

And with that thought he was ready to leave. They'd worked out the days he'd spend with his son and he didn't need anything else from her.

He got up from the table and carried his cup to the sink. "Thanks for the coffee and the cookie," he said.

She rose and together they walked to the front door. "I guess we'll see you Tuesday afternoon," she said.

He turned to face her and the scent of apples and spices suffused him. She stood close enough to him that he could feel the heat from her body radiating outward to warm him. Desire punched him hard in the gut.

He felt like he had when he'd been sixteen years old and she was fifteen and all he wanted was a kiss from the girl who had stolen his heart. The urge to capture her lips with his was nearly overwhelming.

Her eyes flared deep gold and she took a step backward. "Good night, Knox."

"Good night," he replied and stepped outside into the dark of the night. As he hurried to his car in the driveway, he didn't know if he hated her for lying to him or if he hated her because as crazy as it was, he still wanted her.

Monday morning at nine o'clock, Allison sat at her desk in the Rafferty Construction Company's office on Main Street.

Outside the glass partitions that made up her office space was the blood and guts of the business. Lumber in all sizes and types stacked the walls of the large space. Bath and kitchen tiles were in another section, along with anything and everything that might be needed to renovate a home.

At the moment two of her best men were building custom kitchen cabinets, and the sounds of power miter saws and hammering were as familiar to Allison as her own heartbeat.

Much of her childhood had been spent in the shop area, watching men build things from wood and talk about plumbing and wiring. It had never been her intention to take over the business. She'd wanted to be a nurse, but her father's illness and his desire for her to take over for him had changed her life plans.

Now she couldn't imagine doing anything else. This business was in her blood, a continuing tribute to the father she'd loved so much.

She sat up straighter in her chair as foreman George Carlson walked in. He headed straight for her office, a deep frown cutting into his broad forehead.

"We've got a problem on the Wilkenson place," he said as he sat in the chair before her desk.

"What's the problem?" The Wilkenson home was a large two-story on Main Street that had been in foreclosure for nearly a year. New owners had finally bought the place but before moving in they'd wanted an extensive renovation. Allison had bid on the job and three days ago they'd been given the go-head.

"I delivered a load of lumber there yesterday and this morning I discovered that it had been ruined. Somebody took a saw to it and made a bunch of kindling." He narrowed his brown eyes. "And that same somebody also spray painted what wasn't cut up, and you know who's probably responsible."

She sighed. Yes, she knew the likely culprits. Rafferty Construction had been in a fierce competition for business with Brothers Construction, Inc. That company, run by brothers Brad and Bob Billings, had also bid on the Wilkenson project and had lost the job to Allison. This wouldn't be the first time the two sore losers had caused problems on a site.

"Call Sheriff Jeffries and get him out to the house to make a report," she said with a sigh.

George snorted. "Bud Jeffries couldn't find a criminal if one crawled up his pant leg."

Allison fought against a smile. "We still need to make an official report," she replied.

"Yeah, I know. On another note, are you going to fire Chad today?"

"You're the one who told me he needs to go."

"He does," George said firmly. "He's a drunk and he's become more and more dangerous on the jobs because of his drinking. I don't want him on my team, and I know Larry feels the same way."

She nodded. "I called him at eight this morning and told him I wanted to see him in here at ten."

"Hopefully that will be early enough that he hasn't started hitting the bottle," George replied. He stood. "I'll give the sheriff a call and take care of filing a report."

"Thanks, George. You know I appreciate you."

He flashed her a quick smile and then headed out the door.

Every day Allison thanked her lucky stars for her two foremen. George Carlson and Larry Smith had been loyal and good workers for her father, and she was grateful that when the weight of the business had fallen to her, they'd been there to counsel and guide her.

She slumped back in her chair. Anger surged through her as she thought of the vandalism on the job, but she knew the odds of Sheriff Bud Jeffries finding and arresting the culprits were minimal. Not only was Bud one of the laziest men in the entire town of Shadow Creek, he was also good buddies with the Billings brothers.

She'd only been in the office an hour and already she was exhausted. It didn't help that she was functioning on too little sleep. Thoughts of Knox had kept her tossing and turning all night. Thoughts of Livia somehow discovering she had a grandson hadn't helped. She had no idea how Livia might use that information, but she knew not to underestimate the wickedness of Livia Colton. Hopefully the woman stayed as far away from Shadow Creek as possible.

There had been a moment the night before when she thought Knox was going to kiss her. What had appalled her was the realization she had wanted him to.

It was as if no time had passed and she was still crazy for him. How many times did Knox Colton get to break her heart before she stopped wanting him?

She'd had no desire to be with a man for the past ten years. She'd been too busy taking care of her father, stepping up to run the business and being a single parent. There had been no time to even think about dating. Besides, she hadn't wanted to bring any man into Cody's life who might just be a temporary thing.

It galled her that Knox waltzed into town and within minutes of being around him all of her hormones came to life and raged out of control.

Damn his handsome hide. When he'd asked her if she was interested in "resuming where they'd left off" with him, there had been a small voice in the back of her head that had whispered, *Why not?*

All she wanted from Knox was for him to be a real

and present father to Cody. Other than that, she wanted nothing to do with him. She would admit to herself that she still entertained some desire for him, but that was a place she didn't intend to go ever again.

Hurt me once, shame on you. Hurt me again, shame on me, she told herself. Knox was strictly off-limits. She'd be an absolute fool to trust even the tiniest piece of her heart to Fort Knox again. They had been star-crossed lovers who'd had their chance together and they'd both blown it.

She straightened as Chad Watkins walked into the shop. As if Knox hadn't thrown her for a loop, she now had vandalism and the firing of a man to deal with.

Chad Watkins was thirty-five years old, but his drinking had aged him. He threw himself into the chair opposite her, his blue eyes watery and red rimmed and his nose covered in broken blood vessels. The faint smell of whiskey and body odor drifted off him.

"What's going on?" he asked.

"Chad, I'm sorry, but I'm afraid I'm going to have to let you go," she replied. No sense in making pleasant small talk with him, she thought.

He stared at her for a long moment. "Let me go? You mean you're firing me?" He looked at her incredulously. "Why?"

"Your drinking has gotten out of hand and it's affecting your performance on the job. I've had many complaints and I just can't overlook it any longer. I'd like to encourage you to seek some help."

"I don't need any help. I need this job." He glared

at her as if she were personally responsible for all the woes in his life.

"I'm sorry, Chad..."

"You're going to be sorry about this." He got up from the chair, his eyes narrowed in anger. "What about severance pay?"

"I'll give you two weeks," she replied.

"Two weeks? How about you give me ten thousand dollars?"

Allison stared at him in disbelief. By law she didn't have to give him a penny. She'd thought she was being generous in offering him the two weeks. "That's certainly not going to happen," she replied stiffly.

"I'll definitely make you sorry for this. I'll sue you and I'll own this stupid company. You just wait and see. I'm going to turn your world upside down."

Before she could say another word, he stormed out of the office and slammed the door so hard the glass walls shuddered. "Well, that went well," she muttered aloud.

She wasn't really worried about his threats. She suspected Chad was nothing more than a blowhard who would console himself with a bottle or two of booze and would eventually find another job. At least he didn't have a wife or a family depending on his paycheck.

The rest of the day passed fairly uneventfully. George checked in with her to let her know a police report had been made on the damaged wood. He agreed with her it was a good idea that any supplies brought to the site in the future would now be stored inside of the house rather than outside. Hopefully that would solve the problem of any further damage.

At three o'clock she left work to head home. One of the advantages of being boss was that she could knock off early and be there for her son when he came home from school.

She hadn't wanted Cody to be a latchkey kid, and everyone who worked for her knew that she left the office early each afternoon, but was available by cell or home phone if anything important came up.

It took her only ten minutes to get home. When she'd bought the house less than two years ago, it had needed a lot of work to update and make it into the place of her dreams.

She'd left the major updates to her team of men, but she had personally spent hours sanding down the oak woodwork and floors. The end result had been worth all the hard work.

She loved so many things about the house…the bay window in the living room, the large wraparound porch and, most important, the large fenced yard that included several mature trees that were perfect for climbing.

If they had any slow months this summer, she intended to pay the men to build Cody a tree house. She'd thought about having it done last year, but had never accomplished it. One of the trees was perfectly formed to hold such a structure and she knew Cody would love it.

Instead of sitting at the kitchen table to wait for Cody to come home, she moved outside to sit on the porch swing. It was a gorgeous afternoon, but she was grateful for the weight of her sweater against a faint cool March breeze.

She moved the swing back and forth and her head

once again filled with thoughts of Knox. The night before she'd ached with his pain as he'd told her about his forced sabbatical because of his mother's escape from prison.

When she and Knox had begun dating in high school, Livia had pretended to approve of the match, although Allison had suspected she didn't approve of Allison's blue-collar background.

Nobody had been more surprised than Allison when she'd been awarded a scholarship to Boston University. The opportunity was too good to dismiss. It wasn't until she had to pull out of school to nurse her father that she'd discovered her scholarship had been made available to her thanks to the charity of Livia Colton. A friend of hers who worked part-time in the bursar's office had told Allison.

Livia had gotten her wish to break Allison and Knox apart through distance, but the minute she had returned to Shadow Creek, they had resumed their romance... until he'd left her.

All thoughts of Knox fled her mind as she saw Cody in the distance heading toward home. He walked with his best friend, Josh Inman, who lived on the next block.

This was the first year Allison had allowed her son to walk the three blocks from the school bus stop to their home. He'd begged her to be allowed to walk home instead of her picking him up, and she'd finally relented.

Josh veered off the sidewalk for his house and Cody hurried forward. He spotted her on the swing and waved and her heart swelled with overwhelming love. He was such a good boy and only very rarely pushed boundaries.

When he reached her he pulled his fire-engine-red backpack off his back and tossed it onto the porch, then sat next to her on the swing.

"Good day?" she asked. She took a deep breath, loving the scent of sunshine and all things young boy that filled her nose.

"Great day," he replied. "Tony Mantelli brought his hamster for pet day and it got loose. All the girls jumped up in their chairs and screamed and Stacy Burrwell's cat was going crazy in the cage and Danny's dog was barking. It was totally awesome."

Allison laughed. "Did Tony ever get his hamster back?"

He nodded. "Mrs. Jackson finally caught it and got it back in the cage." He kicked his feet to move the swing a little faster. "I wish I had a pet." He slid her a sly glance.

"And I'll bet I know what kind of a pet you'd like to have. It's bigger than a dog and smaller than an elephant."

Cody grinned at her. "And it has a mane and hooves."

"Cody, having a horse is a huge responsibility."

"I know, but I'm ready for it, Mom. I always do my chores on time and I get good grades. I'm responsible and Miss Jade will tell you I'm great with the horses. Just please tell me you'll think about it."

"Okay, I'll think about it," she replied. "And what I'm also thinking about is walking to the Cozy Diner for dinner this evening. It's a beautiful day."

"Hmm, spaghetti Monday." Cody rubbed his stomach.

Allison got up from the swing. "Homework?"

"Yeah, a little."

"Let's get to it so that you don't have to worry about it when we get home from eating."

It was just after eight that evening when she and Cody left the diner for the six-block walk back home. Clouds had moved in, making the darkness of night come faster than usual.

"I'm so full," Cody moaned as they began the trek home.

"Me, too, and I didn't have a big piece of chocolate pie like you did," she replied.

"No, but you totally pigged out on the garlic toast. Besides, the chocolate pie was worth it. It was delicious."

Dinner had been pleasant. They'd visited with friends and neighbors and enjoyed the good food the diner always provided. "You know what the best thing about eating out is?" she said.

"No dishes," Cody replied.

"That's right," she agreed with a laugh.

The neighborhood sidewalk was darkly shadowed as the clouds hid the moon. Their footsteps rang out in unison in the otherwise still of the night.

She was definitely feeling the lack of sleep from the night before and all she wanted now was the comfort of her bed and a night with no dreams.

Her body tensed as she thought she heard the scuff of a footfall behind them. She whirled around, heart pounding, to see nobody sharing the sidewalk with them.

Had she only imagined it? They had only gone a couple more steps when a rustle sounded. Once again she turned around, her heartbeat accelerating even faster.

She saw nobody. However, there were bushes and trees right next to the sidewalk where somebody could hide, and her intuitive senses were screaming that somebody was following them.

"I'll race you to the house," she said to Cody. She couldn't explain the fear that suddenly torched through her, she could only respond.

Her heart still banged an unsteady rhythm as Cody shot just ahead of her. "Winner gets a cookie before bedtime," he exclaimed.

She ran, making sure Cody stayed just ahead of her. He could win the race and have his cookie, but she intended to see that nobody sneaked up on her son.

The house had never seemed so far away and she'd never felt the kind of abject fear that coursed through her as they raced to safety.

"Ha, I win," Cody said as he reached their front porch two steps ahead of her.

Allison fumbled her keys out of her purse and quickly unlocked the door. She pushed him through the doorway. "Get upstairs and get your pajamas on and then you get your cookie reward."

As he headed for the stairs, Allison remained at the front door. She looked down the sidewalk from where they had come. Had somebody been following them or had it only been a trick of her imagination?

A dog barked in the distance and a chill walked up her spine. She quickly closed the door and locked it, then leaned with her back against it as she waited for her heart to resume a more normal pace.

If there had been somebody out there, it was possible it was Chad being drunk and stupid and hopefully no harm had been really intended. Still, that thought somehow didn't chase away the simmering fear that remained with her long into the night.

Chapter 4

Knox arrived at Allison's house at three forty for his visit with Cody. The plans he'd had for them for the afternoon and evening were a washout due to the rain that had pelted the area since before dawn.

Thank God it had tapered down to just a fine mist as he left his car and raced for Allison's front porch. She met him at the door and let him inside, where awkward greetings were exchanged.

"Cody should be here in just a few minutes," she said.

He looked out the door. "Since it's raining, maybe I should take the car and go pick him up."

"I wouldn't do that if I were you."

He turned to look at her.

She smiled. It was the first real smile he'd received

from her since he'd accosted her at Jade's stables and it warmed him from the chill of the rain.

"I've been told by Cody that nine-year-old boys don't mind walking in the rain," she said. "He's also told me quite firmly that he isn't a baby anymore."

"Then I'm glad you stopped me from doing something to insult his budding manhood," Knox replied.

Before he could say anything else to her Cody ran through the door, bringing with him muddy shoes and boyish laughter. "Hi, Knox," he said as he kicked off his shoes. "Sorry about the mud, Mom."

"Hi, Cody," Knox replied. "I had some plans for us outside this afternoon but the rain has changed everything."

"That's okay. Maybe we should just stay here and play some games. I've got some awesome video games and Mom mostly stinks at all of them." Cody flashed his mother an apologetic grin. "You know it's the truth, Mom."

"Okay, I'll admit I'm fairly lame at video games," she replied with a grin.

"And maybe we could order pizza for dinner," Cody said. "It could be a really fun night."

Knox looked at Allison. He wasn't sure she would consider his presence there all evening a really fun night. She gazed at her son and smiled. "Of course you two can hang out here, and pizza for dinner sounds great, but before you start any video games you need to go upstairs and change out of those damp clothes."

"Okay, I'll be right back." Cody headed up the stairs

and Allison's smile disappeared as she turned to face Knox once again.

"If this is inconvenient for you I can always take him to Thorne's or Mac's," Knox said.

"Cody being here is never an inconvenience to me."

"I wasn't talking about him being here, I was talking about me," he replied wryly.

"You're a necessary evil," she said.

"Said the kettle to the pot," he replied. "Why am I the only bad guy here?"

A dusting of color filled her cheeks. "I guess you're not…yet."

He released a sigh. "At some point you're going to have to trust me, Allison."

"It's going to take time." She reached up as if to grab a strand of her hair, but it was in that charming, slightly untidy knot at the nape of her neck and she dropped her hand back to her side. "Cody can get the video games set up and whatever else you might need. I'll be upstairs until dinnertime."

As she began to climb the stairs, Cody came back down, and within minutes he and Knox were in the living room with game paddles in their hands as an earnest rain began to pelt the windows.

With a gun Knox could outdraw most men, but he quickly discovered that he was no match for a nine-year-old's nimble fingers on game paddles. The first two football games they played, his team lost to Cody's by a landslide. Cody's triumphant cries of victory didn't last when he put in a gun range challenge and they exchanged paddles for plastic weapons.

A wooden fence appeared on the television with bottles lined up. Knox cleared them before Cody got off his first shot. "Wow," Cody said, his eyes glittering brightly as he high-fived Knox. "That was awesome. You shoot like a superhero."

Cody set his gun in his lap and gazed at Knox. "My dad is a superhero."

Knox froze. "A superhero?" he finally said.

Cody nodded. "That's why he can't be here with me. He's doing important work keeping the world safe and catching bad guys. There are a lot of bad guys." He stared down at the gun in his lap. "I just wish for one day he could forget about the bad guys for a little while and come here and say hello to me."

What in the hell had Allison done? He'd wondered what she had told Cody about his father and now he wished he'd asked her before. Why on earth would she have told Cody that outrageous story?

"Let's play another game," Knox said as a new anger toward Allison burned in his belly. What had she been thinking?

They played video games until six when he called the local pizzeria and made their order to be delivered. While they waited for the pizza, he and Cody set the kitchen table with paper plates and napkins.

When the meal arrived, Cody shouted up the stairs to his mother and she came down to join them. Knox swallowed his anger, not wanting a hint of it to show while the three of them ate together. But there was no way he was leaving this house tonight before he spoke his mind to her.

He'd ordered a large meat-lovers for them to share. He waited until Cody and Allison took their first pieces and then he served himself. Automatically he picked off the pepperoni on his slice and placed them on Allison's plate. It was a habit deeply ingrained from when they'd been a couple.

"How did you know Mom loves pepperoni?" Cody asked.

"I know a lot of things about your mother," Knox replied. "We went to high school together."

"You did? Tell me some other stuff you know about her," Cody asked as Allison handed him his napkin to wipe off a string of mozzarella cheese that clung to his chin.

"I know her favorite color is purple and when she laughs too hard she gets the hiccups." His gaze locked with hers and for the moment his anger was gone, replaced by haunting memories.

"She likes pizza, but she loves cheeseburgers with lots of dill pickles and mayo," he continued. What he couldn't say was how soft and inviting her lips were when she kissed or how her hazel eyes changed colors when she was fired up with desire. "She also isn't much of a chocolate eater, but give her a bag of chips or a loaf of French bread and she'll tear them up."

Cody laughed in delight and then looked at his mother. "That's all true! Now, Mom, tell me some stuff you know about Knox."

She finally broke eye contact with Knox and instead smiled at her son. "He was the star of the high school football team. He had great moves on the field, but he doesn't dance very well."

Cody shot a glance at him and giggled.

"He's very loyal to his brothers and sisters and when he laughs too hard all the dogs in the area howl." Her eyes twinkled with a teasing light. "And don't ever ask him to sing to you because he can't carry a tune worth a darn."

Knox found himself laughing and for a moment it felt good to be there with her and his son and sharing some humor. The rest of the meal passed with easy conversation and was filled with more laughter. At one point Allison laughed hard enough that she got the hiccups, to the utter delight of her son.

Knox had forgotten how much he enjoyed her sense of humor and how delightful he'd always found the way her mind worked. And just that quickly he closed off to her as he remembered what she'd told Cody about his father. What on earth had she been thinking then?

The meal finished and cleanup was done and then Cody and Knox returned to the living room to play some more games. Rain still bounced off the windows and it felt as if in no time Allison came back downstairs to tell Cody it was bedtime.

"Would you like for me to come up and tuck you in?" Knox asked before the boy went up the stairs.

He held his breath, surprised by how much he wanted to tuck the sheet around his son's neck and tell him to have sweet, wonderful dreams.

Cody's eyes brightened. "Sure, I'd like that a lot. I'll

call you when I'm ready." He bounced up the stairs and disappeared from Knox's view.

He turned to face Allison who had come downstairs to get Cody for bed. "You don't mind, do you?"

"No, it's fine," she replied.

"And after he's in bed you and I need to have a talk."

"About what?" Her eyes filled with an instant wariness.

"You can come on up, Knox," Cody's voice drifted down the stairs.

"I'll tell you when I finish tucking in my son." He turned from her and headed up the stairs.

Great, what now? Allison wondered as she watched Knox climb the stairs and disappear at the top. Whatever he wanted to discuss with her had put that cold chill back in his eyes.

As days went, this one had already been pretty crummy. Not only had George reported that three windows on the Wilkenson home had been broken overnight, but she'd also received a flurry of unpleasant text messages from Chad.

He'd threatened to turn her into OSHA, the IRS and any other number of government authorities. Although the business was in compliance with every one of those agencies, she couldn't afford a ton of legal costs incurred by frivolous lawsuits or government inquiries.

She still hoped he was just blowing off steam and would eventually stop with the texts. However, the whole thing had put her a bit on edge.

The only thing that had taken Chad and the new vandalism out of her mind for a little while had been the laughter they'd all shared over pizza.

It had been so unexpected. In a million years she'd never dreamed that she and Knox would be able to laugh with each other again. But he hadn't been amused when he'd gone upstairs to send Cody off to sleep.

She went back into the living room and sank down on the overstuffed brown sofa to wait for Knox's return. There was no question that her son was developing a huge case of hero worship for Knox. Did it worry her? She had to admit it did a little bit.

She just didn't want Cody's fragile heart to be hurt in any way. It should be a little girl that gave him his first heartbreak, not his father.

Her muscles tensed at the sound of Knox's footsteps coming back down the stairs. She'd stayed out of the way this afternoon and evening so that he and Cody could spend quality time together. From upstairs it had sounded like they'd had fun. What on earth could he have to discuss with her now?

He entered the living room and immediately she felt the heavy tension that wafted from him. "Did you get him tucked in?" she asked.

"I did." He sat in the wingback chair opposite her and stared at her with his beautiful but cold blue eyes. "What on earth were you thinking when you told Cody that his father is some kind of a superhero who is off fighting crime?"

Allison physically felt the blood drain from her face. "I didn't know what else to tell him."

"I'm surprised you didn't tell him his father was dead."

She sat up straighter. She refused to allow his harsh gaze to cow her. "Three years ago a close friend of Cody's lost his father in a car accident. Cody was distraught for his friend and while he was crying he asked me about his own father. That certainly wasn't the time for me to tell him that his father was dead, so I told him he had an important job fighting crime and couldn't come to visit because he was keeping us all safe." She raised her chin a notch. "Besides, it was the truth."

"Except the part where you didn't tell him that I didn't even know he existed."

She leaned back and released a deep sigh. "Knox, I agree that I've made some mistakes. I thought…" She cast her gaze to the right of him, not wanting to look at him as she continued. "I thought I was doing what was best for everyone in the situation."

"By telling me you got pregnant by another man when we were together? What part of that was best for everyone?"

"You had already left town. The last thing I wanted to do was force you to come back to me by telling you I was pregnant." And then there was the fact that his mother was a convicted murderer.

"I thought you cheated on me."

"I'd never cheat on any man. That isn't who I am." Another sigh escaped her. "Knox, this is all water under the bridge. I'm trying my best to make everything right now."

To her utter surprise tears burned hot in her eyes, tears that were impossible to control. "Look, I've had a really bad day at work and the last thing I need right now is for you to berate me for decisions I made in the past."

She ended her words with an audible sob and raised her hands to hide her face. Good grief, what was wrong with her? Why was she suddenly so out of control?

"Don't cry, Allison. You know I could never stand it when you cried."

The unexpected softness in Knox's voice did nothing to staunch her tears. It only made her feel worse. She'd made such a mess of things when she'd lied to Knox so long ago. But she'd already been hurt by his abrupt withdrawal, and the last thing she'd wanted was to tie him to her when he obviously didn't want to be with her.

She shook her head, feeling foolish as she only cried harder.

"Allison."

His voice was close and when he grabbed her by the hand she allowed him to pull her up and into his arms. It was the very last place she should be, but she leaned weakly against him as her tears continued to flow.

She'd had to be so strong in taking care of her sick father, a baby and a business. She'd had to remain strong for Cody when her father had passed away, but at this very moment she had no strength left; there was only old grief and new regrets.

"Shh." Knox tightened his arms around her. His embrace was wonderfully familiar and despite the years, in spite of his anger with her and her long-ago hurt and anger toward him, his arms felt safe. His shirt smelled of fabric softener and his woodsy cologne as she buried her head against his shoulder.

Slowly the tears began to subside but she didn't move out of his embrace. There had been many times in the past ten years that she'd yearned for a man's arms around her. She'd secretly yearned for *his* arms.

He rubbed a hand up and down her back, the caress not only comforting her, but also stoking a delicious warmth inside her. *Move away*, a little voice whispered in her head. This was madness, to linger in the arms of a man who would never have a place in her life again.

She raised her head with every intention of stepping away from him. But his arms pulled her closer to him and his lips crashed down on hers.

Hot and hungry, his mouth demanded an immediate response from her and she was helpless to do anything but comply. Without her volition her arms rose to encircle his neck as she opened her mouth to him.

The kiss erased all rational thought from her mind. Instead, all of her senses came gloriously alive as his mouth made love to hers. His tongue swirled with hers as his scent suffused her, and the heat of his hands on her back invited her to melt against his broad chest. Their bodies fit together perfectly, as if they had been made for each other.

He finally left her lips to slide his mouth down the column of her throat. As her knees weakened with desire, rational thought slammed back into her. She jerked back from him, appalled by how quickly, how completely, he could break down all her defenses.

His eyes radiated a raw hunger as he held her gaze intently. "Despite everything that has happened between us, I still want you. There's always been something strong between us, Allison, and you can't deny that it's still there."

No, she couldn't deny it, but she also wouldn't admit it to him. "It doesn't matter." She took two steps back from him, needing not only to emotionally distance herself but to physically distance herself, as well.

"That kiss was a mistake. I don't feel that way about you anymore." Okay, maybe she could deny it, but she could tell by the look in his eyes that he didn't believe her.

"In any case, anything like that between us would be foolish and it would only complicate things. We aren't going there again, Knox, and now I think it's time we say good-night."

She breathed a sigh of relief when he nodded and turned to walk to the front door. Her legs were still shaky as she accompanied him.

"I'm sorry about my little breakdown," she said.

He turned to face her and before she could read his intentions he grabbed her and once again planted a kiss on her lips.

It was short and searing and when he released her his eyes sparkled with a knowing glint. "The next time you try to tell me you don't feel that way about me anymore, say it like you really mean it," he said, and then he was gone into the night.

Allison closed and locked the door, then raised a hand to her lips where the heat from his mouth still burned. How had the night gone so crazy, first with her unexpected tears and then with the even more unexpected desire that had exploded between them?

She turned out all the lights on the lower level and then slowly climbed the stairs where the hall light was on at the top. Thoughts of Knox still filled her head as she went past her bedroom and instead stood at Cody's bedroom door.

He was asleep on the top bunk and facing the doorway. A little smile lingered on his face, as if he was enjoying happy dreams.

This was the first night in over nine years that she hadn't been the one to tuck him into bed. She hadn't kissed him on his forehead and told him to have sweet dreams. Her face hadn't been the last one he'd seen before he went to sleep. Tonight Knox had maybe stroked the hair off Cody's forehead and wished his son happy dreams.

She turned and went into her bedroom. In the adjoining bathroom she pulled the pins from her hair to release it and then changed from her clothes to her pink, short-sleeved nightshirt. Cody had bought it last year for Mother's Day with his allowance, and it had a rearing horse on the front with the word *Spirit* in purple.

As she brushed her hair and teeth, her head was still filled with Knox. She shouldn't be surprised by the intense physical attraction the two of them shared. It was part of what had brought them together again and again in the past.

In high school they'd broken up once, but it had only been a couple of days before they got back together. When they'd grown apart while she was in college, it had only taken them a few days after she'd returned to

Shadow Creek for them to pick up their intense relationship.

But there was too much damage between them now to resume anything. Passion meant nothing if it wasn't followed up by trust and the broken bond between them would never be completely repaired. It was imperative that she remember that in the future.

She left the bathroom and vowed she wasn't going to think about Knox anymore. He would always have a role in her life as Cody's father, but that's all he would ever be to her.

She pulled down the spread and got into bed and then grabbed her cell phone which she had forgotten to carry down for dinner. She had twenty new text messages.

u goin.g to pay.

u pay bitch

Bitch

Bitch

Bich

Bith

They were all from Chad and she could only guess that the more he drank, the sloppier the spelling. But the sentiment was the same. Anger…rage…and it didn't seem to be abating with time, but was rather escalating.

The heat that Knox had evoked in her seeped away as she remembered that moment the night before when she'd thought she and Cody were being followed. A chill suffused her.

She knew Chad was a drunk. Now she worried that he was not only a drunk, but potentially dangerous, as well.

Chad stood beneath a tree across the street from Allison's house. The rain had finally come to a stop and he had left the Whiskey Sour to head for home.

He figured by the time he took the long walk back to his small house, he'd sober up. Right now he knew he was drunk, but that didn't stop the hatred that flooded through him as he stared at the dark house across the street.

Allison and her boy would be sound asleep by now. He hoped she was having nightmares. He grabbed hold of a low branch to steady himself.

She was such a Goody Two-shoes. He hadn't liked her from the moment she'd hired him. She was nothing but a self-righteous bitch.

All the men had a beer or two at lunchtime and yet she'd come down on his ass and fired him. She was going to be sorry. He was definitely going to make her sorry.

He released his hold on the branch and started walking up the street, his hatred for Allison Rafferty burning hot in his soul.

Oh, yes, he was going to make her pay. He was going to be her worst nightmare come true.

Chapter 5

Main Street in Shadow Creek hadn't changed much in the ten years since Knox had been gone. The quaint buildings would have been perfectly at home on the set of an old Western movie. The only thing that had changed was some of the businesses.

Where he remembered a barbershop had once existed, the space was now a cell phone store. The ice cream parlor where he and Allison had often gone after school with friends had been turned into a computer repair and printing shop.

However, there were still familiar places like the Shadow Creek Mercantile and El Torero's Mexican Restaurant. Apparently women still got their hair done at Marie's Salon and Spa, and the Whiskey Sour and Aldo's were still the popular drinking joints.

Knox wasn't looking for a drink, although he wouldn't mind popping into El Torero's for some lunch. He'd come into town with a specific goal in mind and he'd found what he wanted at the mercantile.

Two ball gloves and a baseball now rested in a sack in the backseat. Although Cody hadn't mentioned anything about playing catch, wasn't that what fathers and sons did together?

He thought maybe tomorrow night when he picked up Cody they could go back to Thorne's to play some catch and then cook some burgers for dinner. Knox couldn't believe how anxious he was to once again be in Cody's company.

He couldn't imagine what man wouldn't want to be a part of their child's life. Although Knox had no role model for parenting, he was excited to be an involved parent.

Why hadn't his own father felt that way about him? Perhaps Tad Whitman hadn't believed that Knox was his or maybe he had just wanted to get as far away from Livia as possible. It sucked that he had missed out on having a father in his life and it sucked even more that his mother had been nothing short of a monster.

Shoving these troubling thoughts aside, he decided to indulge his hunger for some Mexican fare. He parked his car several spaces down from the restaurant and then got out.

The rain from the day before was nothing but a memory this morning and the sun was bright and warm. Or was it the thought of kissing Allison that had his body temperature elevated?

He'd definitely thought about those kisses long after

he'd left Allison's house the night before. Her mouth had been as hot, as inviting, as he'd remembered.

The visceral, aching desire he'd always felt when around her hadn't dissipated through time. Something about her stirred him like no other woman ever had. That didn't mean he wanted a relationship with her. But he definitely wouldn't mind getting her in his bed again.

He was about to walk past the sheriff's station door when the woman in his thoughts exited the building and took off, walking just in front of him. "Allison," he called after her.

She stopped and turned to face him. He quickly caught up with her. "Are you all right? Is Cody okay?" A surge of concern swept through him. Why had she been in the police station? People only went there if they were in trouble.

"Cody is fine and so am I."

The words were right, but a line of tension across her forehead said otherwise as she reached up and grasped a strand of her hair.

"What were you doing in the sheriff's office?" He told himself that he had a right to know what was going on in her life because it might affect his son.

She dropped her hand to her side and met his gaze with troubled eyes. "I had to fire a man on Monday and since then he's been blowing up my phone with text messages. I thought it was time to talk to Sheriff Jeffries about it."

"I was just on my way to El Torero's. Why don't you let me buy you some lunch?" He wanted to hear more about these text messages. Allison wasn't the kind of woman who got shaken easily, but she was obviously shaken up now.

She looked away and then back at him and he saw her hesitation. "Come on, Ally. A couple of enchiladas always make the world better."

She looked lovely in a tailored white blouse and navy slacks. As usual her hair was pulled back and navy hoop earrings hung on her delicate ears.

She finally offered him a small smile. "Okay, lunch sounds good."

Together they walked into the restaurant. El Torero's was like a million other Mexican restaurants. The interior was dark, the walls were decorated with beaded sombreros and painted murals, and it smelled of spicy salsa, onions and toasted chips.

There was no hostess at the front, only a sign that indicated they should seat themselves. Knox led Allison to the booth where they had often eaten when they'd been a couple.

They had barely settled in when a young woman appeared with water glasses and menus. "I'll be back in just a few minutes to take your orders," she said with a friendly smile before disappearing once again.

"I don't need to look at the menu." Allison set the large plastic menu aside. "Cody and I eat here occasionally and I know I want a number three platter."

"Let me guess…two cheese enchiladas with beans and rice." Knox smiled as she nodded.

"And I bet you're going to order beef enchiladas and a pork burrito," Allison replied.

"Seems like old times." He gazed at her for a long moment. "Now tell me about those texts."

Before she could reply the waitress returned to take their orders. It was only when she once again left the table that Allison released a sigh and set her cell phone on the table. "Here, you can see them for yourself. They came from Chad."

Knox picked up her phone and went to her messages. As he read what the man had written, a new tension began to build inside him. Even though Allison wasn't really his business anymore, the emotions that pressed tight against his chest were the needs of a man to protect his woman.

He turned her phone off and slid it back across the table to her. "Tell me more about this Chad."

"I hired him about eight months ago and for a while he was a fairly decent worker. But over the last couple of months I'd gotten complaints about him drinking on the job or coming to work drunk. My two head foremen had told me they didn't want him working with them anymore, so Monday I had to let him go. Needless to say he didn't take the news well. I ignored the messages until I felt like they got personally threatening and I thought maybe Cody and I were followed when we walked home from the diner."

The knot in Knox's stomach remained tight. "What did the sheriff tell you?"

She frowned. "He said he'd have a talk with Chad and reminded me that Chad was a good old boy with a bit of a problem who was probably just blowing off steam."

"Any man who talks to a woman that way is scum," Knox said. "Do you think this guy might be dangerous?"

Her frown deepened. "To be honest, I don't know. I just thought it was time to speak to Sheriff Jeffries about the messages. You know, better safe than sorry."

The conversation halted as their food arrived. For a few minutes they ate in silence and for the first time since arriving back in Shadow Creek he thought about the incredible strength Allison had to possess.

For the past almost ten years she'd been a single parent and had to take care of her ailing father and keep the business running smoothly.

It would be a daunting task to do just one of those things, but she'd done it all and obviously done it successfully. A new admiration for her winged through him.

"Other than those text messages, the construction company is doing okay?" he asked, breaking the silence that had stretched for too long.

"Relatively okay. Since I took it over we've had some bumps in the road," she replied.

"What kind of bumps?"

She told him about Brothers Construction and the vandalism that had taken place on several of the sites. "I'm convinced they're responsible because it only happens on jobs where I underbid them. Unfortunately, I make reports and nothing comes of them."

"Does Sheriff Bud Jeffries do anything in this town?" Knox asked.

She offered him another little smile. "He eats doughnuts and glad-hands everyone important in town. He's up for reelection in the fall."

"Is anyone worthwhile running against him?" Knox finished the last of his burrito in a single bite.

"Not that I've heard."

He leaned back and watched as Allison finished the last of her meal. "How about a margarita to finish things off?" he suggested when she pushed her nearly empty plate aside. He didn't know why, but he was reluctant to end this unexpected time with her.

"I really shouldn't…but I wouldn't say no to an order of sopaipillas."

"Then the lady shall have sopaipillas." Knox gestured for the waitress and within minutes he and Allison were sharing an order of the fried pastry with dipping honey.

"I bought two ball gloves and a baseball earlier," he said. "Cody doesn't play any kind of organized sports?"

"I'm sure he'll love playing ball with you, but no, he'd much rather spend all his free time at Jade's place with the horses than on any kind of a sports team. He even asked me for a horse the other day."

Knox lifted an eyebrow. "Have you considered buying him one?"

"Not yet, and don't you think about it, either," she replied with a firm tone. "I take things slow, Knox. I want to make sure this horse thing isn't just a whim that will be forgotten next week when he suddenly decides something else is more important."

"A horse would make a fine birthday present."

"Maybe we'll talk about it when it's closer to his birthday."

"When exactly is his birthday?" It was pathetic that

he didn't know the exact date. It had been in the fall when he'd heard she'd had a baby.

"October fifth."

He nodded. "If it's a matter of the expense, I'd be more than willing to help with that."

"I appreciate that, but I'm not ready to commit to a horse just yet." She shoved her dessert plate away and glanced at her wristwatch. "I really need to get back to the office."

"Wait a minute and I'll walk you there." Once again he motioned for the waitress, this time to get their check. Within minutes they were headed for the door, and at the same time Jason Tankard walked into the restaurant.

Allison and Knox had been friends with Jason in high school and Knox greeted the tall, thin man with a friendly handshake. "How have you been, Jason?"

"Good…busy. I own the computer repair and printing place down the street and when I'm not there I'm at home chasing around three little rug rats, a boy and twin girls. I married Rebecca Cook. You remember her?"

"Sure, I do," Knox replied. He had a vague memory of a quiet, dark-haired girl with glasses. Truly, he hadn't paid much attention to the other girls in high school. He'd been so captivated by Allison.

"If I hadn't already heard you were in town, I'd for sure know it this morning," Jason said.

"Really? What happened this morning?" Knox asked curiously.

"There's a big story on all of you Coltons on *Everything's Blogger in Texas*," Jason replied.

Knox's gut tightened. "Guess I'll have to check it

out." He suddenly felt ill. Nothing good ever came from that sleazy gossip site.

"I'd better get some lunch and then get back to the store. It was good seeing you again, Knox… Allison."

"You, too, Jason," Allison replied.

They left the restaurant and this time it was Allison who linked her arm firmly with his. "I have a computer in the office if you want to check it out."

It was odd, that after everything that had happened between the two of them, she obviously sensed his tension. Of all the women in the world he wouldn't have believed that, at this time in their complicated lives, he would find support in her arm entwined with his.

He could have easily pulled up the story on his cell phone, but he was surprised to realize he wasn't ready to tell her goodbye yet.

Allison was thankful nobody was working in the shop when she and Knox arrived at her office. She sat down at her desk and turned on her computer while Knox picked up a framed photo of her father with Cody that she kept on her desk.

"Good picture. Your dad was a good man," Knox said as he put the frame back down. "He probably had nothing but hatred in his heart for me when he died."

Allison looked up in surprise. "Why on earth would you say that?"

"Surely he knew Cody was mine, and I was nowhere around."

The tension that had stiffened his shoulders when he

heard about the blog was now accompanied by a deep frown that slashed across his forehead.

"Knox, I don't know what Dad knew for sure. When I told him I was pregnant, I also told him I was going to be a single parent. He never asked me who the father was and I never told him. I do know how much he loved you when we were dating and I don't think anything that happened over the years changed his feelings for you." She was surprised to see his eyes narrow as if in pain.

"Let's see what that blog has to say," he said, his voice thicker than usual. He moved to stand behind her and placed a hand on her shoulder.

The warmth of his hand instantly evoked thoughts of the kisses they had shared, kisses she'd tried desperately to forget.

"You know this blog is nothing but idle gossip. Most people know not to believe a word of it," she said as she went to her bookmarks and clicked on the one that would take them to the page.

The headline read: Can't Get Enough of the Coltons? We Have the Real Scoop.

He leaned closer to read as she did the same. His hand tightened on her shoulder. The first two paragraphs of the blog entry were devoted to Matthew Colton, Livia's half brother. Matthew was a man who had killed nine people, including his wife, leaving his children to grow up in foster care. He'd eventually died in prison but not before telling everyone that the only thing he truly feared was his ruthless sister, Livia.

But it was the next paragraph that tensed every muscle in Allison's body.

A reliable source tells us Livia's eldest son, Knox Colton, is back in Shadow Creek and apparently he left something behind when he left town to become a Texas Ranger ten years ago…a son. He's been seen squiring the boy around town and spending time with his lover, Allison Rafferty.

The article went on to talk about River Colton being overseas as a marine and Jade's concern that Livia might return to town. Another paragraph talked about Leonor and Claudia and their lives in Austin and New York with intimate details about the two women. The next paragraph was devoted to Thorne and his father.

Knox's anger was palpable in the air. He walked around the desk and sat in the chair facing her, his jaw pulsing as his lips pressed into a tight slash.

Allison wasn't thrilled that her life had been exploited on the blog. She definitely didn't like the idea that now everyone who read the stupid website would know that Knox was Cody's father. She could only hope and pray that Livia remained in the dark about Cody's existence.

"Just let it go, Knox," she said softly, shoving her own whisper of fear aside. "Like I said before, nobody believes what they read on the site."

He leaned forward, his eyes blue fire. "I need to know who is giving out that kind of personal information."

"They're probably just making most of it up."

He shook his head. "You don't understand. Everything in that blog is true. Somebody has to be feeding them things about all of us, things that are personal." He rose to his feet. "I need to get going. I'll see you tomorrow when I pick up Cody."

Before he got to the door, Allison saw Brad Billings enter the shop. She stood and stiffened. Could this day get any worse?

"Who is that?" Knox asked.

"Brad Billings…one of the owners of the construction company who I believe has been vandalizing my sites."

Brad wasn't a tall man, but what he lacked in height he more than made up for in width. Although his arms were thick and muscled, his stomach was big and soft.

He opened the door to the office and stepped in, his brown eyes narrowed as he glared at her. "You need to keep my name out of your mouth," he said.

"Excuse me, but I don't believe we've met," Knox said.

Brad looked at him and snorted. "I know who you are and I'm not talking to you. I'm talking to this mouthy bitch who keeps talking to the sheriff about me and my brother."

Knox stepped up to Brad. "You obviously don't know who I am if you think you can talk to her that way." Knox's voice was deadly calm.

Allison hurried around her desk in an effort to keep things from escalating between the two men. "It's all right, Knox."

"No, it isn't okay," he replied, not taking his narrowed gaze off Brad.

Brad's chubby cheeks flushed and he took several

steps back from Knox. "Look, I don't want any trouble here."

"The only reason you would be here is to cause trouble," Allison replied angrily. "And I'll talk to the sheriff whenever I have vandalism on a job site. If you and your men aren't guilty of anything, then you have nothing to worry about. Now get off my property before I call the sheriff to remove you."

Brad flashed her another glare and then turned and strode out of the office.

She placed a hand on Knox's bicep, unsurprised to find it bunched and ready for action. "Remember in high school when Jake Prann called me a bad name?"

The tension in his muscles eased. "Yeah, I punched Jake in the nose and got a two-week school suspension for fighting." He looked at her with a small smile. "I really wanted to punch that doughboy in his face."

She fought against a laugh and the internal thrill of having a man protecting her. "And I appreciate the sentiment." She dropped her hand to her side. "I don't think he'll be back."

"If he does come back and you're here alone, lock your office door and call the sheriff." He reached up and gently shoved a wisp of her hair from her cheek. "I don't want anything to happen to you." He frowned and took a step back from her. "After all, you are the mother of my son. I'll see you tomorrow."

He was killing her one sweet gesture at a time, a tender caress, a stand of protectiveness and the kisses that had rocked her to her very soul. What did Knox really want from her? Another chance at getting things right between them? She seriously doubted that.

However, she could believe that he might want to seduce her into a hot sexual relationship for as long as he was in Shadow Creek. She turned and went back to her desk.

A habit. That's all they were to each other. An addictive habit as strong as smoking cigarettes, as potent as any drug on the streets.

Knox was definitely her addiction and it was one that needed to be broken. It had been ten years since she'd been in his arms as they made love. She was determined that she wasn't going to go there again with him.

Earl Hefferman sat in a cheap motel room just outside of Austin and read the *Everything's Blogger in Texas* blog entry for the day.

He had a riveting interest in everything Colton. More important, he definitely had a riveting hatred for everything Livia Colton.

He shifted positions on the lumpy bed and groaned as the wound in his side screamed in protest. She'd thought she'd killed him. Instead of paying him what she'd promised when he'd picked her up in the prison construction site and driven her to the Mexican border, she'd shot him and left him for dead.

Well, he wasn't dead. He was very much alive and Livia Colton owed him big-time. He'd been her right-hand man for years. He'd known what kind of woman she was, but despite that he'd never thought she'd turn on him.

He read the blog a second time and then slammed his laptop shut. Music blared from the room next door and he fought the impulse to bang on the wall. He reminded himself the last thing he needed was to draw attention.

Instead he picked up the bottle of prescription pain pills he'd bought from a kid on the streets. He shook one out and popped it into his mouth and then chased it with a swallow of beer.

He couldn't very well show up in any hospital or clinic with a gunshot wound. Too many questions would be asked and he couldn't afford that. It wasn't that long since he'd been on probation. Thank God packing the wound had made it stop bleeding.

He'd already given up enough of his life serving time because of his allegiance and complicity with Livia and her crimes. She owed him. He had no idea where she might be now. She could still be in Mexico or she could be in the motel room next to his.

He wouldn't put anything past her. With her beauty and charm and that soft Texas twang of hers, she could wrap most people right around her little finger.

But not Earl. Oh, no, she owed him, and one way or another she was going to pay. He stretched out on the bed as the effects of the pain pill began to work.

As sleep started to overtake him, he smiled as he thought of everything he had read on the blog about the Colton siblings. All he had to do was figure out how to use that information to get to Livia.

Chapter 6

Knox had spent most of Wednesday afternoon on the phone with all his siblings, trying to figure out how the blog had gotten so much personal information about them.

He hadn't had to call his sister Claudia. She'd called him, outraged that somebody was feeding the blog intimate details of their lives. All the rest of the siblings had denied having anything to do with the story that *Everything's Blogger in Texas* had published.

Knox couldn't imagine who the source of the information could be. Although all of her children had known of the relationship between Livia and her notorious serial killer half brother, it certainly hadn't been something she had told others. It wouldn't have fit into her narrative of being a society queen.

Whoever had talked to the person at *Everything's Blogger in Texas* had shared enough information to suggest they had intimate ties to the family. But who?

By the time Thursday afternoon rolled around, he was more than ready to put all of that behind him and spend time with Cody.

He arrived at Allison's just before the time for Cody to get off the bus and walk the short three blocks home. As he knocked on Allison's door, a restless energy filled him. He didn't know if it was because of the unresolved questions about the blog or because his night had been spent in erotic dreams of him and Allison.

She opened the door, and as always when he caught sight of her a fist of visceral want punched him in his gut. He wanted to hate her, but he couldn't. He wanted to hold a grudge against her, but as she smiled at him and gestured him inside, any ill feelings were impossible to maintain.

And that irritated him.

"When are we going to tell Cody that I'm his father?" he said in greeting.

The smile of welcome that had been on her lips fell away. "Knox, you've only been in town a week."

"Yeah, well I'm thinking about all the years I've already missed with him." He narrowed his gaze on her. "Besides, now anyone who read that stupid blog knows about my relationship with him."

"He's not ready yet." She crossed her arms defensively.

"He likes me well enough," Knox retorted. He wasn't sure why but a part of him wanted to pick a fight with her, to get a bad taste in his mouth where she was concerned. "What if one of his school friends says something to him? I'd rather he find out from us than on the streets."

"He didn't mention anyone saying anything to him yesterday when the blog was published." Her frown deepened. "I know he likes you, Knox, but he hasn't known you long enough to love you…to trust you. I…I wanted that for you before you tell him."

Knox jammed his hands in his pockets, deeply frustrated. Would it be better to wait until Cody loved him to tell him the truth? Surely telling Cody the truth would only made the boy love him faster.

He didn't know what was right or wrong in all this. Was he putting his own needs before Cody's? That's the very last thing he wanted to do. His mother had done that all her life where her children were concerned.

"Okay, we do it your way and wait," he finally said. "But if he comes home from school and starts asking questions because somebody said something to him, then you need to call me right away and we will talk to him together."

"Of course," she readily agreed.

Knox wanted to be angry. He didn't know if the root cause of that emotion was the tell-all blog, his desire to let Cody know who he was, or his ever-present desire for Allison. And he wasn't sure if it wasn't something deeper…something he refused to acknowledge even to himself.

Cody burst through the door, bringing with him sunshine and smiles, and Knox's anger couldn't be sustained with his son's happy presence.

"How was school?" he asked after Cody greeted them and as he put his backpack in the hall closet.

"It was okay. We had a spelling quiz and I got all the words right."

"I knew you were a smart kid the first time I met you," Knox replied.

Cody beamed up at him. "So, what are we gonna do today, Knox?"

"I thought we'd go back to Thorne's and play some catch with a baseball and then build a fire in the barbecue pit and cook some hamburgers and hot dogs," Knox said.

"That sounds cool, but I don't have a baseball or a glove," Cody replied.

"I've got you covered. I've got two new ball mitts and a baseball in the car. One of the mitts is yours to keep."

"That's awesome." Cody's eyes shone.

"And what do you say?" Allison said.

"I say 'thank you,'" Cody replied with a wide grin.

"Go up and get a jacket before you leave," Allison instructed. "It will be cool as the sun goes down."

"I'll be right back." Cody raced up the stairs.

"Hey, mister…slow down," Allison called after him and then looked back at Knox. "You'll have him home by seven?"

He nodded. "Have you gotten any more nasty texts from Chad?"

"No. Nothing today. Maybe Sheriff Jeffries talking to him did the trick."

"What about Brad?"

"No other problems with him, either. Thankfully it's been a peaceful day."

Cody came back downstairs with a navy jacket in his hand. "Okay, I'm ready to go." He turned to look at Allison. "What are you going to do tonight while I'm gone?"

"I don't know, maybe I'll dye my hair pink and start a rock-and-roll band," she replied, her eyes wonderfully warm and sparkling as she gazed at her son.

Cody rolled his eyes and looked at Knox. "Don't worry, she isn't really going to do that. She's probably just going to watch some sappy, girlie movie."

Knox envied their easy, loving relationship. It was love without condition and he had never had anything like that in his life…except maybe briefly with Allison…before she lied to him…before she'd ripped his heart out.

"Let's get going, champ," he said, and after a final goodbye he and Cody headed out the door.

During the drive to Thorne's, Knox asked Cody questions about school, his teacher and his friends. He wanted to know everything he could about Cody's life.

He wanted to know the names of the friends he spent his spare time with and what things interested him other than horses. He needed to know what foods he liked and what television shows he enjoyed. He even wanted to know what his son dreamed about when he slept.

Time.

Allison was right; he needed to be patient and allow the relationship to build naturally. He just hoped Cody didn't hear about him being his father from someone else.

The way he felt about Cody only magnified the utter dysfunction in his own family. His father hadn't wanted him enough to fight for him and Livia had only wanted him when it was convenient to trot him out for a photo op. Knox would take a bullet for Cody, but he knew without doubt if faced with a gunman his mother would have used Knox as a shield.

He and Cody played catch in Thorne's pasture for about forty minutes or so and then saddled up two of Thorne's horses for a short ride.

He made sure that the horse Cody mounted was a gentle mare and he was proud to see how the boy sat easily and relaxed in the saddle. Cody was obviously a natural.

They rode slowly, chatting about anything and nothing. They were almost back to the stables when Cody asked him if he had a girlfriend.

"No girlfriend for me," Knox replied.

"And you aren't married, right?"

"Right. Why?" He looked at Cody curiously, but Cody refused to meet his gaze.

"I was just wondering. You know my mom isn't married and she doesn't have a boyfriend." Cody then shot a quick glance at him. "My mom is really pretty and she can cook real good, too. Don't you think she's pretty, Knox?"

Uh-oh. Knox definitely smelled an attempted matchmaking going on. Aware that he should tread lightly, Knox took a moment before replying. "Yes, your mother is very pretty, Cody. But I'm not looking for a girlfriend right now."

"Why not? Don't you ever get lonely, Knox?"

Over the past ten years, loneliness had been a constant companion. Sure, Knox had made lifetime friends with some of his fellow Rangers, but friendship hadn't filled the core isolation that had plagued him since he'd left Shadow Creek behind.

"I think Mom is lonely," Cody continued before Knox could reply. "She's got me, but I think she really needs a boyfriend."

"Maybe she'll find one someday," Knox replied, hoping that would put an end to any further idea Cody might have of playing Cupid.

Still, Knox was vaguely surprised that the thought of Allison with another man bothered him more than a little bit. Seeing her again, being around her again, had definitely stirred up some old feelings…feelings he didn't want to have.

It was while they were eating dinner with Thorne that Cody brought up the subject of a horse of his own. "Maybe Mom would listen to both of you if you'd talk to her. I'm ready to have my own horse, and I'd ride him and brush him and take real good care of him."

Thorne raised his hands with a laugh. "Don't get me involved in this."

Cody looked at Knox. "Then you could talk to her, Knox. She likes you and she'd listen to you. You saw how good I ride. You know I'm ready for a horse of my own."

"I can't promise anything but I'll put in a good word for you," Knox said.

"Thanks," Cody replied. "Now could I have another hot dog?"

They finished up dinner and cleanup and by then it was time to take Cody home. "I thought maybe you'd like to spend Saturday with me at Jade's," Knox said as they pulled into Allison's driveway. "I know you usually work there on Saturdays, so your mom and I thought we could hang out there together."

Knox parked the car but didn't turn off the engine. "It's okay with me if it's okay with you. Aren't you coming in?" Cody asked.

"Not tonight," Knox replied.

"But I thought you were gonna put in a good word for me…you know, about a horse."

Knox smiled at his son. "And I promise I will, but tonight I need to get back to Thorne's. I'll be back here bright and early on Saturday and maybe I can sneak in a good word or two for you then."

"Okay. Thanks for a great day and I'll see you Saturday."

Knox watched his son as he raced to the front door. It was only when Cody was inside the house that he backed out of the driveway and headed back to Thorne's.

He hadn't gone inside to see Allison because he wanted to go inside and see her. The talk about loneliness and boyfriends had left him feeling oddly vulnerable, and there was no way he wanted to see her with the hollowness that blew through him at the moment.

He definitely didn't want to think about Allison being lonely. There had been a time when they'd filled each other up, made each other whole.

She'd mourned the absence of her mother and he'd mourned the absence of a kind and loving parent. Besides their overwhelming sexual chemistry, they had been the best of friends.

But those times were long gone and there was no going back. It was probably just nostalgia making him want Allison again.

He'd dated several women in the last ten years and had looked for that chemistry, that basis of friendship with each woman, but the ideal mate he'd sought had been elusive.

When his mother was caught, he'd return to his job in El Paso. He'd come back to Shadow Creek for vacations and whenever he had time off to see Cody, and he'd have his son visit him there whenever possible.

There was no reason for him and Allison to have a relationship other than what they needed for the well-being of their son. He didn't need to come inside the house and talk to her when he picked up or dropped off Cody.

He could want her all day long, but taking her to bed without any plans to have her in his life wasn't fair to her and ultimately it wasn't fair to him.

There was only one thing he had to keep in mind. Fort Knox didn't need anyone in his life except the son he hadn't known existed.

Allison hurried through the front door and into the kitchen, where she deposited her purse on the table. It had been a hellacious week and if she was completely honest with herself, she'd admit that she didn't mind that Knox was picking up Cody for their Thursday evening together.

She could use the hours they were gone to completely relax and get the bad taste that work had left out of her mouth. They'd had to make another police report that morning about more vandalism on the Wilkenson place, and she'd had to spend a half an hour on the phone assuring the new owners that there would be no delays on the work being completed according to the timeline they'd agreed to.

She'd also had to move two of her men from another job to the Wilkenson one to make sure she hadn't made a false promise to the owners.

She sank down at the table and looked at her watch. Knox should be arriving at any moment, but she didn't expect him to come inside the house.

Both Saturday and Tuesday, when he'd picked up and dropped off Cody, he hadn't come inside. She should be relieved that he apparently was seeking some distance from her, and it irritated her that rather than feeling relieved she was more than a little bit disappointed.

Cody had come home from his time with Knox bubbling with happiness. It was obvious the two were growing very close. Maybe it was time for her and Knox to sit down with Cody and tell him the truth.

Just maybe it was time for her to trust that Knox would always make Cody a priority in his life. They had been lucky so far that Cody hadn't heard any rumors after the blog had outed Knox as his father. If anyone was talking about it in the community, then they were talking behind her back because nobody had said a word to her.

She got up from the table, walked over to the window and stared out at the sky blue birdhouse that hung from one of the tree limbs. Next to it hung another birdhouse. It had once been a bright pink, but had weathered over the years to a pastel.

She'd been ten when she and her father had built that one together. She remembered sitting at the kitchen table and listening as he told her how to fit the wood together and how important it was to nail them together tightly so the birds would have a nice, dry home.

She'd felt so warm, so loved as his big hands had covered her smaller ones to guide her, as she'd breathed in the scent that belonged to her father alone.

Father.

Cody needed to know that he had one who loved him. She saw the love that shone from Cody's eyes when he talked about Knox. Yes, it was definitely time to make it official.

She turned away from the window and walked to the front door. She peered outside to see Knox's car sitting in the driveway.

She went out the door and walked to the car, intensely self-conscious as he watched her. No man's gaze had ever filled her with the heat that his did. He could make her feel completely naked with a languid glance from those bright blue eyes.

He rolled down the car window as she approached. "What's up?" he asked.

"I was wondering if you want to come inside. I think

maybe it's time for you and me to sit down and have a little talk with Cody."

His eyes instantly lit up with warmth and a hope that touched her heart. Allison suddenly remembered the absolute wonder, the overwhelming joy she'd felt when the doctor had first placed Cody in her arms. She was now sorry that she'd deprived Knox of that miracle moment.

"You think he's ready?" he asked.

"I think we're all ready," she replied. She stepped aside as he opened the door and got out of the car.

"It's crazy, but I feel as nervous as I did the first time I asked you out for a date," he said once they were in the house.

She looked at him in surprise. "You were nervous when you asked me out?"

He smiled at her, the warm, wonderful smile that she remembered from that day so long ago. "God, yes. It took me a full week to work up my nerve."

"The smooth Knox Colton? Trust me, it didn't show." She sat on the sofa and he took the chair opposite her.

"Do I look nervous now?" He raised a hand and swept it through his short hair.

This unexpected vulnerability, the show of nerves she'd never known him to possess, once again shot an arrow of sweetness through her heart. His uncharacteristic openness only spoke of his love for his son.

"You look fine, Knox," she replied.

He leaned forward. "Do we need to come up with a story about why I haven't been around before now?" A frown danced across his forehead. "I don't want him to believe anything or anyone was ever more important to me than him."

Fear suddenly replaced the warmth that Allison had been feeling. If they told him the truth, that she hadn't informed Knox about Cody, then would Cody hate her for keeping his father from him? Would this build a new relationship between Cody and Knox and at the same time destroy hers with her son?

"Allison, I don't want you to take the fall for this," he said as if reading her mind. "I definitely don't want this to ruin the relationship you have with him. There's no reason he needs to know everything that transpired between the two of us at that time. Why don't we just tell him that I was off fighting crime and you didn't know where I was or how to contact me to tell me about him?"

"That works for me if it works for you," she replied in relief. There was really no reason to assign blame in this situation; besides she wasn't the only one to blame for the circumstances that had led them to the here and now. In any case, there was no reason to burden a child with adult things.

Knox checked his wristwatch. "He should be here anytime. Maybe the three of us should go to dinner together tonight to celebrate."

As much as she would like that, she didn't want Cody to get the idea that somehow, someway they were going to all be one, big, happy family. She didn't want to fool herself into believing they could ever be a family again.

"Thanks, Knox, but I think the occasion calls for a father-son celebration," she replied. She wasn't sure whether he was relieved or disappointed that she didn't intend to join them.

He stood from the chair and glanced at his watch once again. "You want to come outside and wait for him with me?"

"Okay," she agreed. They stepped out the front door and she took a seat on the swing, vaguely surprised when he joined her there.

"Still no more texts from Chad?" he asked and kicked his foot to move the swing back and forth.

"No texts, but the last two days he's been sitting on the bench in front of the post office across the street from my office and staring at my building. It's like he's reminding me that he's still around and he's still angry."

Knox put a foot down to stop the swing. "Did you call the sheriff?"

"For what? It isn't against the law for a man to sit on a bench." It had certainly been unsettling and more than a little bit creepy, but there was really nothing she could do about it.

"You want me to punch him in the nose?" He asked the question lightly, but the intensity of his gaze on her let her know he'd do it in a minute if she asked.

She laughed. "I appreciate your chivalry, Mr. Colton, but I would hate for Cody to have to visit you in jail, and there's no doubt in my mind Chad would press charges against you."

"Speaking of Cody, where is he?" Knox got up from the swing and moved to the edge of the porch where he could look up the sidewalk.

Allison looked at her wristwatch. "He's only five

minutes later than usual. Some days he's as much as fifteen minutes later because either the bus was slow to leave the school or the bus driver pulled over to the side of the street to yell at the kids if they got too rowdy."

Knox shot her a warm smile. "I'm just more than ready to be his dad for real." His smile fell and he held her gaze. "Whether I return to the Rangers or not, Cody is always going to be a priority in my life. I promise you that."

"Whether you return? Is there some question of you not returning?"

He frowned. "No, of course I'm eventually going back. I just want you to know that no matter where I live, no matter what I do, I'll always figure out a way to be a good father to Cody."

"That's all I want from you, Knox," she replied. But there was a little part of her that could still drown in the blue waters of his eyes and a big chunk of her heart that would always belong to him.

He nodded and then turned and looked up the sidewalk once again. He shifted from one foot to the other, obviously impatient.

Several more minutes passed without them speaking. Allison took the opportunity to drink in the sight of him as he continued to keep his focus up the street.

Today he wore a long-sleeved black polo shirt with dark-colored jeans. He looked so tall, so physically fit and overwhelmingly handsome. He didn't have his hat on, and his light brown hair gleamed in the sunlight.

She could admit to herself that she still wanted him

and she knew he would welcome her into his bed once again. But, the stakes were too high now.

If they did fall back into old habits, then her heart would be as shredded as it had been ten years ago when he'd called her to tell her he needed a break from her. And with her shredded heart she would hate him and that's the last emotion she wanted to feel for the father of her son. They had to remain civilized and smart for Cody's sake.

She looked at her watch once again and frowned. Cody should have come home by now. This was the latest he'd ever been. A flutter of concern shot off inside her. She got up from the swing and walked over to stand next to Knox.

"He's definitely late today," she admitted.

"Could he have stopped off at a friend's house?" Knox asked.

"Our number one rule when I agreed to let him walk home from school was that he come straight home from the bus stop." The concern pressed a little tighter against her chest.

"You do realize that sometimes little boys break the rules," Knox replied.

"He's never broken the rule before."

"There's always a first time," he countered.

Would Cody stop at a friend's house, knowing that Knox would be here waiting for him? Even if he forgot that Knox would be here today, would Cody really risk her anger by doing something he knew was wrong?

Perhaps. *He's only nine*, she reminded herself. He

wasn't fully cooked yet. "Maybe he stopped in at his friend Josh's house and lost track of the time."

"Where does Josh live?" The darkness in Knox's eyes mirrored the worry that suddenly gripped Allison by the throat.

"In the next block. I'll just go inside and call Josh's mother." She was vaguely aware of Knox following just behind her as she went into the kitchen and got her cell phone out of her purse.

Surely Cody was there. Maybe Josh had gotten a new video game or a brightly colored fish for his aquarium and had invited Cody in to take a look. Little boys didn't always think about the time.

"Marianne," she said when Josh's mother answered the call. "It's Allison. I was just wondering if maybe Cody stopped by after school."

"No, he's not here, Allison."

"Can you ask Josh if Cody was on the bus to come home?"

"Josh woke up with a fever this morning and so I kept him home from school. He wouldn't know if Cody was on the bus or not," Marianne replied.

"Oh, okay, thanks, Marianne." Allison hung up and stared at Knox, her brain attempting to work out a logical scenario. "He's not there. Maybe he missed the bus and is still at the school," she said. "Or maybe he got into trouble and is in the principal's office right now."

"Wouldn't somebody from the school have called you if that was the case?"

"Maybe somebody tried and I didn't hear the phone." She picked up her cell once again, but no calls had come in while she'd been outside. She then went to the desk to check her landline. No messages and no missed calls.

Don't panic, she told herself. If she panicked, she wouldn't be able to think clearly. Surely Cody would walk through the door at any minute, apologizing for being late and begging her not to be mad at him.

"Let me drive up the street and see if I see him anywhere," Knox suggested. "While I'm doing that, why don't you call the school and see if for some reason he's still there?"

He strode out of the kitchen and Allison dialed the number for the school office. As she waited for the phone to be answered, wild thoughts flew through her head.

What if he hadn't been in school all day? She'd seen him out the front door that morning but there was no way for her to know if he'd actually made it to school. Surely if he'd been absent without her calling him in sick, somebody would have checked with her to see why he wasn't in class.

For the first time ever she prayed that Cody had gotten into trouble in school, that he was now ensconced in the office waiting to learn his punishment.

"Shadow Creek Elementary." Lauren Patten's professional voice pulled Allison out of her thoughts.

"Lauren, it's Allison Rafferty. Could you tell me if Cody is in the office?"

"No, I saw him get on his bus as usual this afternoon. Is there a problem?"

"He hasn't come home from school and I thought

maybe he'd gotten into trouble or something." Allison's heartbeat accelerated.

"Cody never gets into trouble. I'm sorry I can't help you, Allison, but I know for sure he got on the bus to go home."

Allison murmured a thank-you and hung up, her heart now beating so fast she was half-breathless. At that moment Knox returned and in his hand he had a bright red backpack… Cody's backpack.

"Where did you find that?" Her chest ached as she stared first at the bag and then at him.

"In a front yard down the street." He tossed the backpack on the sofa. His jaw ticked and his eyes were narrow slits of blue fire. "Call the sheriff. I think somebody took Cody."

Somebody took Cody?

As his words penetrated her brain, Allison's knees buckled and she would have hit the floor if Knox hadn't reached out to catch her.

Somebody took Cody.

The words echoed in her brain in a horrifying refrain.

Chapter 7

"We need to get out there and look for him, Knox. Maybe he fell somewhere and hit his head, or broke his leg." Allison grabbed Knox's forearm, her fingers icy cold and her eyes wide with alarm. "Maybe he's lying unconscious in a yard up the street right now. We've got to find him." Her voice held more than an edge of hysteria.

Knox took her by the shoulders firmly. It was obvious she was in complete denial to the idea that Cody might have been taken by somebody. "I checked the yards, Allison. He isn't there. Can you think of any other friends he might have gone to play with?" he asked.

"I don't know...maybe Tim. Cody has gone to his house for playdates before." Her face was almost as white as her blouse.

"You call anyplace you think he might have possibly gone and I'm going to call the sheriff." Knox knew without a doubt that she wasn't going to find Cody at any friend's house.

He'd gotten off the bus and there's no way he would have just dropped his backpack to the ground and wandered off. Somebody had grabbed him. Knox knew it with a gut instinct. Somebody had kidnapped his son, and the faster the sheriff and his men got involved, the better the odds of finding him.

Knox should have never picked up the backpack. He'd had enough law enforcement training to know better. But the horror of seeing it on the ground had circumvented all good sense. He'd grabbed it up and held it to his chest...not a response of a trained Texas Ranger, but rather that of a desperate father.

He made the 9-1-1 call and they waited for the sheriff to arrive. He paced the floor while Allison sat on the edge of the sofa, her eyes half-glazed with fear, and there was nothing he could do, nothing he could say to take the fear away. It resonated in his gut, as well.

She grabbed the backpack and opened it. "Maybe there's a note or something inside that might tell us where he's gone."

She pulled out a couple of textbooks and a notebook. She thumbed through the notebook but apparently didn't find anything that might tell them where Cody had gone. She set the backpack next to her and gazed at him with frightened eyes.

Minutes ticked by in agonizing silence. Knox was intensely aware that each minute was a minute lost in searching for his son. The burn of anger in his belly couldn't compete with the taste of fear in his mouth.

What was happening? Who might be responsible for Cody's absence? He swallowed hard against the fear, not allowing it to completely consume him.

Allison now gripped her cell phone so tightly in her hand that her fingers were white. Her home phone receiver was in her lap. He knew she was hoping for a call from somebody, from anybody, letting her know that Cody was all right and would be home soon.

Knox moved to the front window and stared outside. Where in the hell was the sheriff? They needed to form a search party immediately. They needed to get people out on the streets asking questions and hunting for Cody.

He would be out there right now, interviewing all the people who lived on the block where he'd found the backpack, if it wasn't for the fact that Allison looked as if she was hanging on to her sanity by a thread.

"It's got to be Chad," she finally said, breaking the painful silence. "He said he'd screw up my life, and what better way than this?"

If Chad had taken Cody in an effort to get back at Allison, then the man better not hurt his son in any way. If he did…then Knox would kill him without blinking an eye.

"Would he have gotten into a stranger's car?" he asked.

"Never. I've had all those talks with Cody. We even have a safe word in case of an emergency when somebody else might have to pick him up for any reason."

"We need to just wait for Sheriff Jeffries," Knox replied. "I'm sure he'll check out Chad." It was now almost an hour from when Cody should have been home, over twenty minutes since Knox had called 9-1-1. Didn't anyone in this damned town care that a little boy was missing?

He was just about to make a second call when the sheriff's car finally pulled up in the driveway. He watched as Sheriff Bud Jeffries got out of his car.

The lawman looked to be in his middle forties. A bit of scalp shone through thinning blond hair as he slowly ambled toward the front door.

Knox despised the man already. He wanted sure, determined footsteps to carry help their way. He wanted a man with a mission in his eyes…the mission to find a missing child who should have been home an hour ago.

Knox opened the door to allow him inside. "Knox Colton," he said grimly as Allison joined them just inside the door.

"Sheriff Jeffries," he replied.

"Sheriff, Cody didn't come home from the bus stop," Allison said. "And Knox found his backpack on the ground between here and the bus stop." Tears welled up in her eyes. "Somebody must have taken him. We think he's been kidnapped."

"Whoa, let's not jump to conclusions here," Bud replied with a small laugh. "How long has he been gone?"

"Almost an hour now," Knox responded tersely.

Bud ran a hand down his shirt front, where the buttons strained across a slightly paunchy belly. "It's a beautiful day outside. Maybe he and a couple of friends are playing together and forgot all about the time. It happens a lot."

"Cody knows he's supposed to come straight home from the bus stop," Allison replied as she swiped at an errant tear that fell on her cheek.

"Ah, but sometimes boys will be boys, right?" Bud replied with a rueful smile.

Knox's hands curled into fists at his side. Dammit, he wanted the sheriff to be as frantic as they were. He wanted the man to feel a sense of urgency. Something was wrong; otherwise Cody would be there.

"Allison has checked with all his friends. He isn't with any of them. As she told you, I found his backpack on the ground between here and the bus stop. Cody would have never left his backpack anywhere," Knox replied evenly. "You need to get some men out here and set up a search."

Bud's brown eyes narrowed slightly. "I don't take my orders from a Colton."

Knox stepped back in surprise and his blood boiled, but he maintained his control with tremendous effort. After all, they needed this man and his resources right now.

"Then consider me just an ordinary taxpayer," Knox replied curtly.

Bud took a step back from him and grimaced, as if aware that he might have crossed a line.

"You need to check out Chad," Allison said. "I showed you the horrible texts he sent to me. He swore he'd make me pay for firing him." A sob escaped her and Knox placed an arm around her shoulder.

"We've got a child missing under suspicious circumstances, given that his backpack was on the ground where it shouldn't have been," Knox said.

"Ms. Rafferty, was your son upset with you for any reason when he left for school this morning?"

Allison stared at him as if in disbelief. "No, Cody wasn't upset with me or anything else in his life. He's a happy boy and if you think he ran away, then you're dead wrong. He didn't run away," she replied.

"Time is passing by with no answers. For God's sake, do something," Knox said in open frustration.

Bud frowned. "I'll get a couple of deputies out here to canvass the area and I'll head over to Chad's to check him out. In the meantime, let me know if you hear from Cody. I wouldn't be a bit surprised if he showed up here anytime after having a bit of an adventure with a friend."

"He's not taking this seriously," Allison said once Jeffries had left the house. The tears she'd obviously tried to hold back since they had called 9-1-1 now fell in earnest down her cheeks. "Where's our son, Knox? Where can he be?"

He grabbed her to him and she buried her head in his chest as she cried. "We'll find him, Allison. I promise we'll find him and bring him home safe and sound."

As she continued to weep, he hoped and prayed that he hadn't just made a promise he couldn't keep.

"We questioned everyone who was home between here and the bus stop," Deputy Wendall Kincaid explained.

"Nobody we spoke to saw anything suspicious and none of them saw Cody," Deputy Jim Baker added. "But most people had no reason to be looking out the window at the time the bus stopped."

Allison stared at them wordlessly, willing them to say something different, wanting desperately for one of them to tell her that Cody was safe and sound in the back of their patrol car. "So what happens now?" she finally asked.

"Do you know your son's school bus driver?" Wendall asked.

"We already called her," Knox said. "She told us that Cody was on the bus and got off at his stop as usual this afternoon. He was walking down the sidewalk toward home when she pulled away."

"And when he went to school this morning, he didn't say anything that might indicate to you that he planned to stop somewhere after school?" Wendall looked at Allison.

She searched her mind frantically to remember everything that had happened that morning before school. She'd fixed Cody pancakes for breakfast and they'd laughed at her attempt to make them in the shape of horses. He'd told her he had a math test that day but he was confident he'd ace it. It had been one of their routine, normal morning conversations.

"Nothing," she replied desperately. "Cody knew that Knox would be waiting here for him this afternoon and he was looking forward to spending time with him."

"Have either of you spoken to Sheriff Jeffries? He

was going to check out Chad Watkins, who has made some threats against Allison," Knox asked.

"We haven't been in contact with him since he radioed us and told us to get over here," Wendall replied.

"So what happens now?" Allison asked again. "Can't you get more deputies to look for him? Maybe you should check with the Billings brothers. They've been giving me a lot of trouble lately."

Her brain was frozen with a horrifying disbelief that this was happening. It was past dinnertime. Cody should be sitting in a restaurant with his father celebrating their newfound relationship. Or he should be here and she'd make grilled ham and cheese sandwiches with chicken noodle soup...one of his favorites.

"I'm sure Sheriff Jeffries is going to put more men on this, but in the meantime maybe you should contact some of your own friends to search for him," Jim said sympathetically.

"We're going to go back and knock on more doors and see if we can find somebody who might have seen Cody after he got off the bus," Wendall added.

Allison stumbled backward to the sofa and sat as Knox walked with the two deputies out the front door. She was in a horrible nightmare and the only thing that would wake her up was the sound of Cody's voice, the sight of him right here where he belonged.

She wanted to run outside. She needed to race up and down the streets and knock on doors, calling his name until he answered her, and yet she was afraid to leave here in case somebody brought him home or he called her to come and get him.

Kidnapped. Was that really what had happened to him? The word had no place in her reality. If Chad had taken him to teach her a lesson, then what was it she was supposed to learn? And when would he bring him back?

Tears once again burned hot at her eyes, but she consciously swallowed against them. She couldn't fall apart right now. Her son needed her to be strong.

She jumped up off the sofa as Knox came back inside. "I don't know how seriously the sheriff is taking it, but those two deputies seem to be taking it very seriously," he said.

"Wendall has a boy a year younger than Cody," she replied. "And Jim has two little girls." Both of them were parents. They'd know what she was going through. They'd do everything they could to get Cody back for her.

"I called Thorne and Mac to come over and help with a search. Maybe you could make a pot of coffee?"

"Of course," she replied, grateful for something, for anything to do besides fall completely apart. She went into the kitchen and prepared the coffee. As she waited for it to brew, she stared out the window.

It wouldn't be long before dusk would fall and after that the darkness of night. Surely he'd be home before his bedtime. Surely she'd get to tuck him in tonight as she had so many times before. When night came, he needed to be in his bed with the stars on his ceiling shining down on him. She had to believe that.

She closed her eyes as she remembered the sweet kiss on the cheek Cody had given her that morning before he'd left for the bus stop and how they'd laughed at her silly-looking pancakes. She'd give anything she possessed to hear his laughter once again, to feel his kiss once again.

If he had made a mistake and gone to play and lost track of the time, she wouldn't be angry with him as long as he came home.

The coffee had just finished making when Sheriff Jeffries arrived once again. The fact that he didn't have Cody in tow increased the despair inside Allison.

"Unfortunately I haven't been able to locate Chad," he said. "He's not at his home and he isn't in any of the bars. The bartender at the Whiskey Sour said he was in earlier and left about three thirty. I've instructed my men to stop him if they see him."

"What about the Billings brothers?" she asked. "Have you spoken with them?"

Bud frowned. "Why would I talk to them?"

"You know they've been vandalizing my jobs," Allison replied, her voice slightly raised.

"I know no such thing," Bud replied. "I know you've had some vandalism and that you suspect them, but we haven't found any proof that they're responsible. Besides, Brad and Bob aren't the kind of men who would take a kid."

"But Brad is the kind of man who would threaten a woman in her office," Knox replied. She could feel the tension that rolled off him.

"Yeah, Brad told me about his knucklehead move to talk to Allison in her office," Bud replied with a wry grin. "I told him not to pull something like that again."

"So maybe he decided to take Cody instead," Allison replied. "Sheriff Jeffries, you have to take this seriously."

"I am taking it seriously," he replied and puffed up his chest. "I've told all the men on the streets to look for the boy."

"Cody. His name is Cody," Knox replied evenly. "We're planning on getting together a search party with friends and relatives. Do you want to coordinate it?"

"I'm overseeing the search by my own men and attempting to find Chad. I can't be at ten places at one time," Bud replied defensively.

Lazy, Allison thought bitterly. Even now, with a child missing from his home, Bud didn't want to commit himself to working too hard. There had been many in town who had been complaining about Bud's indolence.

"Wouldn't it help your men to have a picture of Cody?" Knox asked, his voice the deceptive calm that she knew hid a wealth of anger.

Bud rocked back on his heels. "I was just about to ask for one."

"Allison, do you have an up-to-date photo of Cody?" Knox asked gently.

The request suddenly made this even more horrifyingly real. When was the last time she'd taken a picture of her son? She couldn't remember. God, she hadn't taken enough pictures of him. She should have been taking one of him every single day.

"The latest one is his school picture," she finally replied. "I have some in the kitchen desk drawer." She went into the kitchen, sat down at the desk and pulled open the drawer that held the envelope of her son's school pictures.

Her fingers trembled as she withdrew a sheet of four five-by-seven prints. One was missing. She'd cut it off and framed it the day he'd brought them home. It was on the stand next to her bed where she could gaze at it first thing in the morning and right before she went to sleep.

She stared at Cody's image. He'd insisted he wear his favorite blue plaid shirt, which made his bright blue eyes appear even bluer. His wide smile invited everyone around him to smile, as well.

A lump formed in the back of her throat. *Don't cry*, she commanded herself. To cry meant she had abandoned hope, and that was all she had right now. A warm hand fell on her shoulder. She looked up to see Knox, his gaze riveted to the pictures.

"Do you have any wallet-sized?" he asked.

"Is that what Sheriff Jeffries wants?"

"That's what I want. I want to carry a picture of my son in my wallet." A wealth of hunger, of love was in his voice.

If she focused on his emotion, she would have a complete and total breakdown. She pulled out a pair of scissors and cut a wallet-sized photo for him and the bigger one for the sheriff.

"You'll keep us posted as to what you find out?" Knox asked Bud as he handed him the photo.

"Of course, and you let me know if the b…Cody shows up here. I'm assigning Deputy Kincaid and Deputy Baker to sit here with you. They'll be back here in a little while." With that Bud left.

For a long moment Allison and Knox stared at each other, and in that moment his eyes were completely unguarded and the pain that shone there mirrored her own. She wanted desperately to fall into his arms, but that wouldn't make Cody magically appear.

"Do you really think he's been kidnapped?" she asked softly. Her brain flashed on the fact that Livia Colton was someplace running free. Was she behind this? Oh God, she couldn't even think such a terrible thing right now.

He released a deep sigh and jammed his hands in his pockets. "To be honest, I don't know what to think." His eyes were shadowed but the vulnerability that had been there moments before was gone. "But we have to consider that it's definitely a real possibility."

"He said the bartender told him Chad left the bar at around three thirty. He would have had time to take Cody," she said.

At that moment a knock fell on the door. Knox answered to allow in Mac and Thorne. "Thanks for coming," Knox said. "I'm not sure exactly what the sheriff is doing, but I figured we needed to get some people out searching."

Mac frowned. "If I know Bud Jeffries, he's doing as little as possible."

Allison listened as Knox filled them in on finding the backpack in the next block over. She assumed Knox had told Mac and Thorne about Cody being his son in the last week.

Everyone froze as the house phone rang. *Let it be*

Cody, Allison prayed as she hurried to pick it up. Knox's hand crashed down on hers just before she answered.

"Put it on speaker," he said urgently.

She realized he thought it might be a ransom call. A surge of nausea rose up inside her as she picked up the receiver. "Hello?" Her voice was a mere whisper.

"Allison, it's Lauren Patten from the school. I was just wondering if Cody ever got home okay."

Allison expelled a shuddery sigh, unsure if she was disappointed that it wasn't a call from a kidnapper or relieved that it was the school receptionist. "No, Lauren, he hasn't come home yet. We've gotten the police involved but we'd appreciate anyone who wants to join a search party for him."

"I'll see who I can round up," Lauren replied.

"We've got about an hour and a half or so left of daylight," Knox said when Allison hung up the phone.

"We'll head out," Thorne said and then left the house with Mac.

Once again Allison and Knox were alone with their despair, a living, breathing third person. "What do we do now?" she finally asked bleakly.

"We wait."

The two words thundered in Allison's head. How long before they had an answer? How long before she could clutch her precious boy to her chest and feel his heartbeat against her own? How long before Cody was home where he belonged?

Chapter 8

By seven thirty, the house was filled with well-meaning people and Deputy Wendall Kincaid, who sat at a chair in the kitchen and fielded calls from fellow officers and tried to coordinate the neighbors and friends who had shown up to search.

Allison was in the kitchen, making sandwiches and more coffee for those who had come to help. She appeared efficient and in control, unless Knox looked into her eyes, which held her intense, screaming despair.

Knox was just grateful she had something to do to keep her busy and a couple of friends to chat with her and offer support. He paced the floor, waiting for something to happen, and finally climbed the stairs to Cody's bedroom.

He stood in the threshold and stared at the top bunk.

He'd tucked Cody into bed with a pat on the shoulder and Cody had placed his hand on Knox's cheek.

I'm glad you want to spend time with me, Knox, he'd said. *I really like being with you.* Knox had tucked the sheet around his neck and wished him happy dreams. He wanted to do it again. He wanted to tuck his son into bed tonight and tell him how much he loved him, how happy he was that Cody was his son.

The room held the scent of little boy and big dreams. Knox's gaze shifted to the miniature horses on the shelves. His heart swelled in his chest, making it difficult to draw a breath. The glow-in-the-dark stars on the ceiling would soon be shining, but Cody wasn't here to see them.

Where are you, son? How can I find you and bring you home where you belong? There was no way he believed Cody had run away. Cody loved his home and his mother, and Knox hoped he had started to love him.

Before a wealth of emotion could grab him by the throat, he left the bedroom and headed back down the stairs. As darkness began to fall, a frantic restlessness filled him.

He was a Texas Ranger, not accustomed to sitting around and waiting for answers. He was usually out pounding the pavement and turning over rocks to find answers.

Finally he couldn't stand it any longer. He needed to get outside and do his own search before night fell with its deep darkness and secrets.

He strode into the kitchen to talk to Allison. She

stood at the sink with her hands immersed in soapy water as she washed several coffee cups.

"I can't just hang out here anymore. I need to go out and look for him," he said.

He hated how white, how strained her features were. "I should come with you," she said as she grabbed a towel to dry her hands.

He shook his head. "You need to stay here in case we get a phone call."

"It's important that you be here, Allison," Wendall said from his seat at the table. "If Cody comes home, he'll need his mother."

"Yes, of course. You're both right. I should stay here," she quickly agreed. She twisted the towel so tight her fingers were white. "You'll call if you find him?"

Knox shot the deputy a grateful look and then gazed at Allison once again. "Of course I will. I'll be back later," he said.

He left, torn between the need to be in the house and be an emotional support for her and his own need to do something…anything, to find his son. At least she had some friends here, he reminded himself as he walked out the front door.

Rather than take his car, he took off on foot to retrace the route that Cody would have taken from the bus stop. Although he knew the deputies and some of the other searchers would have come this way, he walked slowly, methodically checking not only the sidewalk but in the yards he passed, as well.

Was it possible Cody had chased a stray dog and had somehow fallen into a ditch or a hole and couldn't get help? Had he seen something of interest and left the sidewalk and gotten tangled up in a vine or a bush?

When he reached the place where he'd found the backpack, he stopped. This was the spot where something unpredictable had happened. Had a car pulled up? Had somebody jumped out of that car and grabbed Cody? Had he dropped his backpack as some sort of clue or had it been torn off him in some kind of a struggle? The very idea caused a rising nausea inside him.

The asphalt of the street didn't show a clue, nor did the yards he had passed. It was as if Cody had taken off his backpack and then had simply disappeared into thin air.

Kidnapped. There was no question in Knox's mind that somebody had taken his son. But who? Had it been Chad or one of the Billings brothers? Or was it his mother?

The thought thundered in his brain. Was it possible that Livia wasn't in Mexico anymore but rather right here in Shadow Creek? Why would she take Cody? It certainly wouldn't be because of a grandmother's love and desire to see her grandson. Livia didn't do anything out of love.

Knox crossed the street and headed back to the house, once again checking yards for any clue that would lead him to his son.

When he reached the house, he frowned as he saw the local news channel van parked in front. That was the last damn thing they needed right now. That would only complicate things with throngs of people showing up just to watch whatever might be happening. *But news reports might also unearth some witnesses*, he reminded himself.

He pulled his keys from his pocket and got into his car. Very soon it would be too dark for any kind of a successful search.

He'd gotten Chad Watkins's address from a reluctant Wendall earlier in the evening and it was there he headed. Jeffries hadn't called to let them know whether or not he'd found and questioned the man.

He drove the streets slowly and attempted to shove away the black thoughts that attempted to choke him. The idea of somebody intentionally keeping his son from him, from Allison, shot an icy chill through him.

At least there were now dozens of people helping to search. And at least nobody had found Cody's body. He gripped the steering wheel tightly as that thought filled his mind. He couldn't go there…he just couldn't believe that Cody might be dead.

Chad lived on the western outskirts of town. He saw the patrol car parked at the curb and an old Chevy in the driveway as he got to Chad's address. Apparently Bud Jeffries was sitting on the house.

He pulled up behind the patrol car and parked. The house was small with a lawn full of weeds and overgrown grass. It screamed of a need for maintenance, the gray paint peeling and one of the gutters hanging off the roof. There were no lights on inside.

He got out of his car and approached the driver side of the patrol vehicle. Bud rolled down the window. Instantly the scent of onions and French fries drifted out.

"I've been here since I talked to you," Bud said. His

seat was reclined and he had a wrapper in his lap hold-ing a half-eaten hamburger and a handful of French fries. The sight of the man enjoying a meal while his son was missing enraged Knox, but he carefully kept his temper in check.

"He'll eventually wind up back here," Bud said. "His car is here so he can't have gone far."

"Have you checked inside the house?"

"I knocked on the front door…knocked hard enough to wake the dead, or a drunk, but nobody answered."

"Maybe you should go inside," Knox replied.

"Can't do that. I don't have a search warrant and no real evidence to get one. I walked around the place and didn't hear anything from inside. He's probably passed out under a tree or in a bush. It wouldn't be the first time."

Then why are you just sitting here feeding your fat face? "Do you plan to stay here all night?"

"I don't know what plans I have from minute to min-ute." Bud picked up a large plastic soda cup and took a drink. "I had a couple of my men check out Brad and Bob. They were both at their homes and were shocked that Allison would even think they could be capable of taking the boy. There's no reason to believe they had anything to do with it."

Knox looked at Chad's house and then back at Bud. "Does Chad own any other property around town?"

Bud laughed. "That boy hardly owns this property. His parents lived here for years but they were killed in a car accident several years ago and Chad moved in. He owes back taxes and is barely hanging on here."

"You'll call us as soon as you speak with Chad?"

"I will." Bud took another drink of his soda.

Knox wanted to reach through the window and pull the man out of the car by his ears. Why didn't the sheriff feel a sense of bigger responsibility? A little boy was missing and night had fallen.

Without saying another word Knox got back into his car. The fact that he needed to turn on his headlights tortured him. Cody was someplace in the dark…scared and without his parents. How had this happened, and who was responsible?

He hated to go back to Allison's without bringing Cody home. He didn't want to see the fear, the utter misery in her eyes. He also wasn't ready to mention the possibility that his mother might be behind it. Right now he couldn't figure out a motive for her and Chad was a far more likely suspect.

Once again he drove slowly, looking at each of the houses he passed, wondering if Cody was in one of them. Could he trust Bud that the Billings brothers didn't have a hand in this? Was it possible Chad was holed up someplace with Cody?

He finally got back to Allison's house. Most of the cars that had been there earlier were now gone, and the news van was just pulling away. People had to get back to their own lives, tuck their children into bed with extra hugs and the gratefulness that it wasn't one of their own missing.

Wendall Kincaid's patrol car was still parked in front of the house, along with another one, and Thorne's truck also remained.

He walked into the house to the scent of fresh coffee and voices coming from the kitchen. Wendall had been joined again by Deputy Jim Baker. Allison's home phone sat in the center of the table with what looked like an ancient recording machine hooked up to it. The two deputies were chatting with Thorne and Mac, who both leaned with their backs against the counter.

Allison sat at the table, a cup of coffee before her as she stared out the window into the darkness of the night. She turned to look at him when he entered the room. For a brief moment hope leaped into her eyes, but it quickly died as he silently shook his head.

"Knox, we've walked the streets and checked yards, and we finally came back here because we don't know what else to do to help," Mac said. His dark brown eyes radiated concern and deep compassion.

"I appreciate everything you've done, but it's getting late. I don't know where else to tell you to search. Go home," Knox said.

"Are you sure?" Thorne asked. "You know we'll stay as long as you need us."

"I know that, but I'm positive," Knox replied. "I'll walk you out."

The three men left the house in silence. "You'll let us know if there's anything else we can do?" Mac asked when they reached their vehicle.

"I will," Knox replied.

Thorne clapped a hand on Knox's shoulder. "You know we're here for you."

"I know, and I appreciate it." A cold wind of desperation swept through him. "The hardest part is this helpless feeling I have. I don't know where else to look for him. I don't know who might have him and why."

"You've got two good men in there helping out," Mac replied. "Wendall and Jim are good at their jobs."

"Unlike their boss," Thorne added darkly.

"Jeffries is sitting on Chad's place," Knox replied. He tamped down his irrational anger at the thought of Bud feeding his face and relaxing in his car seat.

"You think Chad is behind this?" Mac asked.

Knox hesitated. "I don't know. If he's the drunk everyone talks about, I'm not sure he'd be coherent enough to pull off a kidnapping. I just hope like hell my dear mother isn't behind this."

Even in the darkness of night, Knox saw the surprise on the other men's faces. "Why would Livia have anything to do with this?" Mac asked.

"Who knows why she does what she does?" Knox replied, aware of the bitterness that crept into his voice.

"She'd be a fool to come back here," Thorne said. "She'd find no help whatsoever in this town. Everyone here hates her. They even took her name off that fancy hospital she built."

"Yeah, I'm sure you're right," Knox said. "Now go on, get out of here."

"Are you coming back to my place?" Thorne asked.

"Not until my son is home safe and sound," he replied firmly. A few minutes later he watched until their taillights disappeared from view. He turned around and stared at the house.

The porch light was on…a beacon in the surrounding darkness. But there was no light inside of him. There was nothing but darkness and a growing rage against whomever had taken his son.

He now prayed for a ransom demand. He now wanted to believe that Cody was the victim of a kidnapping for ransom and not some sort of stranger abduction. Those rarely got solved and almost never ended happily, but he and Allison might have a fighting chance against somebody who wanted to bargain for Cody's return.

He entered the house to find Allison seated on the sofa. Her face was wan, her eyes burning with intensity. "I refuse to cry," she said. "If I cry, it means something bad has happened and I can't allow my thoughts to go there."

Knox sat next to her and took one of her hands in his. Her fingers were icy and trembled against his. "This is all my fault," she said. "I should have never fired Chad." Her lower lip quivered and she reached up with her other hand to worry a small strand of her hair.

"We don't know for sure that Chad is responsible for anything yet, and you can't blame yourself for firing a man who drank on the job."

She squeezed his hand. "I'm so afraid, Knox."

"I know." God, he felt so helpless. "Sheriff Jeffries is sitting on Chad's house. We should know if Chad is responsible for this before the night is over."

They remained on the sofa as the night deepened, holding hands, with their love for Cody binding them together. The soft voices of the deputies in the kitchen were the only sound in the house.

Knox didn't even know what a ransom demand would look like. Would it come as a text on Allison's cell phone? Would a note be put in the mailbox? How would a kidnapper contact them?

"Let's go get some coffee," he said when it was almost midnight. He knew neither of them would sleep through this long night.

Allison nodded and together they got up from the sofa and went into the kitchen. Wendall and Jim still sat at the table, their faces lined with tiredness.

"Don't you have men to spell you?" Knox asked as he poured two cups of coffee.

"We aren't going anywhere until Cody gets home," Wendall said.

Allison took her coffee cup and sat at the table. Knox sat next to her. Her inner strength amazed him. Other than her brief breakdown earlier, she'd remained relatively calm throughout the long hours that had passed.

Knox burned with frustration. There were no clues to follow, no discernible leads and only a weak motive at best. The recording and tracing wires were hooked into Allison's phone and all they could do was wait. And if a ransom call didn't come in, then Knox would lose hope.

The minutes ticked by and with every one Knox felt a tightening in his stomach. There was no silence as great as that left behind by a missing child.

And then the phone rang.

Chapter 9

Allison's heart leaped into her throat. She looked first at Knox, and then at the phone on the table. Surely nobody would be calling at this time of night to see if Cody had come home. It was midnight, too late for a well-meaning person to call. Besides, the caller ID box displayed private caller instead of a phone number.

The phone rang a second time. "Answer it," Wendall said as he pushed buttons that would record any conversation that took place.

She was suddenly more terrified than she'd been throughout the entire night. The phone rang a third time.

"Allison, answer the phone," Knox said urgently.

Her hands trembled as she picked up the receiver and breathed a faint hello.

"I have your son." The voice boomed throughout

the kitchen. It was impossible to tell whether it was a male or a female. It was obviously digitally distorted.

Knox moved closer to Allison as her hand tightened on the receiver. "Please…please don't hurt him," she said. She fought back the tears that tried to choke her. "Who is this? What do you want?"

"There's a lightning-struck crooked tree on the west side of town. Bring a million dollars there at midnight tomorrow night. I'll exchange the boy for the cash. Twenty-four hours, and the money better be there. Come alone. If I see a cop, the boy dies."

Knox grabbed the phone from Allison. "We're not giving you a dime unless we get proof of life," he said. "We don't even know if you really have Cody."

Allison stared at Knox in horror. She couldn't believe they were asking for proof of life where their son was concerned. The nightmare just kept getting worse.

"He's wearing a pair of jeans and a long-sleeved T-shirt with a horse on the front."

Allison gasped. Oh, God, that was exactly what Cody had been wearing when he'd left for school that morning.

"We still want proof of life. Do you hear me?" Knox continued. "No clock starts ticking until we know our boy is alive and well. And if you hurt him in any way, I'll hunt you down and kill you."

There was a long pause. "You'll hear from me soon." The phone went dead and Allison collapsed into her chair, her heart fluttering so fast she could scarcely catch her breath.

"Knox, that's what Cody wore to school this morning, his black horse T-shirt," she said half-breathlessly. "So, now we know. Somebody really kidnapped him."

"Maybe," Knox replied. "Or maybe that call was just from somebody who saw Cody today and is trying to cash in on his disappearance."

Wendall got up from the table. "I'll just step into the other room and give the sheriff a call to catch him up to speed. He'll get somebody on tracing the source of the call."

"Play it again," Knox said to Jim as Wendall left the room. "I want to see if I hear any background noise."

Knox listened to the phone call four more times and by then Allison wanted to slam her hands over her ears and never hear that horrendous voice again.

"It could be a hoax," Wendall said when he came back into the room.

"That's one of the reasons I asked for proof of life," Knox replied. "It's the only way to know if the call was real or not."

Allison didn't know what was worse, the call being a hoax or real. If it was fake, then they still didn't know what had happened to Cody. If it was real, it meant that some evil person had her son. Who? Dear God, who would do this?

"I'll get the money," she said. "Somehow, someway, I'll figure out how to pay to get him back." A million dollars. She could sell her business. She could mortgage the house. She'd do whatever it took to get Cody back home.

"We aren't paying," Knox said firmly.

"We have to," she protested. "It might be the only way we get him back safely."

"We're not going to give a kidnapper a single penny. We're going to find the bastard and get Cody back," Knox replied with deadly intent shining from his eyes.

"How?" She felt a rising hysteria. "How are we going to find him, Knox? We don't know who he is. We have no idea where he's taken Cody." She released a sharp laugh she didn't even recognize as her own. "We don't even know if it's a male or a female." Once again, fear that Livia might be behind the kidnapping grabbed her by the throat.

"I'll figure it out." A knot of tension pulsed in Knox's jawline.

Allison was about to argue with him but a knock fell on the door and once again her heart thudded with anxiety. "That's probably Sheriff Jeffries," Wendall said. He left the kitchen to answer the door and then returned with the sheriff trailing behind him.

"I want to hear the ransom call," Bud said.

Allison listened yet another time to the horrendous phone call. When it was finished Bud looked at her. "Do you recognize the voice?"

"I don't think you'd recognize it if it were your own mother," Knox replied impatiently. "It's obvious that it's been distorted."

"I know that," Bud snapped with a scowl. "But maybe she recognized the cadence or the particular word choices the caller used."

She shook her head. "I don't recognize anything about the caller." She was vaguely surprised by Bud.

She'd always thought he might be a stupid man as well as lazy. He'd just changed her mind about the stupid part.

"There's no way to know if the caller really has your son. Once you get some sort of proof of life, then we'll figure out how we intend to handle this," Bud said.

"What about a tip line?" Allison asked. Tragically she'd seen enough of these cases on television shows and in the news to know that usually a dedicated phone line was used for people to call in if they knew or had seen anything that might yield a clue.

Bud frowned. "These kinds of cases always bring out the crazies."

"It only takes one caller to be right about something they saw or heard," Knox said.

Bud released an audible sigh. "I'll head back to the station now and get that set up. I'm planning on a news conference here in the morning. We'll flash the number across the air and see what comes in." Bud shifted his gaze to his two deputies. "I'll send a couple of men over here so you can go home."

"If it's all the same to you, we'd like to see this thing through," Wendall said. "We'll be fine. We'll spell each other through the night."

Bud shrugged. "Works for me." He looked back at Knox. "I'll get an AMBER alert out. Call me if anything happens. I want to be kept up to date."

"What about Chad?" Knox asked.

"Nobody has seen hide nor hair of him." Bud frowned. "I've got somebody sitting on his house. I still suspect he's passed out in some alley or in a bush and will eventually be home. His car was in the driveway, and he doesn't own any other vehicles, so he hasn't gone too far."

"Have there been any reports of any stolen vehicles?" Knox asked.

"No, nothing like that. All I can tell you right now is that everything that can be done is being done. I'll check in with you in the morning." And with that the sheriff left.

Allison stood. "Maybe I should make another pot of coffee." Making coffee, that's how she'd gotten through the long afternoon. She didn't know what else to do, and she was desperate to do something, anything to take her mind off the phone call.

"I think we all could use some rest," Knox replied.

Rest? How could she rest when Cody wasn't home? Although her eyes were gritty with a need to sleep, her brain raced so fast she couldn't imagine it quieting.

"But what if we get another phone call? I should be here to answer," she protested.

Knox got up and moved to place his hands on her shoulders. "Ally, I don't think we're going to hear anything more tonight. And if the phone rings, I'll answer it. Why don't you go upstairs and get some sleep? You'll need all of your strength for tomorrow. Cody is going to need you to be levelheaded and rested when he finally comes home."

She searched his features, noting the light lines that creased down the sides of his face, the overbrightness of his eyes. "What are you going to do? You look like you could use some rest, too."

"If it's okay with you, when I'm ready, I'll just stretch out on the bottom bunk in Cody's room."

She nodded. "I'll go up and lie down, but I'm sure I won't sleep. I'm not sure I'll ever sleep again until Cody is home. Just please let me know if anything happens."

He squeezed her shoulders and then dropped his hands to his sides. "Go on, go rest and I'll see you later."

With a weary nod to the other men, she left the kitchen. She climbed the stairs slowly, her feet feeling as if they weighed a thousand pounds. When she reached the top, she went directly into her bedroom.

She thought of going into Cody's room, but she didn't think she could handle it right now without completely losing it. Smelling his scent, feeling his presence when he wasn't there, was just too great a heartache for her to bear right now.

She turned on the lamp on the nightstand and then stretched out on her bed facing the framed picture of her son. *Cody...where are you? Who has you?*

The questions not only worried in her head, but also painfully squeezed her heart. When Knox had left her years ago, she'd thought her heartache couldn't be worse than it was. But this...this created a whole new kind of pain in her chest, one that felt as if she might not draw her next breath.

Everything that could be done was being done, she reminded herself. That's what the sheriff had told them. If the phone call was really from a kidnapper, then eventually they'd get some sort of proof of life. Bud had said they'd figure things out from there...but what was there to figure out?

She just wanted her son back.

Tears burned at her eyes and she squeezed them tightly closed. She wished Knox was up there right now, holding her tight against his broad chest as the rest of this torturous night passed. She shoved the thought away, knowing that was probably the very last thing she needed.

Cody awoke from a nightmare. In his dream somebody had been hiding behind a tree and had jumped out at him and pressed a stinky rag over his mouth and nose.

He opened his eyes, expecting to see the glow-in-the-dark stars that always comforted him if he woke up in the middle of the night.

There were no stars…only darkness. And even though it was dark, he knew he wasn't in his top bunk. It felt like he was on a cot like he'd slept on one time when his mom had taken him camping for a weekend.

His stomach rolled and goose bumps crawled over his skin as he realized it hadn't been a nightmare, after all. This was terrible and it was real.

He wanted to cry out for his mother, but he knew with certainty she wasn't anywhere around. There was no way she would let him sleep on a cot that smelled so yucky or in a place that was so cold. She made sure he had plenty of blankets on his bed and they always smelled like wind and sunshine.

And he was so hungry. The last time he'd eaten had been in the school cafeteria and they'd served some yucky, soggy fish sticks and runny mac and cheese. His mom would never let him go to bed hungry.

As he remained with his eyes open, he realized it wasn't completely dark as he'd first thought. A shaft of moonlight drifted through a small window high above his head, allowing him to make out a set of wooden stairs across the room that led up.

A basement. He was in some sort of basement. Who had put him there? He didn't even remember seeing the person who had put that cloth over his face. He'd sneaked up behind him. Whoever had done this was a very bad person.

His stomach ached with his hunger and he was so very cold, but more than anything he was terribly afraid. He'd never been this afraid before in his entire life. He'd watched a zombie movie one time when he'd spent the night at Josh's house, but even that hadn't scared him as much as he was now.

Was the person who had taken him upstairs? Maybe if he just climbed up the stairs he could get out of here. Maybe the bad person was asleep and Cody could sneak past him and get out of this place. Maybe if he got outside he could find his way back home or at least find somebody to help him.

He moved his legs and then froze. Something was around one of his ankles. He sat up and leaned over to see what it was. It was something hard and attached to it was a length of chain. He had no idea how long the chain was, but he wasn't going to get out of bed in the dark and find out.

He tried to get out of the ring, but it was too tight for him to slip his foot through and get free. He then tugged on the chain, but the other end of it was in the wall and he couldn't get it to release.

Tears leaped to his eyes. He was in trouble. He was in really big trouble. His heart pounded frantically and he squeezed his eyes tightly shut.

He didn't want to cry. Only babies cried and he wasn't a baby anymore. He didn't know how long he'd been in this basement, but it was obviously nighttime outside.

He knew his mom and Knox would be looking for him. His mom had lots of friends. There were probably hundreds of people searching for him right that very minute. And the sheriff and all his men would be hunting for him, too.

These thoughts helped him be a little bit less afraid, but not much. Maybe his father would come and find him. His dad chased bad people and put them in jail. Maybe his dad would realize Cody needed him now more than ever and he'd rescue him.

He held on to that thought as he drifted back to sleep.

Knox stood in the shower and allowed the beat of hot water to massage his tense muscles. It was just after dawn and he'd managed to sleep in fits and starts for about two hours.

He was grateful that when he'd peeked into Allison's room a few minutes before she'd been soundly sleeping. She'd need the rest to face the day ahead.

He'd stood for several long moments in the doorway, just watching her, and wondered how they had screwed everything up so badly between them. And how they had come to this place where apparently somebody had taken their son.

His mother. It had to be her. If the phone call had been real, then this was all about money. Livia Colton was on the run from the law and the first thing she would need would be plenty of cash. There was no doubt in his mind that she'd kidnapped Cody for monetary gain. It was who she was, and he'd never hated anyone in his life as much as he hated her.

And how would Allison feel about him if it did turn out to be his mother? He shoved the troubling question out of his head.

He turned off the shower and grabbed a towel. He intended to call Thorne later and ask him to bring some clothes to him. Knox had no idea how long he'd be there and he didn't intend to leave unless Allison told him to go or until Cody came home.

He dressed in the same jeans and polo shirt he'd worn the day before and then left the bathroom. He paused in Allison's doorway, grateful that the sound of the shower hadn't awakened her.

She looked beautiful in the faint dawn light that lit the room. Her features were relaxed and her hair was a silky cloud around her head.

He had no idea how long this ordeal might last. She'd been so strong the day before, but there was no way to guess when she might reach a breaking point. Hopefully the sleep she'd gotten would keep her strong.

He was about to leave her doorway when she emitted a small gasp and her eyes flew open. "Cody," she said in a pleading whisper that broke Knox's heart. She then sat up and her gaze landed on him.

He walked over to her bed and sat at the foot. She sat up and pushed strands of hair out of her eyes. "I slept," she said, her voice filled with heavy guilt. "My son is missing and I went to sleep."

"Allison, don't beat yourself up. Your body needs sleep, no matter what's going on. I even dozed off for a couple of hours." He couldn't help but notice she smelled of warm woman and fresh apples.

"So nothing else has happened?" she asked.

He shook his head. "Nothing." He stared at her for several long moments. "I was just wondering earlier how we got things so screwed up between us."

She turned her head toward the window, the morning light caressing her pretty features. "Oh, Knox, we tried so many times, but we just could never get it right." She turned to look at him once again. "The only thing we got right was making a beautiful baby who has grown into a wonderful, loving boy." Her voice cracked on the last word. "I just want him home."

He reached out and took one of her hands. "We'll get him home." He paused for a moment, and then continued. "I think it's my mother." The confession was difficult for him, even to a woman who knew what kind of person Knox's mother was. Shame coursed through him, a shame his mother had made him feel many times before in his life.

Allison's eyes widened. "Oh, Knox, you really can't believe that. I know Livia has done a lot of horrible things, but surely you can't believe that she would kidnap her own grandson for ransom. I…I don't want to believe that." Still, she had to admit, more than once the possibility had jumped into her head.

"I think she saw that blog on *Everything's Blogger in Texas* and realized I have a son, and she saw it as a perfect opportunity to get money. It takes a lot of cash to stay on the run from the law." His gut churned despite the hollowness inside him.

She stared at him, her lower lip trembling with emotion. "Do you think she'd hurt him?"

As always, thoughts of his mother welled up a black despair. "I think she's capable of anything," he finally replied.

She slowly shook her head and pulled her hand from his. "I just don't believe it. I don't believe your mother somehow got back here to Shadow Creek and took Cody. I still think it's Chad…or maybe one of the Billings brothers."

He would allow her this moment of denial, mostly because he was afraid that if it really was his mother he had no idea what lengths Allison would go to when Cody was returned. He knew she'd do whatever possible to keep Livia out of her son's life, but would she take Cody away from him, too? It didn't matter what she believed. What would kill him more than anything was if he had unintentionally brought danger to Allison and Cody. If he hadn't come back here, then the blog probably wouldn't have been written and Livia wouldn't know about Cody's existence. If the kidnapper turned out to be his mother and something horrible happened, he didn't know how Allison would ever forgive him, and he didn't know how he'd ever forgive himself.

"I'm going to head downstairs and whip up some breakfast," he said as he got up from the bed. If he lingered there any longer with the scent of her swirling in his brain, he'd want to reach for her. He'd want to escape his own black thoughts in her slender, warm arms.

They hadn't been able to get it right in the past and he didn't think there was any way they'd get it right in the future, especially if Livia was behind the kidnapping.

"I'm going to take a quick shower and then I'll be down," she replied.

He left her room and headed down the stairs. The scent of freshly brewed coffee filled the air as he headed to the kitchen.

Jim and Wendall were at the table with coffee cups in front of them. "Good morning," Wendall said. "I hope you don't mind that we helped ourselves."

"I don't mind a bit." Knox walked over to the counter and poured himself a cup of the fresh brew. "Did you two get any sleep last night?"

"We both got a couple of hours," Jim replied. "The sofa is very comfortable."

"Either one of you thought about running for sheriff in the fall?" Knox asked.

"Not me," Wendall replied with a short laugh.

"Or me, either," Jim added. "I like what I do right now. I don't need the headache."

"Speaking of headaches, the kidnapping made the news. *Everything's Blogger* has it up on their site," Wendall said.

"I wish I knew how in the hell they get their information." Knox pulled an egg carton out of the refrigerator. He fought against the impotent frustration and anger that had filled him since he'd awakened in Cody's lower bunk bed.

"I wouldn't be surprised if Sheriff Jeffries contacted them," Jim said. "The site mentioned a press event here at eight this morning."

Knox looked at the clock. It was just after six. Would a press release help or hurt things? He couldn't know. "What do you think about some scrambled eggs and toast?"

"Sounds good to us," Wendall replied.

As Knox got busy whipping eggs with milk, he wondered when they'd hear something from the caller. If that person really did have Cody, then how would they get proof of life? Would a picture appear in Allison's text messages? On his? Had the call been from the real kidnapper? Maybe it really had been nothing but a hoax, but then what had happened to Cody? So many questions with no answers. If he focused on them, he'd be insane.

The eggs were in the skillet when Allison appeared. She'd obviously showered and changed her clothes, and her hair was in a neat bun at the nape of her neck. She wore a pair of jeans and a tailored white blouse with a navy blue blazer. She looked strong and in control.

She returned the deputies' greetings and then poured herself a cup of coffee. "Can I help?" she asked Knox.

"No, I've got this. Just sit and relax." He popped slices of bread into the toaster. It felt so wrong to be doing something as mundane as fixing breakfast when his son was missing.

He needed to be strong for Allison, and he wanted to stay strong for Cody, but he had to continue to swallow against thick emotion that rose up in the back of his throat.

He'd dreamed of making breakfast for Cody. He'd imagined his son sitting at a table and filling the kitchen with his wonderful laughter while Knox whipped up French toast or bacon and eggs.

The fact that he'd had none of those kinds of moments with his own father only made him hunger to have them with his own son. He needed to make certain that everything he had longed for as a fatherless boy he gave to Cody. They were fantasies he still wanted desperately to become a reality.

They ate in relative silence. Allison picked at her food, not really eating but instead moving the eggs from one place to another on the plate.

Knox didn't have any appetite, but he ate like a soldier needing fuel for whatever lay ahead. He tried desperately to keep himself from feeling anything.

After all, he was the unemotional Fort Knox. He wasn't accustomed to emotion. He wasn't used to feeling fear and rage and love and regret, but all those roiled around inside him.

Seeing Allison in bed had definitely screwed with his head. Despite the trauma of a missing son, he'd wanted her. He wanted her even now.

The ring of the phone shattered the silence.

Allison's eyes widened but she didn't hesitate like

she had before. She grabbed the receiver and said a firm hello.

"I have the boy." It was definitely a female voice, although it didn't sound like Knox's mother.

"What do you want?" Allison asked as her gaze locked with his.

"I want you to sacrifice a black cat by the light of a full moon."

Allison frowned. "Excuse me?"

"And then you should dance naked in a circle around a tombstone in the cemetery."

Knox took the receiver from Allison. "I've got the police heading to your house right now," he said angrily. "Don't call this number again." He slammed down the receiver.

"It came from a local number. I'll call dispatch and let them do a reverse lookup and get somebody over there," Wendall said.

"Who would do something like that?" Allison asked as Wendall stepped out of the kitchen. "What kind of a person would make a phone call like that to parents with a missing child?"

"Probably a lonely old woman who will be perfectly happy if the police show up at her house, because she'll then have somebody to talk to," Jim said.

"In that case I don't know whether to be outraged at her or sad for her," Allison replied.

"Since the news is out about Cody's disappearance, you can probably expect to get some crank phone calls," Jim replied.

Knox looked at Allison as she sank back down in the

kitchen chair. The strength that she had displayed since she'd come downstairs appeared to have seeped away.

Her shoulders drooped and she closed her eyes. When she opened them again, she cast Knox a weary glance. "I don't know if I can do this," she said softly.

"Of course you can," he replied firmly. "You were strong enough to raise him all alone for the last nine years. You're strong enough to do whatever needs to be done for him now."

And just that quickly he was angry with her. "I need to go make some phone calls," he said, not wanting to air the raging emotions that filled him. He strode out of the kitchen and out the front door.

The morning air was cold, but he scarcely noticed with the heat of anger coursing through him. She'd had nine years with Cody and he'd only had less than two weeks with him.

Cody didn't even know that Knox was his father. He should have insisted Allison tell him on the very first day that Knox had realized Cody was his son. Dammit, Allison should have let him tell Cody before now. What if he never was able to hear Cody call him Dad? What if he never got to cook breakfast for his boy?

He sank down on the porch swing, his legs suddenly feeling too weak to hold him upright. He told himself it was the brightness of the rising sun that caused tears to well up in his eyes. But the sun had never made so many tears and his chest had never been so knotted, so tight.

He'd spent the last ten years not caring about anyone but himself. His heart, his emotions, had been easy to manage because he hadn't had many. But now he was overwhelmed.

He pressed his eyes tightly closed in an effort to staunch the tears. But as the thought of never seeing his son again exploded in his mind, he lost it.

Tears oozed from his eyes and he angrily brushed them away, only to have more trek down his cheeks. Somewhere in the back of his mind he knew his anger should be directed at the kidnapper and not at Allison, but right now he was irrational and just damned angry at the world.

Chapter 10

"A news van just pulled up out front," Knox announced when he returned to the kitchen.

Allison studied his features carefully, unsure what had sent him out of the house a half an hour earlier. His cool blue eyes were shuttered, giving away nothing of his inner thoughts. His shoulders were set in rigidity, and tension radiated out from him.

The doorbell rang and Wendall got up from his chair. "Do you all want to talk to the press? Make a statement of any kind?"

"I don't," Knox said and then looked at her. "But go ahead if you want to."

"No, I don't want to give the kidnapper the pleasure." Allison had seen the parents of kidnapped or missing children standing at press conferences, begging for mercy as they wept in despair. She didn't want to be one of those parents, unless she was convinced it would somehow help them find Cody.

"Then I'll get the door and tell them to stay off your property." Wendall left the kitchen.

"I imagine Sheriff Jeffries will want you two standing next to him when he holds the press conference," Jim said.

"I have no intention of sharing his limelight," Knox replied.

"He's not a big fan of the Coltons anyway," Jim replied and then clamped his mouth shut as if he'd said too much.

"I'd already gotten that impression from him," Knox replied drily. "I guess he's of a mind that one bad apple spoils the whole barrel."

"Or he's just an ass," Allison said.

A burst of laughter escaped both Knox and Jim. The sound was surprisingly welcome, despite the pain that racked her heart. "Sorry," Jim said as he cut his laughter short.

"It's okay." Allison smiled at the deputy who had sat through the long night with them and now wore a faint weariness in the depths of his green eyes.

Wendall returned to the kitchen. "I told all the people outside to stay out of your yard and if any of them knocked on your door for a statement or interview I'd arrest them."

"Thank you. Have you heard anything from Sheriff Jeffries this morning?" Allison asked.

Wendall shook his head. "Nothing, but I expect him to be here anytime."

She moved over to the window and stared outside. She was trying to hold on to her sanity when all she wanted to do was crumple to the ground and scream for her son.

The house didn't feel like her home, not without Cody running up and down the stairs, not without his laughter filling all the dark corners. This home was now an empty, alien place and would remain so until she got her son back.

Her brain still couldn't quite wrap around the fact that two uniformed deputies had taken up residence here and that a news van was parked outside and curious neighbors were gathering in the street and along the sidewalk.

The only modicum of comfort was Knox's presence. He was the only person she knew who felt what she did, who had the same burning emptiness inside, an emptiness that wouldn't be filled until Cody was back home again.

And even he couldn't feel the depth of despair that she did. He'd only had two weeks to love Cody; she'd had over nine years. She'd carried him for nine months; she'd given him life, and her womb now ached with his absence.

Knox had shocked her with his confession that he thought somehow Livia was behind the kidnapping. One of the reasons Allison hadn't contacted him when she'd found herself pregnant was her desire to protect Cody forever from Livia Colton. It hadn't mattered to her that the woman was in prison. She'd known then that she couldn't underestimate Livia's reach, despite the bars that surrounded her. She preferred to cling to the belief that a stupid drunk had taken her son rather than contemplate the possibility of it being Livia.

Another knock on the front door called her away from the kitchen window. Wendall got up to answer and she trailed behind him as Knox walked over to the counter to pour himself another cup of coffee.

She'd expected Sheriff Jeffries, but was surprised to see Jason Tankard at the door. Wendall turned to look at her. "Should I let him in?"

"Please," she replied.

"Allison, I'm so sorry about your son," Jason said as he grabbed her hands in his. He released her hands as Knox came into the room. "I want to help. You know I own the printing shop. If you'll give me a picture of Cody, I'll get posters made up by this afternoon, and then we can get them up everywhere in town."

Surely that would be a good thing. Maybe somebody somewhere would see the poster of Cody and come forward with some information that might help. "Let me get my checkbook," she replied.

"Absolutely not," Jason said firmly. "This is on me. I haven't forgotten how kind you were to us when your company built the addition on my house. All I need is a picture and I'll take care of the rest."

The control that she'd worked so hard to maintain slipped slightly. "I'll be right back."

It took only minutes for Jason to leave with Cody's picture in hand, and by that time Sheriff Jeffries arrived. He appeared well rested and with an eager gleam in his eyes as he discussed the imminent news conference. He seemed surprised that neither of them wanted to join him.

"Are you both sure?" he asked. "It's usually good to have the parents make an appearance."

Knox looked at her and then back at the sheriff. "We're positive. Did Chad ever show up at his home?" Knox asked.

"Not yet," Jeffries replied.

"What are you doing to find him?" Allison still wanted to believe it was quite possible that her ex-employee had taken Cody for revenge. He'd demanded ten thousand dollars on the day she had fired him and he'd asked her for money in many of his nasty texts. What better way to get it from her than to take her son and exchange him for cash?

"I've still got a man sitting on his house." Bud looked out the front window, as if eager to get before the cameras rather than answer any of their questions.

"Do you have a BOLO out on him?" Knox moved to stand next to Allison, as if presenting a united front against a common enemy.

"Not yet. I was giving him a chance to come home," Bud said defensively.

"What about the caller last night? Was somebody able to trace the phone call to find out who made it or where it came from?" Knox asked.

"We're still working on it. Look, I need to get out there. They're waiting for me," he said and gestured toward the window.

He went out the front door and Allison found herself leaning against Knox. He felt as strong and as steady as a tree trunk.

"He is an ass," she murmured softly. "He should be doing door-to-door searches throughout the entire town. He should be doing something more to find our boy."

Knox roughly grabbed her and pulled her to his chest, his heart beating rapidly against her own. She tamped down the rising emotions that threatened to drown her.

It was at that moment, with unimaginable fear screaming wildly inside her and Knox's arms around her, that she realized she was still as deeply in love with him as she had been years ago.

Instead of bringing her any kind of comfort or joy, the knowledge only deepened the feeling that she was helplessly alone.

She pulled away from him. "When are we going to get proof of life?" she said, needing to focus only on her son.

He jammed his hands in his pockets, his eyes dark blue and turbulent. "I don't know. At this point I don't even know if that call was a hoax or not. I have a feeling Shadow Creek doesn't have the kind of resources they need for something like this. We should have already gotten an answer as to who made that phone call."

"It was real. It has to be real. I have to believe that. Otherwise we're no closer to knowing what happened to Cody than we were when he was an hour late coming home from the bus stop."

"All we can do is wait, Allison," he replied.

"This waiting is going to be my complete undoing." She wanted to fall back into his arms. Only in his arms did she feel slightly warm, and she'd had a cold chill rushing through her for the past twelve or so hours. "I'm going to go make some more coffee. It's going to be a long day."

Within hours the house felt more alien than ever. More deputies drifted in and out as well as neighbors and friends with offers to help in any way they could.

Food began to appear, brought by well-meaning people who looked at Allison with pity. Casseroles and sandwich meat, buns and even cakes…it was as if somebody had died. While she appreciated everyone's support, she hated the funeral-like pall that hung in the air.

George stopped by to offer support and to assure her that work was continuing as usual on all the jobs and he'd keep things running smoothly as long as she needed him.

And each time the phone rang, Allison had a small heart attack, but the only calls that came in were from people to see what they could do to help.

By one o'clock her nerves were shot. She curled up on the chair in the living room, closed her eyes and tried to tune out all the sound in the house.

She immersed herself in all thoughts of Cody. She'd been in labor with him for fourteen long hours. He'd come into the world screaming and kicking. He'd continued to scream until the moment the doctor had placed him in her arms.

He'd immediately calmed and his gaze had locked with hers and as she'd looked into his bright blue eyes she'd thought of Knox. She'd quickly shoved Knox out of her head to focus solely on her baby against her breasts.

She'd been in awe, certain that he was the most beautiful, the smartest baby ever born. Her head now filled with special moments in time…the sweet scent of him after a bath, the softness of his hair and the sound of his laughter. He'd brought a joy she'd never known into her life.

The memories were rich in texture and clarity and she tried to hang on to them, but all too soon they ebbed away and she was just a frightened woman sitting in a chair while men in the kitchen plotted what needed to be done next. She opened her eyes and her heart once again ached with a bubbling terror no mother should ever have to feel.

Knox's raised voice penetrated through her thoughts. He sounded angry. She got up from the chair and went into the kitchen where Knox stood at the counter.

He looked like a man about to explode. His muscles were bunched and his features were strained. "Just give me their damned addresses," he said to Wendall.

"What's going on?" she asked.

"I want Brad and Bob Billings's addresses," Knox said.

"Sheriff Jeffries said he had somebody check them out," she replied.

"I don't trust anything that man says," Knox retorted. "I don't intend to take his word for anything. I need to check things out for myself."

"I thought you believed your mother kidnapped Cody," she replied.

"Your mother?" Wendall said. Both he and Jim looked at Knox in surprise.

Knox's eyes narrowed. "I do, but this is a process of elimination. I want to make sure that Chad doesn't have Cody and the Billings brothers are innocent." His hands clenched and unclenched at his sides as he once again looked at Wendall.

"Knox, it's not a good idea for you to confront them," Wendall said. "They're potential suspects."

"It wasn't a good idea for somebody to take my kid," Knox replied tersely. "If you won't give me their addresses, I'll just ask somebody outside. I'm sure somebody in the crowd will give me the addresses in a matter of minutes."

Wendall released a deep sigh and gave him the addresses. A few minutes later Allison walked with Knox to the front door. She didn't try to stop him, but before he flew out the door she placed a hand on his forearm.

"Don't get yourself put in jail," she said. "I...I need you."

The darkness in his eyes lightened a bit and he reached up and stroked a finger down the side of her face. "Call me if anything happens and don't worry, I'll be back."

And with that he was gone.

"Mr. Colton, can we get a statement from you? Do you know who might have your son?" A reporter attempted to shove a microphone into his face.

"Hey, Fort Knox, can you tell us what's going on?" another person yelled.

Knox pushed past them all and headed for his car as the reporters continued to shout questions after him. He needed to start thinking like a Texas Ranger and not like a father. He didn't trust Bud Jeffries to find his own way out of a paper bag. It wasn't a matter of competency but rather what Knox suspected was a large streak of laziness in the man.

Besides, he'd needed to get out of the house and to do something proactive. He'd also wanted to escape from Allison and the confusing emotions she wrought in him.

A part of him wanted to be angry with her, but whenever she gazed at him, whenever she touched him, he couldn't sustain his ire. She'd said she needed him. Yes, she needed him now, with Cody missing and her heart aching, but he didn't trust that need for him would remain when Cody came home.

According to what little Wendall had told him, Brothers Construction worked out of Brad's house on the edge of town, while Bob Billings's home address was just off Main Street. Knox headed to Bob's first.

It didn't take him long to locate it. He parked in front of the attractive, beige, two-story house and sought to find the cold, hard shell that was Fort Knox. He couldn't interview these men with the emotional turmoil of Cody's father; rather he needed to talk to them with a cool, calm head.

He had no idea if Bob Billings was home. There was no car in the driveway and since it was Friday it was quite possible the man was at his brother's house taking care of the construction business.

No stone left unturned, Knox told himself as he got out of the car and walked to the front door. Bob Billings answered on the second knock. He was taller and thinner than his brother, but his eyes held the same glimmer of a bad temper as Brad's had when he'd confronted Allison.

"I'm…" Knox started to introduce himself.

"I know who you are," Bob interrupted him. "And I know why you're here, although you're way out of line."

"Maybe," he agreed. "Mind if I come in?"

Bob opened the door wider. "Be my guest."

Knox stepped inside.

"Bob, who is it?" a female voice called. An attractive brunette stepped into the foyer. Her eyes widened and then softened with obvious compassion. "Mr. Colton, we're so sorry to hear about your son."

"This is my wife, Lila," Bob said. "Look, I know Allison thinks I have a problem with her, but I don't. I keep the books for the business and Brad takes care of the actual work. I'm not in control of whatever Brad and his goons do, but I know my brother and his men would never sink so low as to take a child."

"I wish we knew something to help you," Lila said. "There's nothing we'd like better now than to hear that your son is home safe and sound."

Knox believed them. He'd been in law enforcement long enough to have a fine-tuned ability to recognize liars, and Bob Billings and his wife appeared to be completely truthful.

"Thanks for your time," he said and then turned on his heels and left Bob and Lila's house. He then headed west to where the official Brothers Construction business was located, on the same property where Brad lived.

West side of town…where Brad lived, where Chad had his home and where a lightning-struck crooked tree was the exchange point for a million dollars. Coincidence? He didn't know what to think.

On his way to Brad's place he drove by Chad's once again, grateful to see a patrol car parked in the driveway. At least Bud hadn't lied about keeping an officer on Chad's place. Where was the drunk? Had he stayed sober long enough to kidnap Cody? It was damned odd that nobody could find him.

Brothers Construction was located on the outskirts of town. Brad's home was small, ranch-style and behind it were several outbuildings.

Tension welled up in Knox's stomach. Was his son being held captive in one of those outbuildings? Was he about to find Cody and take him home? God, he wanted that. He wanted it so badly he was half-sick.

He parked in the driveway and stalked up to the front door. There was no way he was leaving there without looking in each and every one of those outbuildings.

He knocked and waited, his tension rising. He knocked again, this time more loudly. The door finally opened and a blond-haired woman answered. "Can I help you?" she asked with a friendly smile. She had a dish towel in her hand, and the scent of something cooking wafted out of the doorway.

"I'm looking for Brad."

"I'm his wife, Mary. He's out in the shop. Is there anything else I can help you with?" She appeared surprisingly pleasant, considering the fact that she was married to the hot-headed man who had barged into Allison's office.

"No, thanks, I'll go find Brad."

He just couldn't believe that Cody was someplace in the house where a walk-through by anyone official would easily find him. He next headed around the house, where a fairly large building was located with a sign reading Brothers Construction hanging over the doorway. He opened the door and walked inside.

The place was filled with building supplies, but Knox's gaze zeroed in on Brad Billings, seated at a desk near the back. Brad saw him approach and got to his feet. "What in the hell do you want?" he demanded.

"I think you know why I'm here," Knox replied with a coolness that belied the bubbling cauldron of anger inside him.

"And I think I'll just escort you out of here," Brad said and moved around the desk. "And if you don't leave I'll call the sheriff and have you forcefully removed."

"Fine, you can escort me out of here." There was no way Cody was inside this building, and Knox was happy to step back outside to check the other two smaller outbuildings.

Knox walked out the door first, but instead of heading in the direction of the house where his car was parked in the driveway, he walked over to a smaller tin building.

"Hey, what do you think you're doing?" Brad protested.

Knox's heart banged against his ribs as he pulled open the door and peered inside. His breath came out of him on a whoosh. The building was filled with table saws and other tools of the trade, but no frightened little boy waiting to be rescued.

He turned and headed in the direction of a smaller shed with Brad nipping at his heels like a pissed off bulldog. His heart nearly stopped as he saw the combination lock on the shed door. He turned to face Brad. "Open it," he demanded.

"Go to hell," Brad replied, his face as red as a tomato.

Knox took a step toward him. "If you don't have anything to hide, then open the door."

Brad glared at Knox for several long moments. "You're crazy if you think I'd take a kid."

"Then call me crazy and open the damn door."

Brad released a sigh and stepped up to the combination lock. He unlocked it and threw open the door to show a riding lawn mower and other equipment, along with a shelf of spray paint.

"I told you I had nothing to do with kidnapping Allison's snot-nosed kid," Brad said.

Knox's fist met Brad's nose and blood immediately squirted out. "That's my son you're talking about," he said.

"You're crazy," Brad yelled as he pinched his nostrils tightly together. "Get off my property now before I have you arrested."

Knox complied. He got into his car as some of the

adrenaline that had spiked inside him began to ebb. He hadn't intended to hit Brad. He hadn't even known he was going to until it had happened. But he'd do it all over again, considering the man's disdainful words about Cody.

He'd just parked back in Allison's driveway when his cell phone rang. His heart banged against his ribs as he dug it out of his pocket to answer.

"Claudia," he said in surprise. It was rare for his sister to call. She'd left for New York City when she turned eighteen and she'd never looked back.

"Knox, I just heard about your son. I'm so sorry and I wanted you to know my thoughts are with you and Allison."

"Thanks, Claudia. We appreciate the emotional support," he replied.

"Have there been any clues to his disappearance?"

He considered telling her about the ransom call and his belief that Livia might be behind it, but he opted not to say anything. "No, no real clues."

"As soon as I finish some things up here, I'm planning to come back to Shadow Creek. I've just got a lot on my plate right now."

"That would be great, Claudia," he replied, although he doubted she would ever return there. She hadn't been back in all the years she'd been gone. They spoke for a few more minutes and then ended the call.

Knox remained seated in the car for several long moments. The news van was still parked out front with a few people standing on the sidewalk.

It was now twenty-four hours that Cody had been

missing…twenty-four torturous hours. He was beginning to lose faith in the one phone call they had received. If that had been the real kidnapper, then why hadn't they already received proof of life?

He got out of the car and hurried into the house, where several women were in the kitchen with the deputies and Allison. "Knox," she said in obvious relief at the sight of him. "Anything new?"

"The Billings brothers are clean, as far as I can tell," he replied. He leaned closer to her. "Brad called Cody a snot-nosed kid and I punched him in the nose. I couldn't help myself, Allison."

"Did he call the sheriff?"

"No, he just told me to get off his property. What about here? Is there anything new?"

"We've gotten several phone calls. One man reported that he saw Cody standing on a corner in Austin." Allison's eyes were deep pools of anguish.

"We contacted the authorities in Austin to check it out," Wendall said and then shook his head. "Another caller said they saw Cody shopping in the Shadow Creek Mercantile. An officer responded but nobody in the store had seen Cody."

"You never know how many crazy people live in a town until something like this happens," Knox replied.

"According to Sheriff Jeffries the tip line has also received several calls and every one is being followed up on," Deputy Baker added.

"We now have posters," Allison said. "Jason dropped them off about an hour ago and several people are working to get them up all over town."

"I put them up along Main Street," one of the women standing by the table said.

The idea of Cody's smiling face on a missing child poster tortured him. And he knew Allison felt the same way. She wore her agony in the taut lines of her face, in the fragile cast of her shoulders.

"Thorne came by with clothes for you. I put them in Cody's room," Allison said.

"Thanks." Knox jumped as his cell phone rang again. He stepped out of the kitchen to answer it. It was Mac.

"I just thought you'd want to know that Leonor is back in town," Mac said. "She arrived here about an hour ago and asked if she could stay in the apartment above the stables."

Knox was stunned. "Did she say why she's here? I thought she was happy in Austin working at the museum."

"She didn't tell me why she's here and I told her she could stay in the apartment for as long as she needed. I just thought you might want to know."

"Thanks, Mac. I appreciate it."

"Anything new about Cody?"

"No, nothing."

"Let me know if there's anything I can do," Mac said.

"I will." The conversation ended and Knox sat in the chair, his thoughts on his sister. After Livia had been arrested, Leonor had completed her art degree and moved to Austin for an unpaid internship at a museum. She'd worked hard and eventually became curator.

More important, out of all the children Leonor had been the closest to Livia. She'd turned a blind eye to

Livia's faults for years and had defended her to the bitter end.

So why was she here in Shadow Creek now...when his son had been kidnapped? Did she think Livia was here in town? The timing of her return here was damned strange.

The next few hours passed far too quickly. Somebody brought in pizza and others checked in to get more posters to distribute. Allison remained in the kitchen, talking to several women Knox didn't know while he paced the living room floor.

It was obvious from how many people had called or come to offer support that Allison was well liked and respected in the town. They were people her business had served, or from the church and the school. She'd obviously touched a lot of people's lives with her kindness.

Then it was dusk and once again it was just the deputies and him and Allison as another long night began to fall.

Knox sat in a chair in the living room and watched Allison pace from the sofa to the front window and then back again. Instead of her usual grace, she moved like a jerky robot.

"Was Cody a good baby?" he asked.

She stopped and turned to look at him. Her eyes were wild with fear, but the wildness slowly dissipated as she held his gaze. "He was a very good baby." Her voice was soft. She walked back to the sofa and sank down. "He was good-natured and only fussed when he needed a diaper changed or was hungry."

"How old was he when he took his first step?" Knox

was suddenly ravenous to know everything about all the years he'd missed.

"He was eleven months when he started walking. He did everything early. He was such a smart baby boy."

As darkness fell outside the window, Knox listened as Allison recounted every milestone their son had reached so far in his life. He heard about his first word, his first smile and when he got his first haircut.

They were immersed in all things Cody when the phone rang. Allison shot out of the sofa and Knox stumbled up from the chair. They both raced into the kitchen where Wendall was ready with the recording device. It was another private caller.

Allison jerked up the receiver. "Hello."

"I know where your boy is," the female caller said. "He's in a shed on the old Miller property. I was driving by and saw somebody dressed all in black shove the boy inside. I couldn't tell if it was a man or a woman."

"Who is this?" Allison asked, her gaze locked with Knox's.

"I saw the posters of your boy and I'm just a concerned citizen." The line went dead.

"I know the Miller place. I'm going to check it out." Knox headed for the kitchen door.

"Wait, I'm coming with you," Allison replied.

"Allison, if this is the real deal, then it could be dangerous," Knox protested.

"Don't tell me I need to stay here. I am coming with you. Just give me a minute." She ran out of the kitchen and thundered up the stairs.

"I'm going with you both," Wendall said and rose

from the table. Knox and Wendall got to the front door when Allison came running back down the stairs, a gun in her hand.

"Where did you get that?" Knox asked in stunned surprise.

"I've had it for a couple of years and I know how to use it." A steely strength radiated from her eyes. "Let's go get our son." She stormed out of the door ahead of the men.

This was a woman Knox had never seen before, a slightly dangerous woman who almost stole his breath away with her love for her son, with her determination to do anything necessary to get him back.

They got into Wendall's patrol car and as they drove away from the house a cold wind blew through him. With Leonor's sudden appearance in town, he was more convinced than ever that his mother had Cody. Knox knew better than anyone what Livia was capable of… and that scared the very hell out of him.

Chapter 11

The patrol car couldn't go fast enough for Allison. She sat in the backseat, leaning forward and straining against the seat belt as if to hurry Wendall faster.

Her gun was a familiar weight in her lap. Five years before, her father had encouraged her to buy a gun and learn how to shoot it. He'd known that he wouldn't be around forever and had wanted her to be able to protect herself and her child.

She'd wanted a gun. With Knox's dangerous mother, she'd felt better knowing the weapon was in the house. She'd spent hours on the range, making sure she was comfortable shooting it and she kept it locked in a box in the highest dresser drawer near her bed.

She'd never really believed she could shoot somebody until this moment, but she would easily kill for

Cody and have not a single regret. She would walk through a firestorm if that's what it took to get her son back safely.

Knox had grabbed his own gun out of the glove compartment of his car before they had left, and she had no doubt that he felt the same way she did when it came to saving Cody.

The old Miller place was on the southern outskirts of town. John and Marlene Miller had lived there for as long as Allison could remember, but three years ago John had passed away and then last year Marlene had followed, and the ranch had been empty since then.

The couple had no children, and last Allison heard the house and the land were still in some sort of litigation between John's sisters and brothers. It had remained empty since Marlene's death.

She was grateful that nobody spoke, that the car was filled with nothing but the aching anticipation of finding Cody. The night had never seemed so dark and the minutes had never felt so endless as in this drive to nowhere in hopes of a miracle.

Although in the back of her mind, she knew this might be nothing but another crank call, this one had sounded so real. She had to believe this was it, and that before the night was over Cody would be in her arms once again.

The caller had said she couldn't tell if it was a man or a woman. Was it Livia? She didn't want to visit the sins of the mother onto the son again, and she hoped if Livia was behind all of this Allison wouldn't blame Knox. But at this moment she wasn't sure that she wouldn't.

"Kill the lights," Knox said, breaking the silence as they approached the Miller driveway.

Wendall shut off the car lights and instead of turning into the driveway he pulled to a halt on the side of the road. "I should call for backup," he said.

"You've got a Texas Ranger and a pissed off mother in the car. I think that's all the backup you need," Knox replied curtly.

Allison followed his gaze out the window, where the moonlight was bright enough to see an old, wooden shed a little distance from the dark house.

Was Cody in there? Was he crying out for her right now? Her stomach clenched and she fought the impulse to explode out of the car and run to the shed.

"What's the plan?" Wendall asked.

"We go in slow and quiet. We have no idea who exactly is in the shed," Knox replied. "The last thing we want is any kind of a hostage situation."

Hostage situation? Allison shuddered at the very thought. How many times on the news had she seen such situations with the hostages not making it out alive?

Within minutes they were out of the vehicle. Knox led with his gun drawn, and she and Wendall brought up the rear.

The yard was overgrown and thick with weeds as they moved slowly, each footstep unable to keep up with the pace of her thundering heart. The cold night was silent around them, but a fragile hope whispered with a warm breath inside her.

Let him be there. Let him be there. It was a mantra that repeated itself over and over in her brain.

When they got closer to the small structure, Knox turned around and motioned for Wendall to go to the left. "You stay behind me," he whispered to her.

She nodded, but held her gun at the ready. Now all she could hear was the sound of her heart beating loudly in her ears. She kept her gaze on the shed door, praying that Cody was behind it and that he was all alone.

Knox eased up to the door and pressed his ear against the wood. Wendall moved to stand just behind him. Knox shrugged, indicating that he heard nothing from inside.

As she saw there didn't appear to be any lock on the door, some of her hope withered. Why would anyone put a nine-year-old boy in a shed with no lock? Unless he was tied up and gagged. The vision that suddenly exploded in her mind nearly cast her to the ground.

Wendall pulled a flashlight from his belt and as Knox grabbed the door handle and yanked it open, Wendall flashed the light inside.

The last of her hope hissed out of her and she stumbled backward as Knox cursed. Nothing. The shed was completely empty. She turned and headed to the car, her body and her mind completely numb.

She got into the car, pulled her seat belt around her and then leaned back and closed her eyes. She couldn't think anymore. She was utterly and completely empty inside.

A few minutes later the men joined her and Wendall started the engine to make the long drive back to her house.

She remained strangely numb after they arrived home, where Jim told them the phone had remained silent and there was nothing new. She carried her gun upstairs and put it away and then returned to the living room and sank down on the sofa.

"Allison, are you okay?" Knox's forehead wrinkled in obvious concern as he gazed at her.

"I'm fine." Her voice sounded distant even to herself.

"It sounded so damned credible," he said angrily.

"It did, and we had to check it out," she replied. She got up from the sofa, still feeling oddly detached from the world. "I think I'm going to go up to my bedroom for a little while."

He jumped out of the chair. "Allison, are you sure you're all right?"

She cast him a faint smile. "I will be."

Once again her feet were ridiculously heavy as she climbed the stairs. She just wanted to sleep...to escape from this world without Cody. She didn't know what to do to find him. Nobody knew how to get her baby back where he belonged.

Shock. She had a feeling she was experiencing some sort of emotional shock to her system. When she reached her room she didn't bother to turn on a light. She got out of her clothes, pulled on the nightshirt with the horse on the front and then crawled into bed.

Darkness surrounded her, but no place was it as deep as in her heart, in her very soul. She closed her eyes and allowed herself to drift in a place where no thoughts could intrude. She couldn't think anymore because her head would take her to frighteningly dark places. She couldn't handle that. She didn't want to feel anymore, either.

She must have slept, for when she opened her eyes the house was silent. A glance at her clock told her it was just after midnight.

A piercing ache shot through her entire body. The blessed fog that had previously fallen over her was gone, leaving only raw, painful emotions to shoot through her.

She got out of bed and moved to the window. Chad still hadn't shown up anywhere and she was convinced he had Cody. It was just too coincidental that he and Cody had disappeared at the same time. She just couldn't believe what Knox believed, that his mother had made her way back there from Mexico to kidnap their child. She was so afraid to believe that was what had happened.

Tears began to ooze from her eyes, tears she'd been unable to shed when Knox had opened up the Miller shed door to reveal nothing. Pain gnawed at her stomach and her chest felt too small to contain her aching heart.

She needed…she wanted…something to ease some of this killing pain. She needed…she wanted Knox. She swiped the tears off her cheeks and turned from the window. She didn't care what was right or wrong right now. Knox would make her warm, even if just momentarily.

She left her bedroom. She had no idea if Knox was awake or asleep, downstairs or in Cody's room. All she knew was she wanted his strong arms around her.

She wanted him to kiss her until she was mindless and the pain inside her subsided, if only for a few minutes.

With shafts of moonlight to guide her, she went down the hallway to Cody's room, where Knox was stretched out on his lower bunk and the glow-in-the dark stars on the ceiling were lit with brilliance.

"Allison?" he said immediately, letting her know he hadn't been sleeping.

"Knox, I need you." She didn't wait for his response but instead turned and went back to her bedroom and into the bed.

Moments later he appeared in her doorway and hesitated there. "Allison, what do you need?" he asked.

"I need you to make love to me. I need you, Knox."

"Are you sure that's what you want?" His voice was soft, yet filled with gruff tension. "I know the night has been difficult and I don't want us to go there and then you hate me for it afterward."

Was that what would happen? Would she regret what happened between them tonight? Every time they'd made love in the past, she'd expected him to keep loving her, to be committed to her, but she had no foolish expectations now.

This was a one-night deal, driven by emotions she couldn't even name and couldn't begin to process. "I promise you that isn't going to happen, Knox."

In three long strides he was next to her bed. He pulled his shirt over his head, his taut chest muscles gleaming in the shaft of moonlight that danced through the window. He then took off his jeans, leaving him clad only in a pair of navy boxers.

He was beautiful. He'd always made her ache with desire at the sight of his naked body, and that hadn't changed over the years.

She scooted over and he slid into the bed with her and immediately drew her into his arms. His mouth found hers and he stole her breath and then gave it back to her in a searing kiss.

His hands caressed up and down her back and tangled in her hair, evoking flames of desire whenever he touched. Within minutes, her ache for him was so huge it left no room for any other thought but this single moment in time.

Yes, this was what she had needed. A mindless coupling with the man she loved, the man she had a feeling she would always love.

"Ally," he breathed against her neck as his lips nipped teasingly on her skin.

The nickname brought up past memories of their lovemaking. He'd been her only lover, but she knew with certainty that no man would ever move her the way he did.

She completely surrendered to them and him, aching with the need to alleviate the utter emptiness that threatened to engulf her. She needed a mindless respite from the fear for Cody that had been a living beast inside her.

Her hands caressed his muscled back, the familiar contours both comforting and enflaming her. His heart beat rapidly against hers as she pressed against him.

He suddenly pulled back from her, his eyes glittering as he held her gaze. "Are you sure, Ally? I need for you to be absolutely sure before this goes any further."

The fact that he was giving her a chance to halt things before they went to the place of no return only made her want him more. Instead of verbally answering him, she sat up and pulled her nightshirt over her head and tossed it across the room.

At the same time, he took off his boxers and then with a deep groan he pulled her to him, and she gasped at the intimate contact of her naked skin against his. She'd forgotten. She'd forgotten the exquisite joy and the fiery heat of soft need meeting with hard hunger.

"Ally," he whispered against her throat as he grabbed her buttocks and drew her more intimately against him.

She was lost in him…in the scent of him, in the familiar feel of his nakedness against hers. "Love me, Knox. Love me like you used to," she moaned.

In response, he slid his mouth down the length of her throat, across her collarbone and then down to capture one of her taut nipples. He licked and teased and tormented first one and then the other, making her crazy with desire. His hardness pressed against her thigh and she reached down to stroke the velvety length.

A husky groan escaped him and that only fueled her want of him. He caressed down the length of her body with fluid motions, and when he lingered along her inner thigh she raised her hips in need.

And then he was there, his fingers moving against her as a fluttering heat built up wild and untamed inside her. Her climax crashed down on her, leaving her gasping and boneless.

He moved between her thighs then and she cried out his name as he entered her. Clutching his shoulders, she met him thrust for thrust. He stroked long and deep inside of her. They moved slowly at first, but it wasn't long before frantic need changed the languid pace.

Once again, waves of pleasure coursed through her, each bigger than the last until she crested a peak and went over the edge. At the same time, he reached his own climax and shuddered against her.

They remained locked together and not moving for several long minutes. It was only when their breathing returned to normal that he rose up and stroked her hair away from her face and then kissed her long and deeply, stirring her on a whole different level.

Magic. They had always been magical together. The screaming fear that had been inside her wasn't completely gone, but it had quieted at least for the moment. Without saying a word, she moved away from him and slid out of bed and then padded into the bathroom.

She stared at her reflection in the mirror. The taste of him still lingered on her mouth and the scent of him drifted off her skin. She wouldn't take this back even if she could, even though she knew it was just another stupid mistake.

When she returned to the bedroom, Knox had pulled on his boxers and picked up his shirt and jeans from the floor. "You don't have to leave," she said. "Stay with me, Knox. Stay with me until morning." *Yet one more stupid mistake*, she thought. In for a penny, in for a pound.

He dropped his clothes and got back into the bed. She joined him there and he pulled her into the crook of his arm. She relaxed against his warmth and closed her eyes. She didn't want to think. She didn't want to feel. She just wanted to sleep with the warmth of Knox's kisses remaining and a prayer for her son on her lips.

Knox awoke before dawn, his body spooned around Allison's warm back. He remained still, his head filled with the sweet scent of her as thoughts of their love-making drifted through his mind.

It had been as good as it had always been, perhaps even better after all the years that had passed. He'd forgotten the pleasure of making love with her. She'd always been a passionate partner, and that hadn't changed. Despite the fact that they had been lovers in the past, this time had felt new and had been intensely satisfying.

They fit together as well now as they had when they'd been in high school and had become lovers. He had a feeling no matter what happened between them, no matter what happened in his life, she would always be in his blood.

He had no illusions that suddenly now they were going to be a couple again. Hell, he didn't even know if that's what he wanted. What he did know for sure was that she'd needed him last night to sweep away her pain, as he had needed her.

He frowned as he thought of their son. Where could he be? If the ransom call had been real, then why hadn't they received proof of life yet? The fact that there had been no follow-up on the phone call shot a shiver of dread through him.

The questions that whirled around in his mind begged for answers. The one thing that he hadn't wavered on was if this had been done for money, then he was certain his mother was behind it. Damn her rotten, narcissistic, sociopathic hide.

Knowing he wouldn't be able to go back to sleep again, he slowly moved away from Allison and got out of bed. Thankfully he didn't awaken her.

He picked up his clothes from the floor and went into Cody's room, where he grabbed clean ones and then headed for a shower.

It was Saturday morning and he suspected more people would turn out to help today. But what could they do? Walk the streets that had already been walked? Put up more posters, even though there were plenty already plastered around town?

According to Wendall, the sheriff was coordinating things from his office. What things? There were no clues, no leads to follow, so what in the hell was Sheriff Bud Jeffries coordinating besides his nap times?

Steaming more from his own thoughts than the hot water, he finished rinsing off the minty soap, shut off the shower and then dried off. He had no idea what might happen today, but he desperately needed something to. The waiting was not only tearing him apart, but Allison, as well.

Wendall and Jim were drinking coffee as Knox joined them in the kitchen. "Another day," Wendall said with compassion in his eyes.

Knox poured himself a cup of coffee and joined them at the table. "I just hope something pops today. This sitting around and waiting is killing all of us."

"I wish there was something more we could do,"

Jim replied. "The sheriff put a BOLO out on Chad last night, but so far nobody has reported seeing him, and the AMBER alert hasn't yielded anything yet."

"And I can't imagine where Chad has gone," Wendall added. "If this was just one of his normal benders, then he would have crawled home by now. It's definitely odd that he's just disappeared."

Was it possible that Chad had Cody? "I still find it hard to believe that a drunk could have pulled off a kidnapping and kept Cody for this long without making some major mistakes," Knox replied.

"You still think it's your mother?" Wendall asked.

Knox hesitated a moment. "Yeah, I do, but right now she's as elusive as Chad. I'm sure every law enforcement agency in the entire United States is looking for her, but I haven't heard of any sightings except the initial one in Mexico."

He frowned into his cup and then looked back at the two officers. "We all know the longer this goes on, the less likely there's going to be a happy ending."

Just saying the words out loud shoved a painfully tight emotion into his chest. He jumped up out of his chair. "How about pancakes for breakfast?" he asked. He needed to busy himself. He needed to keep his mind occupied so he didn't focus on the diminishing odds of getting Cody home alive.

He'd just served the two deputies pancakes when Allison appeared, clad in a pair of jeans and a pink T-shirt and with her hair loose and damp around her shoulders; the sight of her surged up a new desire inside him.

"Pancakes?" he asked, wondering how he could want

her again when it had only been hours before when he'd held her in his arms and made sweet love to her. Maybe it was just his need to seek an escape from the darkness of his thoughts.

She shook her head. "No thanks, just coffee for me."

She poured herself a cup and then sat at the table. Knox made himself a couple of pancakes and for a few minutes the kitchen was quiet as the men ate.

"Are you doing okay?" Knox finally broke the silence with an intent look at her.

"I'm fine," she replied.

She might be fine, but she was also distant. Gone was the needy woman of the night before. Her face was slightly wan but her eyes were shuttered against him. She remained silent as the morning wore on in agonizing increments of time.

The phone began ringing just after nine. There was another obvious prank call and some from several of her friends. She told them to contact her on her cell in hopes of leaving the landline open.

At ten thirty, a loud knock sounded at the door. Wendall got up to answer, followed by Knox. When Wendall opened the front door and Knox saw who was on the other side, stunned surprise filled him.

"Let them in," he said.

Fellow Texas Rangers Brett Hager and Dalton James came through the door with determined footsteps and grins on their faces. Instead of their uniforms, they were dressed casually in jeans and long-sleeved shirts.

"What are you two doing here?" Knox asked incredulously.

"We had a little vacation time coming and we heard about your son. We're here to help a brother," Dalton said with a clap on Knox's back.

The back of Knox's throat closed up with emotion. These two men were like brothers to him. They had all spent the last ten years together working side by side. They were both highly intelligent investigators, and seeing them here now twisted Knox's heart with a wealth of gratitude.

Allison appeared in the doorway and Knox made the introductions. They all went into the kitchen, where more introductions were made to Wendall and Jim.

"Get us up to speed," Brett said and he pulled a notepad from his pocket.

For the next hour, the two Rangers asked questions and listened as Knox and Allison and the two deputies filled them in on everything that had happened since the moment Cody was late getting home from the bus stop.

Some of their questions were personal and sharp, but he and Allison answered them without hesitation. It was part of the process to get to the bottom of things.

"So the two of you were here together before the time that Cody got off the bus," Brett said. They both nodded. "So you both have solid alibis at the time of the kidnapping."

Allison looked at Knox, obviously unsettled to realize they might each need an alibi. But, he knew all too well that when a child disappeared, the parents were almost always the first suspects.

"Rock solid," Knox replied.

"And you've talked to these Billings brothers and

been to their homes?" Brett asked. Knox nodded and Brett looked at Allison. "Now tell us everything you can about this Chad character."

The questioning continued for another fifteen minutes and then Dalton looked at Wendall. "That recording equipment you have hooked up is ancient."

"Small town budget," Wendall replied ruefully.

"Well, it just so happens we have some fancy new equipment in the car," Dalton said. "I'll go get it." He got up from the table and left the room.

For the first time in the past forty-eight hours, a new hope buoyed in Knox's heart and he saw the same emotion light Allison's eyes.

These weren't small town sheriffs who ate in their cars with their seats reclined; they were trained Texas Rangers with a fierce determination to find Cody.

Dalton returned and hooked up the new equipment to the landline and then he and Brett took off to take the path Cody took to and from the bus stop. Knox walked them out and then returned to find Allison seated on the sofa.

"I'm glad they're here," she said.

"Me, too."

"You're close to them."

He nodded. "They're two of my best friends and they're great investigators. If anyone can sniff out a clue, it will be one of them." Knox eased down next to her. "I thought about calling them before now, but didn't want to interfere with their work."

He studied her face. Even with the strain that showed in the dark circles under her eyes and lines across her forehead, she still made his heart quicken like no other woman.

"Regrets?" he asked softly. "We didn't even use protection."

She sighed and reached up to worry a strand of her hair. "I've been on the Pill since Cody was born. No regrets, although I admit I had a moment of weakness and it wasn't really a good idea."

He wasn't sure why, but her words shot a bit of disappointment through him. "It's okay to be weak sometimes."

She held his gaze for a long moment and then dropped her hand to her lap. "There was a time when you were my strongest weakness, but I can't go there again."

The doorbell rang and she jumped up to answer it. It was Lauren Patten from the school. She carried a large tray of ham and cheese sandwiches. Allison took the platter from her and carried it into the kitchen and then returned to the living room to talk to Lauren.

"Everyone is talking about Sheriff Jeffries's ineptitude," she said.

"That subject has been mentioned around here more than once," Knox said drily.

"He spends most of his time either sitting at his desk or in his car. He's a disgrace," Lauren replied.

"I think he's an ass," Allison added.

"I just hope he's out of office in the fall," Lauren replied. "This town deserves somebody better than Bud Jeffries. Our crime rate has actually gotten worse since he took office."

"Right now I don't care about any other crime than the one that took Cody from us," Allison said.

"Is there anything…anything at all I can do to help? There are lots of us who want to, but just don't know what to do," Lauren said, her eyes lit with compassion.

"We appreciate the sandwiches," Allison said. "I really don't know what anyone can do other than keep searching."

"The rumor is that Chad has Cody."

"That's what I think," Allison replied.

Knox listened as Allison told Lauren about firing Chad and him demanding she pay him ten thousand dollars. "I told him no way and then he got nasty and swore I'd be sorry. Then I started getting nasty, threatening texts from him."

"That creep. I've seen him weaving drunkenly on lots of evenings when he heads home from the bars," Lauren exclaimed. "Somebody should do something about him."

"Right now, I just wish somebody would find him," Allison replied fervently.

As the two women continued to talk, Knox excused himself and went out on the front porch. He drew in a deep breath of the sweet-scented spring air and wondered if Cody could smell the grass. Was the kidnapper feeding him? Keeping him warm on these chilly nights? He sank down on the swing and willfully shoved these thoughts out of his head.

He still couldn't believe that Dalton and Brett were there to help. It felt like a scene from an old Western movie where the cavalry finally arrives and saves the day.

Could they save the day? Could they find something that everyone else had overlooked? A clue that would lead to getting Cody back?

Lauren left and still Knox remained outside, a fragile, new hope burning bright in his heart. He stood as he saw the two men approaching in the distance. He didn't expect them to return to the house with the mystery solved, and they hadn't.

They joined him on the porch. "Did the authorities speak to everyone who lives on the street?" Dalton asked.

Knox nodded. "And nobody saw Cody."

"And you're certain he got off the bus?" Brett asked.

"Yes, we checked with the bus driver who stated that Cody got off as usual." Knox shoved his hands in his pockets. "I know he was kidnapped. I just don't know by whom."

Knox told the two about his belief his mother might be behind it and then about Allison's belief that it was Chad, who had also disappeared around the same time as Cody.

Both of the Rangers were intimately acquainted with Livia and her crimes, and neither of them dismissed Knox's gut instinct. "According to our sources, everyone still believes Livia is hiding out someplace in Mexico," Brett said.

"But we all know without any eyes on her she could be anywhere," Knox replied.

He looked up the sidewalk, wishing some sort of magic would happen and he'd see Cody running toward him. But of course there was no magic and no Cody.

"You mentioned that the sheriff set up a tip line. Anything concrete come from that?" Brett asked.

"He's got his men chasing down anything that comes in, but so far it's led nowhere," Knox replied.

"Are you planning on coming back to the Rangers when you get Cody back home?" Dalton asked.

"You know as soon as this thing with your mother is cleaned up you'd be more than welcomed back."

"I saw the way you look at Allison," Dalton said. "You aren't coming back, are you?"

Knox looked at him in surprise. Was it that obvious? Was it that apparent that he was still hung up on Allison? "No, I'm not going back," he said. He hadn't even been aware that he'd made that decision until the words had fallen out of his mouth.

He pulled his hands from his pockets and continued, "I don't know what I'm going to do in the future, but whatever it is will be here in Shadow Creek, where I can be a present father all the time to Cody."

Dalton studied him. "And your decision has nothing to do with Allison?"

Did it? Was Knox somehow hoping for another chance with her? A chance to finally get it right and be a real family with Cody? "I don't know," he finally replied. "I don't know what the future holds for me and Allison."

Despite what had happened between them the night before, she wasn't exactly jumping up and down with the desire to get back into a relationship with him.

And he still had a knot of anger when he thought about all he'd missed in Cody's life because of her lies.

How could they possibly get past all the baggage that remained between them?

"Let's get back inside," he said. He didn't want to think about a future with Allison. All he wanted right now was his son back.

Lunch came and went as Dalton and Brett continued to ask them questions. They also listened to the tape of the one credible ransom call that had come in four times. Like Knox, they were unable to discern any background noise. It was just after three when Sheriff Jeffries showed up.

It was obvious when Dalton and Brett began to ask him questions that the sheriff wasn't happy with the Rangers' presence or their interest in *his* investigation.

"I've covered all the bases," he said. "I'm on top of things. I've got my men doing everything they can."

"The last thing we want to do is step on any toes," Dalton said diplomatically. "We all want the same thing, to get Cody home where he belongs."

"We would appreciate it if you could share with us the interviews you've already conducted," Brett said.

"This is my investigation. I just wanted to stop by and check in," Bud replied. He looked at Wendall. "And you will keep me up to date on what's going on here." With that, he left the house and slammed the door on his way out.

"Well, that was helpful," Dalton said with a raise of his blond eyebrows.

"I sure hope somebody runs against him in the fall," Allison replied.

The phone rang, and this time it was Dalton who indicated he was ready for her to answer. Knox saw the tremble in her fingers, the darkness of her eyes as she said hello.

"You have proof of life. Go to www.Cody.com." The caller hung up.

"It was the same person," Allison said as her gaze locked with his. "It was the same person who called here before."

"Get your laptop," he said, his stomach twisting in a thousand knots. A web page…he just couldn't believe a drunk like Chad would have the capability to do such a thing.

"I've got it," Dalton replied as he quickly opened his own laptop. "It will be better if we do this on mine."

It had to be his mother, and Knox prayed that whatever was on the website would finally yield a clue. He'd find and arrest her and get his son back home. And she could rot in prison where she belonged for the rest of her life.

But before that could happen they had to see the web page. His heart boomed triple-time beats as he waited to see what Dalton pulled up.

Chapter 12

Allison's heart fluttered frantically in her chest as she watched Dalton type the address for the web page into the browser that would hopefully show her son alive.

She wanted her son home now, but at this moment what she needed was to see him alive and well. She leaned closer behind Dalton's shoulder.

The page pulled up and she gasped. Tears leaped to her eyes, momentarily blurring her vision until she swiped them away. Cody sat in a straight-backed chair and held the morning newspaper in his hands. His eyes radiated a horrifying fear and although there was no sound, his mouth moved and she knew he was calling out to her.

Although physically he looked okay, his terror shot through her. Oh, God, he needed her. She wanted to reach through the computer screen and somehow get him, hug him tight against her heart.

"This looks like a live stream," Dalton exclaimed. "We need to capture the image." His fingers flew over the keys as tears raced faster and faster down Allison's cheeks.

Knox moved next to her and threw an arm around her shoulders, tension radiating out from him. "Damn," Dalton swore as the site suddenly went black.

Almost immediately the phone rang and Knox grabbed the receiver. "Twenty-four hours, a million dollars at the exchange place we discussed," the robotic voice said.

"That's not reasonable," Knox replied. "We don't have a million dollars here, and there's no way for us to get any large sum of money in the next twenty-four hours. It's Saturday afternoon and the banks are closed until Monday."

"Five hundred thousand by midnight on Monday."

"Two hundred and fifty thousand by midnight on Tuesday," Knox countered.

Allison stared at him in horror. She couldn't believe he was bartering for their son's life and moving the possibility of getting Cody back to another day. What on earth was wrong with him? Had he lost his mind?

"Okay, Tuesday night," the voice replied. "And if I see anybody else anywhere in the area, I'll kill the boy." The phone line went dead.

Knox hung up the receiver and Allison launched herself at him. She slapped him, vaguely registering his shock as his cheek turned red with her handprint.

She pummeled him in his chest as she sobbed uncontrollably.

He grabbed her wrists in an attempt to stop her assault. "Allison, stop! What in the hell are you doing?"

"What in the hell are you doing?" she retorted. She tried to yank her wrists from his hands, but he held on tight, only making her angrier.

He pulled her out of the kitchen and into the living room. He still held her wrists tightly, as if he knew if he released them she'd use them to attack him again.

He was right. She wanted to punch him again and again. In the back of her mind, she knew she was wildly out of control, but she didn't care. She couldn't believe what he had just done.

"We could have gotten him home within twenty-four hours, but you haggled for his life as if he was nothing more than an item at a garage sale or a flea market." The words spewed out of her on choked sobs.

"I had to buy us some time," he replied.

"Time for what?"

"Time for us to find him." Knox's eyes were pools of anguish. "Hopefully Dalton can trace the kidnapper through the web page, but it will take time. We've finally gotten something to work with so we can catch whoever is behind this."

"I don't give a good damn about capturing the kidnapper. You believe your mother is behind this? You know what I think? I think you want to catch her and punish her more than you want to get our son back."

Knox drew in a deep breath and let go of her wrists. He stepped back from her, his eyes positively frosty. "If you think anything is more important to me than getting Cody back, then you're dead wrong. What makes you believe the person who has him isn't going to take the money and kill him anyway?"

A small gasp released from her. Her brain was in chaos, her body filled with so many emotions she couldn't make sense of any of them, and his words only added to the horror.

"We need to find the kidnapper and take Cody back before that money drop ever happens. That's the only way to ensure we get him back alive," he said.

She hadn't thought his eyes could get any colder, but they did as he took another step away from her. "You don't think I want him back here as quickly as possible? I had less than two weeks with him while you had nine years. He doesn't even know I'm his father because you didn't want me to tell him and now I'm afraid I'll never get the chance to. You should have let me know that I was his father the minute you found out you were pregnant."

"I didn't want you to know," she retorted. "You left me. I decided to keep Cody from you because you didn't want me and I never wanted your mother to have the ability to use him to hurt you any more than she'd hurt you in the past," she retorted.

"My mother had just been convicted. We were losing our family home and I was a mess. I had to leave town before I lost my mind."

"You should have run to me, not away from me. If your mother is behind this, then I wish you'd never found out about him." She swiped her tears off her cheeks.

He stared at her for a long moment, their bitter words hanging in the air between them. He then turned on his heels and flew out the front door.

Allison stared after him. So he obviously still harbored bad feelings toward her. She'd thought they had made peace with the past, but his accusations and her own words spilling out on a river of anger told her otherwise.

The past had reared up in ugly words, but she couldn't think about that right now. What stunned her the most was the fact that he wasn't as confident about getting Cody back as she'd thought he was.

And that lack of self-assurance shot a new wave of fear through her. She didn't want to go back and sit in the kitchen where the men were talking about IP addresses and all kinds of computer things she knew nothing about, and she didn't want to sit on the sofa where she might encounter Knox before their intense emotions died down.

One thing was clear, if she'd entertained even the slightest fantasy that they might find a way back to each other, it had just died a sharp, painful death. The baggage was still there between them, and she suspected it would always be there.

Instead she went into the kitchen, where the men fell silent at her appearance. They had probably heard the fight. She and Knox hadn't exactly kept their voices low.

She didn't speak to or look at any of them as she went out the door and into the backyard. She walked over to the tree where she'd hoped to have a tree house built for Cody and clung to a lower branch and wept.

She should have built it last year when she'd first thought about it. Now she had no idea if Cody would ever get to enjoy a tree house.

Had she really been afraid that Cody wasn't ready to handle knowing that Knox was his father? Or had her decision to wait been her own fears speaking? Had she been afraid of sharing Cody's love? Afraid that her son would be angry with her if the truth ever came out?

She cried until there were no tears left, only hiccupping gasps that ripped through her stomach.

She should have let Knox tell Cody he was his father the moment he'd shown up in town. She shouldn't have lied to him years ago when she'd discovered she was pregnant, but she'd felt so alone and had been afraid of Livia. But, no amount of regret could give those nine years with his son back to Knox.

She released the branch and dropped down into the cool grass. She wasn't sorry for her words to Knox about his mother. His hatred of Livia had driven so many decisions in his life, and not all of them had been good.

He hadn't gone to college because he hadn't wanted to leave his siblings alone with Livia. Instead, he'd worked on the family ranch.

He'd gone through a spell of drinking too much their senior year and had blamed his mother. And he'd pulled away from Allison, once again allowing Livia to pull his strings.

She hadn't even realized that's what she thought until the words had fallen out of her mouth. She shouldn't have said anything to him, despite what she'd felt about his relationship with his mother.

She definitely shouldn't have said that she thought getting his mother behind bars was more important to him than getting Cody. It had been a cheap shot that had cut him deeply.

None of that mattered now. What did matter was she'd never felt as alone as she did now.

She realized as she plucked a piece of grass and allowed the cool breeze to carry it away that for the moment she had abandoned hope.

Knox was optimistic that they'd be able to find Cody before time ran out, thanks to the extra time he'd bargained for and the clues they gleaned from the website. But, she didn't feel the same.

She was terrified that when this was all over she'd be completely alone with only a killing grief to endure for the rest of her life.

Cody stared at the bologna sandwich covered in plastic wrap in his lap. It had been tossed to him after his kidnapper had taken a video of him holding up a newspaper.

His kidnapper. He now knew that he'd been taken by the person who wore a long, dark coat and a ski mask. Cody didn't know if it was a man or a woman. The person hadn't uttered a word to him the whole time Cody had been captive, although Cody had asked him questions.

Why did you take me? What's going to happen to me? Who are you? Oh, yes, Cody had asked questions, but the person had not answered. The silence was scarier than any answer the person could give him.

He was still chained to the wall, but the chain was long enough to allow him to walk about the room a bit. He could reach the portable toilet in one corner and an old sink with a plastic cup he used to drink water.

His clothes felt dirty against his skin. He never wore them for this long a time. He needed a bath. A lump rose up in his throat. He needed his mom.

He'd tried to figure out how to escape, but the ring around his ankle was so tight and the chain was too heavy and secured too well to the concrete-block wall for him to get free. The ring pinched his skin, and he'd finally stopped trying to get free when his ankle got sore from him attempting to slide it through the iron loop.

It scared him that nobody had found him yet. He didn't even know if he was still in Shadow Creek. For all he knew, he could be in Alaska. They had studied a little bit about Alaska in school, and he knew that it was a long, long way from Shadow Creek, Texas.

He didn't know where he was and he didn't know who had taken him. How would his mom or Knox or anybody know who had kidnapped him and where he was if Cody didn't know?

Tears welled up in his eyes as he once again looked at the sandwich. This was the fourth one that had been given to him. He hated bologna, but he was starving.

He unwrapped it and closed his eyes, pretending that he was back at home and sitting at the kitchen table and his mom had made him his favorite grilled ham and cheese.

* * *

Knox seethed with an anger he'd never known before as he drove away from the house. How dare Allison talk to him about his mother? She hadn't lived through what he had; she didn't know the emotional turmoil and damage Livia had wrought on all the Colton children.

He headed toward the crooked tree that would be the exchange point on Tuesday night. Now that he knew the ransom demand was real, he wanted to get the lay of the land.

Allison had acted like she didn't think he cared about Cody. The most difficult thing he'd ever done in his life was bargain for his son's life. And if what he believed was true and his mother was behind the kidnapping, then he had no doubt in his mind that she would kill Cody if he could identify her. She would leave no witness behind. That's the way she operated.

He clenched and unclenched his hands around the steering wheel. He was hoping that Dalton and Brett could find out all the ins and outs of the web page and come up with information that would find Cody before Tuesday night.

You should have run to me and not away from me.

Allison's words played and replayed through his mind. Some of his anger was expelled on a deep sigh. Perhaps she was right, but he'd felt so tainted by the whole scandal when his mother had been arrested and charged. He'd been broken, and the last person he'd wanted to see him that way was the woman he loved.

At that time, Jade and Claudia were minors and he'd believed he would become their guardian. He wasn't sure where they were going to live or how they were all going to survive.

Thankfully, Mac had stepped in to take the girls, and he'd even offered Knox a job working as a ranch hand on his property, a job that he'd gladly taken.

Still, he had to admit that Livia had manipulated him more than once over the years, attempting to drive a wedge between himself and Allison. When they'd been dating in high school, Livia had told him she'd seen Allison in town with another guy. Knox had broken up with Allison the next day.

While Allison was away at college, more than once Livia had mentioned that she'd heard through the grapevine that Allison was a very popular young woman among her male classmates.

Livia had made it damned easy for him to believe Allison had cheated on him; she'd made it so easy for him to believe that Cody wasn't his.

He slowed his car as he drove the road that led out of town to the west. He didn't know exactly where the tree was located, but assumed it must be fairly visible from the road for the kidnapper to assume they could easily find it.

Attempting to shove away the heated argument with Allison, he focused his attention out the window. As he left the small town behind, the scenery was more rural, with trees and pastures on either side.

Then he saw it. The tree stood alone, its branches gnarled and blackened from a lightning strike that had happened sometime in the past.

There were no buildings around, no place where a

little boy could be hidden away. There was also not a place where law enforcement could hide to be ready to take down the kidnapper.

He parked along the side of the road and got out of the car. He grabbed his cowboy hat from the seat and placed it on his head.

His stomach twisted in a hundred knots as he approached the large tree. He could only assume the kidnapper intended to pull up in a car and exchange the money for Cody.

So many things could go wrong. He was still convinced their best hope was to find where Cody was being held before the exchange ever took place.

He'd been thinking only of Cody's safety when he'd told the kidnapper Tuesday night. That gave them the rest of the day, along with Sunday, Monday and most of the day Tuesday to figure out Cody's location.

He closed his eyes for a moment and Cody's face filled his head. A father was supposed to protect his son, and it killed him that this had happened. It tortured him that his being there in Shadow Creek and that damned blog had probably alerted his mother to a weakness she could exploit.

At least they now knew that Cody hadn't appeared to have been physically hurt. He wasn't sure what he would have done if his son had shown signs of physical abuse.

At the sound of a car approaching, he opened his eyes and turned to see Sheriff Jeffries's patrol car pulling up behind his.

He remained where he was as the sheriff got out of

his car and approached him. "They told me at the house that you'd taken off. I thought I might find you here."

"Then you know we received proof of life and the exchange is supposed to take place here," Knox replied.

"I watched the tape." The lawman rolled back on his heels and then narrowed his gaze. "So, you really thought it was necessary to call in the Texas Rangers?"

"I didn't call them in. They came on their own. They're good friends of mine and they aren't here in an official capacity." A new gratitude swept through him as he thought of the two men who were using their vacation time to be there with him now.

"As long as they don't get in my way," Bud replied.

Little chance of that happening, Knox thought. It was difficult to get in the way of somebody who was basically doing nothing at all.

Bud looked around and frowned. "Going to be hard to have men out here in place for the exchange. There isn't a hidey-hole in the area."

"I don't want any men in place. We were told that if any law enforcement was seen then Cody would die. I'm not going to take that kind of chance with my son's life."

"You're just going to pay the money and hope for the best?" Bud said with a lifted eyebrow.

"I'm still hoping we'll find Cody before Tuesday night," Knox replied.

"I'm working on it," Bud replied.

"And I appreciate everything you're doing," Knox replied. The last thing he intended to do was put his trust in any of Bud's efforts. If Cody was going to be found, it would be through the work of Dalton and Brett.

"Do you have a plan?" Bud asked.

"Not yet," he admitted.

"If you find out where Cody is being held, I'd better be the first to know. It's obvious he isn't being held anyplace around here. Hopefully, wherever he is, there will be places where we can provide backup."

"I appreciate it," Knox said, although he wasn't sure at this point if his plan included letting Bud know anything they might find. "Was there anything else?" he asked.

He was suddenly eager to get back to the house and find out if the men had discovered anything about the website. He wanted to watch it again and see if he could figure out the space where Cody was being held.

"Just that it's important we keep each other informed on any breaking news on this case. I think maybe another press conference would be a good idea, this time with you and Allison speaking to the public."

"I'll talk to Allison about it," Knox replied as he took off walking toward his car.

"I'll be in touch," Bud yelled as Knox got behind the wheel.

Knox felt as if he'd been beaten as he drove back into town. Hell, he had been beaten by Allison. She'd shocked him with her fury as she'd slapped his face and then pummeled her fists against his chest. But she hadn't hurt him physically.

He felt emotionally beaten, and he knew there was no way he and Allison would come out of this situation as the same people. They would be forever changed, forever scarred by the unrelenting terror, the horror of what they were enduring right now.

The last thing he'd wanted was for the stress to make them turn on each other. They should be clinging together right now, giving and getting strength from one another, not fighting with words as swords.

You should have run to me and not away from me. Once again her words played in his mind. They'd definitely turned on each other in an ugly way, one that he now regretted.

He'd been wrong to guilt her about the fact that they hadn't told Cody about him being the boy's father before the kidnapping. She'd been trying to do what was best for Cody and he'd understood that. He'd delivered a low blow to her and he owed her an apology for that if for nothing else.

The intense anger that had driven him out of the house was gone as he returned. He parked in the driveway and got out of the car, suddenly feeling much older than he had a week ago.

Allison wasn't in the living room or in the kitchen. "Where's Allison?" he asked the men in the kitchen.

"She went outside to the backyard when you left," Wendall replied.

"Knox, we got a screen cap of the website before it went down," Dalton said. "I want you to watch it and give us your opinion."

He had to believe that Allison had gone outside because she'd wanted to be alone. He also had to suspect that he was probably the very last person on earth she wanted to see right now.

He sat in the chair Dalton vacated and looked at the laptop screen. Dalton hit a button and the video of Cody holding the newspaper played. All he could focus on was the fear that radiated out from Cody's eyes, the little body that trembled with terror. Knox wanted to reach into the screen and grab his son and hold him until the fear left both of them.

"Play it again," he said softly, knowing what Dalton wanted him to do.

As the video played a second time, he kept his focus away from Cody and instead studied the boy's surroundings. A bare lightbulb hung down from the ceiling. He leaned closer to the computer screen. The wall just behind Cody appeared to be concrete block.

Although the bare bulb cast a pool of light over Cody's head, there was another faint source of illumination that appeared to be coming from a window set high in a wall to the right of the screen.

"A basement," Knox said with excitement. "He's being held in a basement."

Dalton nodded with satisfaction. "That's what we thought, and the fact that Cody is holding up the Shadow Creek morning paper makes us believe he's being held someplace here in town."

"There aren't that many homes around here that have basements," Knox replied thoughtfully. "They're difficult and expensive to build because of all the limestone. Surely we could get a list of places with basements from city hall?" For the first time, a new hope built inside him. They were getting closer.

"You'd probably have the best luck with the city clerk

who issues building permits, but city hall is closed until Monday," Wendall said.

"Who is the city clerk?" Knox asked.

"Myna Turner," Wendall replied.

Knox frowned and stifled a groan. He remembered the fifty-something woman from ten years before. She'd been one of the loudest mouths dragging the Colton name through the mud and she'd led the successful attempt to get Livia Colton's name removed from the hospital. He seriously doubted that she'd want to do anything to help him. But she might want to help Allison.

Whether she was ready to talk to him or not, he needed her to know this new development. He got up from the chair. "I'll be right back."

He walked out the back door and found her sitting beneath a large tree, the early evening sunshine dappled as it came through the new leaves and cast her features in shadows.

She didn't look up when he approached. She didn't look at him until he sank down in the grass facing her. When she did, her eyes were dark gold pools and her face was wan.

"Last year, I intended to have a tree house built for Cody, but one thing led to another and it never got done. I've been sitting here wondering what on earth was more important than a tree house for my son."

"You know, those kinds of thoughts will just try to destroy you," Knox said softly. He hesitated. He wanted to apologize to her, but he feared she would think he was only apologizing because he wanted her to contact Myna Turner.

"We have a new development," he said, deciding his apology could wait until later.

"What?" Her eyes came alive.

"We believe Cody is being held in a basement someplace here in town."

"A basement?"

He nodded. "What we need is to get hold of Myna Turner to see if she can give us a list of people who have basements around here." He stood and held out his hand to her. "I need you to contact her and ask. It might be the clue we need to finally get Cody home."

She hesitated only a moment and then reached for his hand. He grasped hers firmly and pulled her up from the ground, fighting the impulse to grip her close to him. He had a feeling she wouldn't welcome an embrace from him right now.

Together, they went into the kitchen where the other men were once again watching the video. When it finished playing, Dalton leaned back in his chair with a frown.

"No matter how many times I watch it, no matter how I zoom in on the images, I can't get any more information about the room where the video was shot," he said with obvious frustration.

"But we still believe it was shot in a basement and that that's where he's being held," Brett added.

"I'll call Myna and see if she can help us," Allison said. Her voice was stronger, her eyes more focused as she went to the kitchen desk and pulled out a small, pink telephone book.

She found the number and picked up her cell phone.

Knox watched her intently, hoping…praying that finally they had a solid lead.

"Myna, it's Allison Rafferty. I would appreciate it if you gave me a call back as soon as you get this message. It's urgent." She ended the call. "She wasn't home."

"Does she have a cell phone number?" Knox asked.

Allison shook her head. "I seriously doubt it, I once heard her say that she believed cell phones were the work of the devil. I don't even think she has a home computer."

"Is there anyone else who might be able to get us a list?" Knox asked Wendall.

"Not that I know of. Myna is pretty territorial about her work," Wendall replied.

"Then we can just hope Myna gets back to me quickly," Allison replied.

A sinking sensation filled Knox. The clock was ticking, and there was nothing more they could do than wait for a phone call that might or might not be the first step in bringing Cody home.

Chapter 13

Night fell with a bang of thunder. A tornado watch had been issued for the area until midnight as severe storms moved in. Allison stood at the front window and stared outside, her utter despair back like an unwanted enemy.

It was as if she'd swallowed the storm...the thunder was her cry of anguish, the rain her tears and the lightning rent her broken heart into more pieces.

She'd left three more messages for Myna, but the woman still hadn't called her back. She must be out of town for the weekend because Allison was certain if she got her frantic messages she would have called by now.

Brett and Dalton had left to go to the motel where they had rented rooms for the duration of their stay there in Shadow Creek. They had promised to be back by dawn the next morning.

Knox sat on the sofa behind her, but his restless energy filled the room. They had spoken little during the evening. He'd sat in the kitchen with the other men while she'd wandered the house, as if she might find Cody hiding in a corner or under a bed.

"He doesn't like thunderstorms," she said. "When he was small, anytime it thundered he'd sneak into bed with me. As he got older, we had a routine where we sat in here and we'd put on a movie. He'd eventually fall asleep on the sofa and I'd snooze in the chair."

Lightning slashed the black skies and she stepped back from the window. "He's someplace out there all alone in a storm," she said miserably. "He'll be so afraid."

She heard the faint groan of the sofa cushion and then Knox's warm hands were on her shoulders. She turned around to face him, and his hands remained where they were.

"He's tough, Allison. He'll get through the storm. We're all going to get through this storm."

She knew he wasn't just talking about the weather outside. She leaned into him as another boom of thunder shook the house.

His hands moved to her back and he pulled her into a tight embrace. "I'm sorry, Ally. I'm so sorry about the things I said to you earlier. I didn't mean them, I was just frustrated and needed to vent."

She leaned her head against his chest. "I'm sorry, too." She drew in a deep breath. "We're the last two people who should be tearing each other apart right now."

He stroked a hand down her back, not in a sexual

way, but rather as if comforting a child. "From now on, we won't. The past is gone and all we have is the here and now."

She remained in his embrace, and thunder rolled and lightning flashed outside. Rain began to pelt the windows, like the tears that filled her heart.

Finally, she raised her head to look at him, wanting his calm, steady gaze to further comfort her. He lowered his mouth to hers in a kiss that wasn't all fire and desire, but rather all tenderness and caring. It was exactly what she needed from him.

The rain turned to the sharp sound of hail against glass. When the kiss ended, he cupped her face with his hands. "If Cody is in a basement somewhere, let's hope he can't hear the storm and he won't be afraid."

She nodded and then stepped away from him and moved back to the window. The hail lasted only a minute or so and then turned back into rain.

"I think maybe the storm is starting to pass." She turned away from the window and looked at him once again. A deep frown cut across his forehead. "What are you thinking?" she asked, her worry climbing higher by the troubled look on his features.

"I think Chad's house had a basement."

She walked to him and grabbed his forearm in a tight grip. "Are you sure?" Was it possible Chad had really been home all this time, ensconced in his basement with Cody as his captive?

Knox frowned, his gaze distant. "I can't be absolutely positive, but I think so." He focused back on her again. "I'm going to go check it out."

"Let me get my gun and I'm coming with you."

"Allison, you don't need your gun. I've got your back." He dragged a finger down the side of her face, his eyes as bright blue as she'd ever seen them. "No matter what happens in the future, I promise I'll always have your back."

He dropped his hand to his side and walked over to the window, where the rain had turned to a heavy mist. He whirled back to face her. "Let's go."

She was grateful he didn't even attempt to tell her to stay behind. "Should we get Wendall or Jim?"

"No. I'll tell them we're going out, but they don't need to know where we're going because if there is a basement in that house, then I'm going to do something illegal and get inside, and I'm definitely not waiting for Sheriff Jeffries to show up."

"Should you call Brett and Dalton?" she asked.

"No, I don't want to get them into any trouble," he replied.

Together they went into the kitchen where Jim was half-asleep in his chair and Wendall was reading a book. "We're going out for a little while," Knox said.

"Going out?" Wendall cast a gaze toward the window and then looked back at them. "In this kind of weather?"

"It's been a long day. We need some fresh air. We're just going for a drive and besides, the storms sound like they're moving away," she said.

Wendall narrowed his eyes. "You need some fresh air at almost midnight on a stormy night? Allison… Knox…what's really going on?"

"Nothing you need to worry about," Knox replied firmly. "We shouldn't be too long."

Knox didn't bother with a coat but Allison grabbed her black raincoat from the hall closet and a flashlight she kept on the shelf and then they ran through the mist to his car.

"Wendall knows something is up," she said as he pulled out of her driveway. "Maybe we should have brought him with us."

"He would have been compelled to stop me from breaking in, and the only way he would be able to do that is to shoot me." He flashed her a determined look. "If there's a basement there, then nobody is going to stop me from entering."

"And I'll be right behind you," she replied.

They fell silent, the only sound the swishing of the windshield wipers and the thudding of her heart in her ears. She didn't want to entertain any hope because she didn't want another bitter disappointment. And yet it was difficult to keep hope out of her heart as they drew closer to Chad's place.

"I'm assuming there's still a patrol car parked at Chad's," he said when they were a couple of blocks away from Chad's house. "I'll park a block away and we'll have to sneak through backyards. I'm not in the mood to get shot by a deputy who thinks we're thieves."

"I'd walk through an alligator infested swamp if it was possible that Cody would be saved," she replied fervently.

He pulled up to the curb five houses away from

Chad's. She grabbed the flashlight tight in her hand and he had his gun in his hand as they got out of the car.

The mist was still fairly heavy as they cut through a side yard to reach the back of the houses. Thankfully nobody had a fence so their way was clear to get to Chad's.

A dog barked plaintively in the distance and the only other sound was the faint trickle of rain dripping off leaves and bushes.

The night was dark and she clicked on the flashlight to aid them. Wet grass clung to her shoes and dampened the bottom of her jeans and her hair and face were quickly wet from the mist.

Lightning flashed in the distance followed by a faint rumble of thunder. Her heart quickened its pace as they drew closer and closer to the back of Chad's house.

Did he really have a basement? Or was Knox mistaken? Were they mere yards from Cody? Nobody had gone inside the house despite Chad's seeming disappearance from town. As far as she knew, Sheriff Jeffries hadn't even attempted to get a search warrant.

When they reached the backyard, Knox pulled her near him. "I imagine the officer who's in his car is probably asleep, but we have to be quiet in case he isn't."

She nodded, although if Cody was inside and they got him out, she couldn't promise that she wouldn't scream with happiness.

The mist turned into rain once again. As they crept closer to the house, she saw two window wells, indicating that there was a basement. Her heart nearly exploded out of her chest.

There was no light at either window, but that didn't staunch the flood of hopeful expectation that rushed through her.

The only thing that worried her was the possibility that Chad might be in that darkness with her son. Would he be armed in any way? Did Chad have a gun?

They had surprise on their side, but it wouldn't be easy for Knox to get through one of the small windows, and if Chad heard or saw them, what would he do?

Was he really so unhinged he would hurt a little boy? She could only pray that wasn't the case. When they reached the back of the house, Knox got down on his belly in the wet grass in an attempt to look into one of the small windows.

He put his hands up around his eyes, and despite the cold wetness of the night a bead of sweat trickled down her back. He motioned for her to hand him the flashlight. In one quick motion, he smashed out the window and slid inside like an eel.

She shoved a fist against her mouth as she waited. She wanted to scream to release the tension that had every muscle in her body knotted.

And then his face was in the opening where the window had been. "Nobody's down here. I'm going upstairs to check it out. I'll sneak out the back door. Just wait for me."

This time when she pressed her hand against her mouth, it was to staunch the banshee scream of mourning that threatened to erupt from her. *Nobody's down here.* The words replayed in her head in painful whispers.

Seconds ticked by…minutes as the rain continued to

fall and she waited for Knox. She had no hope that Cody was in the upstairs of the house. This had been yet another wild-goose chase, and she didn't know how many more she could handle before she truly lost her mind.

It seemed like an eternity before Knox finally appeared. He threw an arm over her shoulder and silently they made the long walk back to the car.

Once again, she was empty inside and lost in a desolation that was close to shattering her. They finally reached the car and as he started the engine she began to shiver.

"The basement was nothing but a graveyard for empty booze bottles," he said. "And the upstairs was a hoarder's play land. I don't know what happened to Chad, but there's no way I believe he has Cody."

She didn't speak. She couldn't with her teeth chattering. She wrapped her arms around herself, but that didn't ease the chill that had swept over her.

Knox glanced at her and then stepped down on the gas to get them home faster. "We're almost home. I'll get you warmed up when we get there," he said.

When they reached the house, he parked and then hurried around the car to help her out. She was grateful because her legs felt like two icicles. She was so achingly cold. She couldn't remember ever being this cold in her entire life.

He grabbed her under the elbow to steady her as they went into the house. Wendall greeted them, a frown etched across his forehead. "I thought you two were taking a drive, not a walk in the rain, and what did you do, walk on your chest?"

Allison looked at Knox. He was soaking wet and the front of his shirt and jeans held mud and grass stains. No wonder Wendall was looking at them with such suspicion.

"We need to get out of these wet clothes," Knox said. He kept his hand still on her elbow and guided her up the stairs and into the bathroom, where he let go of her and started the water in the shower.

He yanked his wet shirt over his head and threw it on the floor and then turned to her. "Come on, Ally, we need to get you out of those things and warm again."

Like a docile child, she allowed him to undress her and when they were both naked he pulled her beneath the warm spray of water.

She closed her eyes and leaned against him as the water played over them. He took the bar of soap and rubbed it across her back and then turned her around and soaped her breasts as, slowly, the chill began to leave her.

As she got warmed up again, an overwhelming exhaustion hit her like a brick wall. She grabbed the bottle of shampoo, but Knox took it from her.

"Let me," he said softly. He squirted the apple-scented shampoo into his hand and then worked it into her hair.

Once again, she closed her eyes as his fingers massaged her scalp and eased some of the tension that had been a constant companion since Cody had disappeared.

Tired. She was so very tired. As she raised her head to the water to rinse away the shampoo, he washed himself and then shut off the shower.

He led her out and grabbed a fluffy towel from the linen closet and then tenderly dried her off from head to toe. He picked up the brush from the counter and gently brushed her hair.

When he was finished, he grabbed her nightgown from a hook on the back of the door and pulled it on over her head.

With just a towel wrapped around his waist, he swept her up in his arms and carried her to the side of the bed, where he set her back on her feet. He untucked the sheet and blanket and held them up so she could slide into the bed.

When she did, he pulled the sheet back up to cover her and gently kissed her on the forehead. "Get some sleep, Ally."

"I don't want to go on these wild-goose chases anymore, Knox." She couldn't do it. She couldn't have hope only to have it destroyed over and over again.

"You don't have to do anything you don't want to do. Now go to sleep and we'll talk about things in the morning." He turned and left her room.

She drew in a tremulous sigh. She couldn't remember when she'd been so tired. Her son was missing and her emotions where Knox was concerned were in turmoil and all she wanted to do was sleep.

And she did.

"The calls came from two separate burner phones," Dalton said to Knox. He and Brett had shown up back at Allison's house at seven the next morning.

"And we're still trying to trace the particulars on the

web page. Whoever is behind this is pretty sophisticated when it comes to hiding their tracks."

"There's no way this is Chad," Knox said flatly. "It's got to be my mother." His stomach clenched. "She would have the kind of skills you're talking about."

"According to the authorities, they haven't been able to find out where she is. They still believe she's in Mexico," Dalton replied.

"She's here. I swear she's got to be here in Shadow Creek," he said.

"There's been no sightings of her here," Wendall said. "I know Sheriff Jeffries has told all the patrol officers to be on the lookout for both her and Chad."

Knox walked over to pour himself a fresh cup of coffee. He was grateful that Allison was still asleep. She didn't need to feel the negativity that was in the air.

They had three days left to try to figure out where Cody was being held and other than the fact that they all thought it was a basement, they had nothing more to go on. He'd spoken to Jeffries about the basements in town and the lawman had said he had no idea who had a basement and who didn't.

Hopefully at some point today, Myna Turner would return Allison's phone call and give them the addresses of everyone who had a basement in town. If she didn't, then Knox would be driving around and checking on each and every house…which would take up too much precious time.

For now, all they could do was wait…wait as they'd been doing for what seemed like forever.

Allison had hit her breaking point the night before.

Finding out Chad's basement was empty had been the last disappointment she could take.

As he'd bathed her, as he'd washed her hair with that delicious apple-scented shampoo, the last thing he'd had on his mind had been sex. All he'd wanted to do was get her warm and into bed for some much-needed sleep.

It was just after eight when she came into the kitchen. She looked more rested than she had throughout this ordeal. There was color back in her cheeks and she offered everyone a genuine smile.

"What's going on?" She made a beeline for the coffeemaker.

"Nothing. We're all just hoping that Myna will get in touch with you sometime today," he replied.

"I'm sure she'll call me as soon as she gets my messages." She poured herself a cup of coffee and then carried it into the living room. He trailed after her and when she curled up on the sofa he sat in the chair facing her.

"You look much better this morning than you did last night," he said.

She smiled. "Thank you for taking care of me. I hit a brick wall, but I feel strong again this morning. Cody would want me to stay strong."

"That's what you have to remember." He watched her sip her coffee and once again remembered the shower they'd taken together the night before.

Her skin had been so soft and she was so achingly beautiful. But he had known she hadn't needed him. What she'd needed was sleep, a respite from everything bad that was happening in her life, and he'd understood that.

She caught his gaze over the rim of her cup. "Stop it," she said.

He sat back in the chair. "Stop what?"

"Stop looking at me like I'm naked and you want to take me to bed."

He couldn't help the small laugh that escaped him. "Sorry, I wasn't aware I was doing that." He sobered. "But I guess no matter what happens in our lives I'll always want you in my bed."

A knock on the door stopped any further conversation. Knox got up to answer. It was Sheriff Jeffries. "We found Chad," he said.

Allison sat up straighter and set her cup on the coffee table. "Where?" she asked.

"In a motel room in Dallas. Apparently, he met some woman passing through town and hooked up with her. A police officer there saw him walking to a nearby liquor store and stopped him." Bud shook his head. "There was no sign of Cody in their motel room, so officially he's off the suspect list."

"Dammit," Knox exclaimed. He hadn't realized until that very moment that he'd half hoped the drunk was guilty. This left him with the horrifying certainty that his mother was behind the kidnapping.

"Wendall told me you believe your mother might be responsible. We've had no indication that she's anyplace in town," Bud said.

"That doesn't mean she isn't here. It's past time for you to do a door-to-door search. You need to be checking any house that has a basement. We all believe he's someplace here in town. You should be tearing the town apart to find him." Knox hadn't realized he had reached a point of explosion until now. In the back of his mind, he realized he was yelling at the sheriff.

He drew a deep breath to steady himself and at the same time Allison got up and grabbed him by the forearm. He knew she didn't want him to alienate the man with his anger. "We have all day today and tomorrow and all day Tuesday. We've got to find him before the time of the exchange."

"I'm keeping busy chasing down all the calls from the tip line. I'm also holding another news conference down in front of city hall at noon today. Hopefully, another plea to the public will yield some results," Bud replied.

"Hopefully," Allison replied without conviction.

Knox turned on his heels and headed upstairs. He couldn't talk to that man another minute. He went into Cody's room and sat down on the floor next to the bookcase holding the prancing horses.

Cody had told him the names of the horses, but he couldn't remember them. Why hadn't he listened more closely? And why wasn't Sheriff Jeffries doing door-to-door searches? What in the hell was the man really doing to find Cody?

He didn't know how long he sat there when Allison came into the room. She sank down next to him on the carpeting. "Do I need to throw you into a cold shower to cool you off?"

"I can't stand that man," he said. "I had to walk away

before I did something stupid." He drew in a deep breath and released it slowly.

"I hit my brick wall last night, and I think you just hit yours," she said. "Come on, Knox. Let's go back downstairs and I'll make some breakfast for everyone. Bacon and eggs and maybe that cinnamon toast you used to love." She got back up to her feet.

He nodded. "Sounds good. I'll be down in just a few minutes."

She left the room and Knox picked up a dark horse from the shelf.

Spirit. Yes, that was it. The dark horse was named Spirit, like the horse on Allison's nightshirt. He set it back on the shelf and picked up another one. He gripped it tightly in his hand, unable to remember what name Cody had given the little animal.

Finally, he set it down and picked up a white horse from the shelf. He wanted to be a knight on a white horse for Allison and Cody. His anger at Bud Jeffries wasn't just because he thought the man was ineffectual as a lawman, but it was also bred of a deep fear that he was afraid to acknowledge.

What if they didn't get Cody back? The horrible question hung in his head. He clutched the little horse more tightly. Oh, God, what if Cody never came home?

How did parents ever survive the death of a child? Just the thought alone squeezed his heart so tight he could scarcely draw a breath.

He had worried about Allison going over the edge, but at the moment he knew he was flirting with drowning in black despair.

He couldn't go there. He couldn't allow it. He had to be strong for the woman he loved and the little boy he was determined to find and bring back.

Placing the horse back on the shelf, he rose from the floor. He'd eat breakfast and he'd keep going…working to find his son and planning what life would be like when Cody came home.

In the meantime, he had to find Fort Knox once again, the man who had no emotion, because the feelings he had now were too great to bear.

It was just after noon when Myna Turner returned Allison's phone call and agreed to meet Knox and Allison at city hall to get the information they needed. Sheriff Jeffries was there, having just finished his news conference.

Myna Turner had to be close to seventy years old and although she gave Knox a curt nod, she greeted Allison with genuine warmth. "Come on inside, honey. I'm so sorry it took me so long to get back to you," she said as she unlocked her office door. "I was visiting my son in Austin and didn't get back in town until about an hour ago and finally listened to my answering machine."

She opened the door and they all followed her into her private office. "Now, you said you want to know about any basements in town."

"That's right," Allison said.

Knox and Bud stood against the wall as Allison sank down in the chair opposite Myna's desk. Myna patted her gray hair, pulled a pair of reading glasses from her purse and then turned on her computer.

"You're lucky that last year we digitized everything.

Otherwise I would be digging through file boxes to try to find what you want." She put on her glasses and then her fingers flew across the computer keys.

Finally, Knox thought. Finally, they were going to get some information they could use. With addresses, he could check each and every basement, and he prayed that Cody was in one of them. He had no idea where his mother played into this, but he was still certain that she did.

If there was anyone in town who could be bought to help her do her dirty work, she would find them. That's what Livia did; she manipulated and used people to her advantage.

"Let's see here…ah, there," Myna said in satisfaction. She typed some more and then a printer on a nearby table began to work, spitting out several pieces of paper.

All of Knox's nerves sizzled as Myna got up from the desk and walked over to the printer. She picked up the papers and held them out to Allison. "There are six houses in town that have basements. Here are the addresses."

"I'll just take that," Bud said and grabbed the papers from Myna's hand. "This is official business."

"And I want to be at each of those addresses while you check them out," Knox replied. "We can start at the first one right now." He held Bud's gaze intently.

Bud puffed up his chest with self-importance. "You can ride along with me and my men as long as you don't get in our way and obey any orders I give you."

Knox bit the side of his cheek. "Of course," he replied. "Myna, thank you so much."

"It was my pleasure. I just hope you find your boy," she replied.

"Allison, you go on back to the house. I'll go with Sheriff Jeffries and I'll call you if we find anything," he said.

She got up from the chair, and Knox doubted that anyone else in the room could discern the body language tells that let him know how stressed she was. Her shoulders were rigid and she rocked on the balls of her feet. At first glance, her eyes appeared calm, but Knox could see beyond, into the turbulence of her soul. He knew she was probably torn between wanting to come with them and afraid of futile searches that chipped away at her heart.

"Go home and wait for me, Ally," he repeated softly. "I'll let you know what we find."

She nodded and within minutes she was in his car to drive home, and he climbed into the passenger side of Bud's patrol car. Bud radioed for another patrol car to join them and once they were in place, they left city hall.

Five houses…five basements, and if Cody wasn't in one of them, then Knox feared he would slip over the edge into madness.

Chapter 14

It was almost midnight when Knox came through the front door. The look on his face told her everything she needed to know. He was utterly beaten, his eyes filled with a pain she well recognized.

"Nothing," he said as he flopped down on the sofa. "We checked every basement and there was nothing."

She sank down next to him and placed a hand on his thigh. "Don't beat yourself up, Knox. I know you're doing everything you can."

"It's not enough. I've never been enough." He looked at her with the shine of tears in his eyes. "I wasn't enough for my mother to love, I couldn't get it right with you and now I can't find my son."

In all the years she'd known him, Allison had never seen him so distraught, so broken. As tears began to shine on his cheeks, a sob escaped her and she wrapped her arms around him.

He pulled back from her just enough so that his lips could meet hers in their shared heartbreak. She didn't know if she tasted the salt of his tears or her own. She did know his lips tasted of anguish as she knew hers did.

When the kiss ended, they remained in each other's arms, not speaking, for words were inadequate to express the emotions they both felt.

They held each other for a long time as the night deepened. The house was quiet around them, a heavy silence that pressed against her chest. It was the silence of grief.

It was after one when they finally released each other. "Knox, go to bed," she said softly.

She had no idea how much sleep he'd gotten over the past three days, but she suspected it hadn't been enough. He'd been up before her every morning and awake much longer through the nights.

She had to be strong now not just for Cody, but for Knox, who had been there for her since this whole ordeal had begun.

"I'm okay," he replied.

"You're not okay. You're exhausted and you need to get some sleep," she said firmly.

He stood and wore his weariness, his defeat in the slump of his shoulders and the slightly glazed look in his eyes. "I really thought he'd be home tonight. When we left city hall, I was so sure we were going to bring him home."

"I know. Come on, Knox, you need to get some rest."

She grabbed his hand and together they went up the stairs to the room with the stars on the ceiling, the room that still held the scent of Cody.

She stood in the doorway as he stripped to his boxers and crawled into the lower bunk. Only then did she approach him. She leaned down and for a long moment their gazes remained locked.

She reached out and ran a hand over his face, like a blind woman learning Braille. Cody had his bright blue eyes, but he'd also inherited Knox's bold brow and his cheekbones.

It was a face she loved. It was a face she had always loved, and she'd seen the shadows of it every time she'd gazed at her son. At this moment, she'd never felt so connected to Knox, but she knew it was the unity of a couple in crisis and she had no thoughts for what might come after this.

"Sleep," she said and then left the room.

She went into her room and undressed. She pulled her nightgown over her head and thought about what Knox had said about his mother.

She hadn't realized until now that there was still a part of him that was a little boy who had yearned for his mother's love. He'd been diminished by the very woman who should have raised him up, neglected by the woman who should have loved him with all her heart and soul.

Allison hadn't truly recognized the scars left in his soul until tonight, when he'd wept in her arms.

Damn Livia Colton. The ripple effect of what she'd done to her children should put her in jail for life. And if she was behind Cody's kidnapping, then God help her.

She got into bed and within minutes she was asleep and in a nightmare. *Mommy, please find me*, Cody's voice cried out through a shadowed landscape. *I need you, Mommy.* The plaintive cries pierced through her heart.

She awakened with a start, her breathing ragged and as if she'd run for miles and miles. A faint light drifting in through the window let her know it was morning. She was more tired than she'd been when she'd gone to bed, but she wearily pulled herself up and got into a shower.

It was Monday morning and she had to face the fact that they probably weren't going to find Cody before the exchange on Tuesday night.

Dalton and Brett had yet to pin down the web page particulars. Both phone calls they'd received had come from different burners and all the potential places where Cody could be held had already been checked.

They were running out of time. The clock was ticking down to the time of the exchange and she now had to be proactive. She got out of the shower and dressed in a pair of black slacks and a white tailored blouse and then stepped into a pair of high heels. Finally she pulled her hair into the tight bun at the nape of her neck and put on a dab of mascara and lipstick.

She had business to attend to today, the final business that would hopefully ensure Cody's safe return. If the kidnapper wanted money in exchange for Cody, then she'd get it.

It was almost nine o'clock when she came down into the kitchen, where the men were all gathered as usual around the table.

Knox looked at her in surprise. "You look nice...?" There was a definite question at the end of his words.

"I'm going to the bank," she said.

He frowned and got up from his chair. He took her by the arm and led her out of the kitchen and into the living room. "What are you doing, Allison?"

"I'm going to speak to Vince Watson. He's the president of the bank and he can take care of what I need to do."

"And exactly what do you think you need to do?"

She raised her chin. "I'm going to get the money we need to get Cody back. I'm going to mortgage this house and pull all the money out of my business account. That, along with my savings, should be enough. Vince knows me. He'll give me the mortgage today and deal with the details later."

"And so when we get Cody back you'll have no savings, no business and a mortgage hanging over your head." He raked his hand down his jaw where the faint stubble of whiskers was evident. "We still have time, Allison."

"The exchange is going to happen tomorrow night. Knox, we're out of time and all out of clues," she replied fervently. "I know what I have to do."

"You can't give the kidnapper what she wants. You can't destroy your life to pay off my mother. She doesn't get to win, not this time." His eyes blazed with barely suppressed fury.

Allison held her ground. She raised her chin. "I won't take a chance on Cody's life."

He grabbed her by the shoulders. "Just trust me, Allison. Trust me this one last time. We're making plans in case we have to do the exchange. Give me one more day. I swear we're going to get Cody back, but you don't have to do this. You don't have to destroy your life."

She stared deep into his eyes. Trust him? There had been a time when she'd given him all the trust she had, but he'd broken that bond. Still, she saw how important it was in his eyes. He needed her to trust him right now. "Tell me the plan," she finally said.

"Come back into the kitchen," he said.

She followed him and when he motioned her into the empty chair at the table, she sat and looked at him expectantly. "She wants to know what we've been talking about," Knox said.

"If nothing pops before tomorrow night, then we've been working out the best-case scenario for getting Cody back and capturing the kidnapper," Dalton explained.

Her breath hitched in her chest. "And what is the best-case scenario?"

"If we don't have anything else to go on by four tomorrow, then I'll go to the bank. I've got about fifty thousand dollars in a savings account that I'll get out," Knox replied.

She frowned at him. "You just told me not to get any money."

"I don't want you mortgaging your future. Besides, consider it child support for the last nine years," he said.

"We don't need the entire amount of money," Dalton continued. "We just need some in a satchel or suitcase to show and before the kidnapper knows all the money isn't there you'll grab Cody."

"You two will be in the front seat of the car and Dalton and I will be in the backseat hidden from view. You make the exchange and get Cody and then we'll take down the kidnapper," Brett said.

A knot of panic lodged in her throat. "But we were told no cops. What if you're seen? The kidnapper said Cody would be killed." Her heart beat a little faster.

"We won't be seen," Brett replied firmly. "If our kidnapper is Livia Colton like Knox believes, then we want to get her into custody and put her back behind bars where she belongs."

"Has everyone forgotten that this should be dealt with by the local authorities?" Wendall asked. "Sheriff Jeffries would be ticked off if he knew you all were making a plan without him being a part of it."

"I would prefer that man stays as far away as possible from the exchange site," Knox replied with narrowed eyes.

"He's got to know that his presence, or any other presence from his men, would put Cody's life at risk," she protested. Oh, God, there were so many things that could go wrong with all this.

She felt like Knox's Ranger friends had a bigger agenda than she did. She just wanted Cody back. They might have arrived there with the specific goal to help Knox find his son. However, she suspected that when they realized it was possible Livia might be involved, their mission expanded.

And could she really blame them? Anyone who managed to recapture Livia would become an instant hero. They would get their five minutes of fame by taking that woman off the streets once again.

"We've got to make sure Jeffries stays as far away from the scene as possible," Knox said to Wendall.

"You'll need to have that discussion with the sheriff," Wendall replied. "He'll listen to anything that's reasonable. Whether you believe it or not, he wants to make sure Cody comes home safe and sound."

"I'll make sure I speak to him tomorrow, if he isn't too busy with more press conferences," Knox replied drily. "I'll let him know our plan and figure out a way to massage his ego."

Jim and Wendall both released small laughs. "He does like his ego stroked," Jim admitted.

"We're not going to stop trying to find him before tomorrow night," Brett said to Allison. "We're just planning ahead in case we don't get any more leads to follow."

Allison nodded at the dark-haired Ranger. But, she knew there would be no more leads. She had no hope that there would be any more information gleaned that would allow them to find Cody before the exchange tomorrow at midnight. All she had was a fragile hope in Knox and his friends that they would do whatever it took to get Cody home.

The morning passed with slow ticks of the clock and a burning frustration inside Knox that had now become as familiar as the sound of his own voice.

Thankfully Allison had gone back upstairs and

changed into a pair of jeans and a purple T-shirt that enhanced the deep gold of her eyes.

He'd been grateful that he'd been able to talk her out of going to the bank. The last thing he wanted was for money to exchange hands unless there was absolutely no other way.

Nobody had appeared this morning to offer support. He knew that most people probably believed Cody was dead by now.

As Dalton and Brett continued to find whatever they could about the website, Knox paced the living room floor, going over everything in his mind.

Somehow, he felt as if he'd missed something... something that might be important. He'd checked the Billings brothers, and Chad had been found innocent. They had looked in every single basement in town and had found nothing. So, what had he missed?

Leonor.

Thoughts of his sister exploded in his head. Was it possible she knew something about this? Had she been in touch with their mother? It was damned curious that Leonor had shown up there at this particular time.

He stopped his pacing and turned to Allison, who sat on the sofa and stared out the nearby window. "I'm going to leave for a little while."

She looked at him with a frown. "Where are you going?"

"Out to Mac's. Leonor is in town and staying at the apartment over his stables."

She sat up straighter. "When did she get here?"

"Sometime on Friday." Damn, why hadn't he gone

to speak to her earlier. He'd completely put her out of his mind from the moment Mac had called him to tell him she was back.

"I know it's a long shot, but it's odd that she'd turn up here now. I just want to go have a talk with her."

Allison got up from the sofa. "Do you think she might know something about your mother?"

He jammed his hands in his pockets. "I don't know what to think about her. But at this point it won't hurt for me to go and talk to her. I shouldn't be long."

"Then I'll see you when you come back."

He nodded and then went out the door. Before heading to Mac's ranch, he parked along the road by the home that had been taken from them.

La Bonne Vie was made up of three hundred acres of beautiful grazing land. It had a natural spring that provided the best water source around for most of the local ranchers.

The gorgeous French country house sat up on a hill with a long drive and a big fountain in front. Inside, there were seven bedrooms, eight baths and a grand stairway that Livia had loved to use to make an entrance at the many parties and galas she threw.

They hadn't just lost their house when it was confiscated for Livia's crimes; they had also lost their family at the same time. Thankfully, Mac had stepped up and brought Jade and Claudia into his home, while the other children had all scattered to the wind.

He'd stayed in Shadow Creek and destroyed the one relationship that might have saved him: Allison. She'd been right when she'd told him that for years his choices had been driven by his relationship with his mother.

It had been the most dysfunctional bond a mother could have with her child, and he'd been more than a little codependent in the madness.

And it was time that he no longer gave Livia any more power over him. He'd wept with Allison last night and through his tears he'd realized just how much he still loved her.

He had never really stopped. No matter where he'd been, no matter what he'd done, she'd always been a part of his thoughts.

But was there enough forgiveness in their hearts to have any kind of a real relationship when this was all over? He couldn't even think about it until Cody was returned safe and sound.

He pulled away from his childhood home and headed for Mac's, focusing his thoughts back to Leonor. It had been years since he'd seen her.

Although she was only two years younger than him, they had never been really close, and the distance between them had definitely grown when Livia had been arrested and Leonor had continued to cling to Livia's innocence.

Mac's ranch bordered La Bonne Vie and had always been a place of comfort for Knox and his brothers and sisters. The modest, three-bedroom house was painted white and boasted a big porch with a swing.

Mac was seated on the swing when Knox pulled up in front of the house. He rose as Knox got out of the car. "Has something happened?" he asked worriedly.

"No, nothing new," Knox replied. He sank down into the swing next to Mac and told him everything that had been done in the past couple of days and about the ransom and proof of life they had received.

"Mac, I'm more convinced than ever that Mother is behind this, and I'm here to speak with Leonor to see if she knows anything about it."

"Surely you can't think Leonor would stay silent if she knew anything about the kidnapping of your son," Mac replied in obvious surprise.

"Honestly, Mac, I don't know what to believe anymore," he replied with weariness. "All I know is I'm trying to leave no stone unturned in an effort to find Cody."

Mac gazed toward the stables. "As far as I know, she's in the apartment. She hasn't left to go anywhere since she got here."

"Then I'll just head over there now." With goodbyes said, Knox headed toward the stables in the near distance. He had lived in the apartment before he'd gone off to join the Rangers, as had Thorne for a while before he'd gotten his own place.

Knox climbed the stairs that led to the apartment, and he had a sudden memory of Allison spending the night there with him.

He'd attempted to cook her dinner and it had been a total debacle. They'd laughed at the raw chicken and overcooked veggies and had ordered pizza instead. And when they'd eaten they had fallen into bed and made love under a flowered quilt, believing that nothing could ever tear them apart.

And then his mother had been arrested and the whole

world had tumbled down. They'd both made mistakes that had guaranteed they would have no happily-ever-after.

He shook his head to rid his thoughts of the past and knocked on the door. She answered and gasped in surprise. "Knox!"

"Hi, Leonor." He pulled her into an awkward hug and then released her. "Mind if I come in?"

"No…of course not." She opened the door wider to allow him inside.

She looked just as he remembered her. Her bright red, curly hair fell to her slender shoulders and was a perfect foil for her pretty green eyes. She'd always hated her freckles and tried to cover them up, but today she was without any makeup and the smattering of freckles made her appear younger than thirty-one.

"How did you know I was here?" she asked.

"Mac told me. Why didn't you call to let me know?"

"I figured I'd take a few days to get settled in." She gestured him toward a small, white table with four chairs. "Would you like something to drink?"

"No, I'm good." He sat in one of the chairs and she eased down opposite him. "What are you doing back here? Last time we spoke on the phone, you didn't mention any plans to return to Shadow Creek."

"I just needed a little break from my life for a while… a little vacation." She leaned forward slightly. "Knox, I'm so sorry about your son. Have there been any breaks in the case?"

"No, and that's why I'm here."

"What do you mean?" She sat back in the chair.

"Surely you don't think I have anything to do with it." Stunned surprise shone from her eyes.

"Not you personally," he replied. He knew Leonor would never do anything like that. "When was the last time you spoke to Mother?"

Her cheeks became dusted with a faint color. "I went to visit her about a week before her escape. I haven't seen or spoken to her since then."

"Did she tell you what her plans were?"

"Heavens, no. I had no idea she planned to escape from prison. Why are you asking me all this?" She studied his face intently and then released a small gasp. "Oh, Knox, surely you don't believe she's behind the kidnapping of your son. She would never do..." She allowed her voice to trail off.

"Whether you believe it or not, you should know by now that she's capable of anything," he replied.

"But surely not this," she protested.

In the depths of Leonor's eyes, he saw the little girl who had desperately wanted Livia's love, the little girl who still clung to the belief that there was something good in her mother. He also saw a woman who knew nothing about Cody's kidnapping.

"I'm sorry, Leonor, I had to ask."

"I understand." To his surprise, she reached across the table and took his hand in hers. "I hope you get him back, Knox. I can't imagine what you're going through right now."

"It's been the darkest nightmare I've ever had," he admitted. He squeezed her hand and then stood. "I've got to get back to Allison. I just had to talk to you, Leonor. I need to talk to anyone who might have some information."

She got up as well and walked him to the door. "Knox, if I knew anything about your son, I swear I'd tell you. I would never keep silent about something like this."

"I appreciate it," he replied.

"Keep me informed?"

"Absolutely," he replied. "When Cody gets home, you and I will take time and really catch up with each other."

"I'd like that," she replied.

Minutes later, he was headed back to Allison's. He had to accept that Leonor was telling the truth. She might have been the last one to cling to the idea that Livia was innocent, but he just couldn't believe that she would collude in any way in the kidnapping of a child…any child.

He drove by La Bonne Vie once again; only this time he didn't even glance at the house. That was his past and there was nothing he could do about the choices his mother had made. She was obviously mentally ill, a sociopath who had put herself above everyone else.

It was important that he finally let go of boyish dreams of a mother's love. He was a man now and the love he needed was that of a good woman and their little boy.

He knew what he wanted in his future; he just couldn't be sure that when this was all over, Allison would want to be a part of it. But they would have no hope of any kind of future together if Cody didn't come home.

* * *

Damn.

Earl Hefferman stomped up the stairs from the basement where the kid was being held. He was sick of drifting like a ghost in the abandoned house; he was definitely sick of listening to the kid cry for his mommy, and now he'd made a stupid, stupid mistake.

He'd forgotten to put the ski mask on when he'd taken Cody a sandwich. *Damn. Damn!* His side had been killing him and he felt like he might be running a fever, and in his intense pain, he'd just forgotten.

When he'd read about Knox having a son, he'd seen the kidnapping of the boy as the best ploy to draw Livia out of the darkness and into the open.

He'd known that wherever she was holed up she'd be watching the news. She'd love all the stories that had been devoted to her since her escape. She'd relish in all the reporting that had turned her from slightly famous to completely infamous.

And he'd thought when he'd made the ransom demand that she'd come out into the open to help get her grandson back. It had been a stupid-ass plan. He should have known that she wouldn't risk her hide for anything or anyone.

And now the kid had seen his face.

He closed the door at the top of the stairs and threw himself on the musty carpeting on the floor in the living room where he'd been sleeping since he'd taken Cody.

He'd been so careful. He'd planned this out so meticulously. This vacant house on the outskirts of town had been perfect. He'd broken a back window and had made it his own. A little squatting didn't hurt anyone.

He'd only left the house a couple of times to drive into town and get some food supplies. Nobody was looking for him, so nobody had paid any attention to him.

The only thing that disappointed him was that Livia hadn't contacted him. He'd called her at the phone number she'd had when she'd escaped into Mexico, but she hadn't answered any of his messages. He'd even texted her a dozen times that he had the kid, but there had been no response.

If he couldn't get to Livia, then at least he'd walk away from this with some cash in his pocket that would help him start a new life.

He was thinking Florida might be nice. He'd rent a house close to the beach. Maybe he'd get out of the life of crime altogether, set up a bar on the beach and serve drinks all day long to hot, sexy women in bikinis.

He winced as he changed positions on the floor. The gunshot wound in his side wasn't healing; rather, it seemed to be getting worse. Surely when this was all over and he got out of town he could find some under-the-table doctor who could fix him up.

Staring up at the ceiling for several long minutes, he imagined what his new life would look like. He sure as hell wouldn't have to answer to any bitch who thought she was smarter than anyone else.

Maybe Livia would still show. The exchange wasn't until the next night. There was still time for her to get in touch with him.

There was now only one new issue. The kid had seen his face and the last thing Earl liked was loose ends. He wasn't about to go back to prison for this. So now what he had to figure out was how to exchange two hundred and fifty thousand dollars for a dead body.

Chapter 15

This night appeared longer and darker than any one they had endured since Cody had gone missing. It was just ten o'clock when Allison curled into the corner of the sofa, her heart so terribly heavy her chest ached.

She should have gone to the bank as she'd planned that morning. Maybe she'd feel better if she had the money in a suitcase ready to exchange for Cody.

But, there was no suitcase filled with money. There were no more clues to follow, and the plan for getting her son back seemed fraught with danger.

All the men were gathered around the kitchen table, plotting and planning for every scenario that might come up the next night. Their voices were just deep murmurs, but she found them oddly comforting.

Maybe she was reaching a strange place of peace.

They had done everything humanly possible. They had searched and cried and now there was nothing left except to meet the kidnapper at midnight tomorrow and pray that everything went as planned.

She looked up as Knox came into the room. He offered her a smile and sank down next to her. "This is almost over, Ally. Hopefully, late tomorrow night, Cody will be back in his bed where he belongs."

"That's all I want in the entire world," she replied.

"Me, too." He leaned back and scrubbed a hand down his jaw. "Dalton and Brett should be leaving in just a few minutes. They plan on coming back here at noon tomorrow and they'll be with us for the exchange."

"Have you spoken to Sheriff Jeffries this evening?"

"I did. He's coming by about seven tomorrow night to discuss the final plans." Knox frowned. "It would be so much easier if he'd just keep his nose out of this. He wasn't interested in working too hard from the very beginning and I think all he's interested in now is another photo op."

"I just don't want him to mess anything up." She wrapped her arms around her shoulders as a chill walked up her spine.

"Before that might happen, I'll punch him in the nose and hog-tie him."

She couldn't help but smile. "You are way too eager to punch people in the nose."

He returned her smile. "Only those who hurt my family," he replied.

His family. Was that the way he saw her and Cody? In one way or another, they would all be family forever.

Even if they weren't together, she and Knox would always have a special place for each other.

There was no question that since he'd been back in town she'd loved having him to lean on and to talk to. She'd loved the protective light that jumped into his eyes when he perceived that she was being threatened.

The ring of the home phone wiped the smile off her face. They both jumped off the sofa and ran for the kitchen.

"Private caller," Dalton said and gestured for her to answer it.

What now? Another stupid prank phone call telling them Cody was in the state capital holding a rally for abused animals? She picked up the receiver. "Hello?"

"Cody is safe." It was a muffled female voice. "The threat against him has been neutralized. You'll find him in the basement in the old Miller place. He needs his mother and his father to come and get him." The phone went dead.

Allison hung up the phone and stared at Knox. "Could it be real?" she whispered half-breathlessly. She wanted to believe. She was terrified to believe.

"We didn't go to the Miller house. It wasn't on the list of places with basements," he replied. "We just checked the shed on the property."

"That place is just outside of the city limits. It wouldn't have been on the list," Wendall said.

She clutched Knox's arm, her heart hammering, and she stared into his darkened blue eyes. "Do you think it might be real?"

God, she wanted it to be. She wanted the caller to

be right. Was it Livia who had called? She couldn't be sure. She tightened her grip on Knox.

"We don't lose anything if we go and check it out," he replied.

She had told him she didn't want to go on any more wild-goose chases, but something in her heart, in her very soul, told her she had to go with him now.

The caller had said Cody's mother and father needed to come and get their son. She'd said that the threat had been neutralized. Allison had no idea what that meant. All she knew was that the caller had said Cody was safe and if that was true then he needed his parents to bring him home.

Within minutes, she and Knox and Dalton and Brett were in the car and headed to the old, abandoned house with the promise that if anything was there, Knox would immediately call Sheriff Jeffries. Wendall and Jim were following in their car.

They had flashlights and guns and a tense anticipation that filled the car as Knox drove as fast as safety would allow.

"Do you think it was your mother who called?" she asked once they were on their way.

He frowned, his hands so tightly clenched around the steering wheel they appeared white in the light from the dashboard. "I don't know. I can't be sure."

"Worst-case scenario, we get there and find out the call was just another hoax," Dalton said from the backseat.

Were they all fools? Rushing to yet another heartbreaking disappointment? Her stomach rolled with nervous tension. She'd been here before…wound up with hope, praying for a good outcome, only to crash down with a bitter despair.

When the dark Miller house came into view, her heart was so big in her throat she couldn't speak. The rush of her heartbeat was so loud in her ears she could barely hear.

Knox parked on the side of the road and then turned in the seat to look at the other men. "We go in quiet. I'll find a door or a window to get inside the house, and you two see if there's a way to get inside the basement from the outside. Don't move in until you hear from me."

He reached over and grabbed Allison's hand. "You stay with me."

They got out of the car and the cool night air blew around her and inside her. She gazed at the shed they'd checked on because of the phone tip. It had been empty. Was this yet another crazy person's idea of fun? Or had they been this close to where Cody was being held and had left him behind?

As Dalton and Brett took off, quickly blending into the night, Knox once again grabbed her hand and together they walked through the overgrown grass and weeds toward the front of the house.

His hand held hers almost painfully tight as they drew closer and closer to the front door. When they reached the small porch, he dropped her hand. He pressed his ear against the door and then tried the doorknob. Locked.

He motioned for her to follow him to the living room

window. He turned on his flashlight and peered inside, then clicked the light off again.

She gasped as he smashed the back of the flashlight into the glass. Immediately, he listened once again. No sound came out of the house. Surely if there was somebody inside, they would have heard the glass shattering.

Already, a wave of bitter disappointment swept through her. The belief she'd had that the call might be real died on the wave of silence that greeted them as they crawled through the broken window and into the dark living room.

Once again, Knox turned on the flashlight, sweeping it around the room. It appeared that somebody had been squatting here. A ratty blanket was on the floor, along with a pile of trash and a bottle of pills.

Some addict who had obviously seen the empty house and had taken up residency to eat cheap bologna sandwiches and drink beer, by the look of the garbage pile. It was just another dead end.

Her disappointment transformed into the deeper emotion of renewed anguish. So where was the squatter now? Had he left or was he someplace in one of the other rooms? Possibly asleep or passed out?

Knox pulled his gun as they left the living room and entered the kitchen. There were three doors, one that led outside to the backyard, one that apparently led to a pantry and one that went downstairs to the basement.

She held her breath as Knox opened that door. The stairs yawned dark and silent before them. For several long minutes, they simply stood and listened to the silence.

"Is anyone down there?" he finally called out.

"Knox?" The little boy voice shouted out. "I'm down here, Knox."

"Cody!" she cried.

"Mom?"

She wanted to run down the stairs, but Knox held her back. "Cody, are you down there by yourself?" he asked.

"There's a dead man down here." The words ended on a sob.

She and Knox thundered down the stairs and he clicked on his flashlight. In the beam of light, she saw her son's beautiful face for the first time in almost four days.

She cried out his name and almost stumbled over a man's body prone on the floor as she rushed to Cody. When she reached him, she gathered him into her arms as they cried together.

The two small windows in the basement exploded inward as Brett and Dalton came in, their flashlights helping to illuminate the basement.

"It's okay," she said tearfully. "It's okay, Cody, we're here," she said as she kissed his forehead, his cheeks and his eyes. She would have liked to kiss each of his fingers and each of his toes as she had when he'd been a little baby.

Safe. Her little boy was safe and in her arms and her heart could scarcely hold the fullness of gratitude and love. She'd been so afraid she'd never hold him again.

"I knew you'd find me," he said. "I knew it." His tears came faster when Knox joined them, embracing both of them with his big, strong arms. For just that moment they were a family, and love for Knox joined her intense love for Cody.

She was vaguely aware of Dalton leaning down to place his fingers on the man's neck beneath the ski mask he wore. "Whoever he is, he's dead," he said as he straightened. "I'll give Sheriff Jeffries a call."

After that, everything blurred together. She was horrified to see the metal ring around Cody's ankle and grateful when Knox found the key to unlock it in the dead man's pocket.

As they waited for the sheriff to arrive, she sat on the cot and held Cody tightly against her side as he told them about the man jumping out from behind a tree and drugging him.

He told them about the darkness and the bologna sandwiches and about the murder of the man on the floor. "He was down here to give me a sandwich and somebody else came down the stairs behind him. That person was dressed all in black and had a ski mask on, too. Then the person stabbed the man in the back."

Cody pressed his face into her side and she bit back more tears. She couldn't begin to understand what had happened there; all she knew was she had her son back and she could finally draw a full breath again.

Knox had never been so happy to see anyone in his life as he was to see Cody. He wanted to sit on the cot with him and Allison, but he also wanted to know exactly what had happened here. There was a dead, masked man on the floor and a murderer on the loose. What in the hell?

More than anything, now that he knew Cody was safe, he wanted to rip the mask off the body and find out his identity, but he knew he needed to wait for the sheriff. The last thing he wanted to do was screw up any evidence that might give him a better understanding of what had happened.

He'd also wanted to grab Cody to his chest and hold him tight, breathe in the scent of his son and tell him that he was his father. But instead he had backed away after only a brief hug and given Cody and Allison space. He had to remind himself that to Cody he was just a family friend and what he needed at this moment was his mother.

The sound of sirens could be heard coming from the distance and hopefully with them would come some answers. "I'll go upstairs and let them in through the front door," Brett said.

"Can we go home now?" Cody asked.

"Not yet, but soon, Cody," he said, once again fighting his need to hug the boy close. As much as he hated keeping Cody in this dungeon another minute, he knew he had to let Sheriff Jeffries take the lead from here.

Jeffries clumped down the stairs with heavy footsteps, followed closely by Wendall and Jim. "Thank God," Wendall said as he saw Allison and Cody on the sofa.

"What the hell do we have here?" Sheriff Jeffries stared down at the dead body. He bent down and grabbed the bottom of the ski mask.

"Wait!" Allison protested. "Please, let me take my son out of here before anything else happens."

"I'll take them upstairs," Wendall said without waiting for Jeffries's okay. "Come on, son. You can tell me all about the little horses you keep in your room."

Knox flashed Wendall a grateful glance. Too bad the compassionate deputy didn't want to run against his boss in the fall. Wendall would have made a sheriff the whole town could be proud of.

Once those three had disappeared up the stairs, again Bud leaned down and grabbed the bottom of the ski mask. He tore it off.

"Earl," Knox said in shocked surprise.

"You know him?" Bud asked.

Knox nodded. "His name is Earl Hefferman. He was my mother's right-hand man. Last I heard, he was someplace out on probation."

"And now he's dead. Have any idea how that happened?" Bud asked.

"I don't have a clue. According to Cody, somebody in a ski mask and dressed in black came down the stairs and stabbed Earl in the back," Knox replied.

"I'll need to question the boy. I'll do that while we wait for the coroner," Bud replied.

"I don't think so," Knox replied with a new weariness. "I'm going to go upstairs and take the boy named Cody and his mother to the hospital and then home with me. It's late, he's had enough trauma to last the rest of his life and you can talk to him sometime tomorrow." Knox turned to head for the stairs at the same time Brett's flashlight landed on something just to the side of the stairs.

"What's that?" Bud asked.

Knox stared at the lacy lavender handkerchief. Was it possible? "It's a handkerchief. My mother used to carry ones just like that."

"So, it's likely that your mother saved the boy and then made the phone call to your house. I need to get more men in the area and let them know who we're looking for. This might be over for you, but it's just starting for us."

Knox crept up the stairs slowly, his mind whirling. Was that really what had happened? Had his mother somehow caught wind of what Earl had done and come to her grandson's aid? It was difficult to believe for, if she had, it would be the first real act of love he'd ever known her to commit.

Wendall, Allison and Cody were seated on the carpeting in the living room. With Wendall's flashlight providing the illumination, it appeared as if the three were gathered for a fun night of storytelling.

"Who is ready to go home?" Knox asked.

"I am!" Cody exclaimed and scrambled to his feet.

"Me, too," Allison added.

Wendall and Allison also stood. "Jim and I have a few things to pick up at the house, but we'll wait until tomorrow."

"Thank you, Wendall. Thank you for everything," Allison said.

"Just doing my job," he replied modestly.

"You did more than your job, and we appreciate it," Knox said.

Within minutes, the three of them were in Knox's car and headed to the hospital and then hopefully home.

Well, not to his home, but to the place where his heart resided.

"Mom, when we get home will you make me some pancakes?" Cody asked. "All I've had to eat is some bologna sandwiches and I don't ever want to eat those again."

Allison turned in her seat to look at him. "Cody, my love, you never, ever have to eat another bologna sandwich, and I will happily make you pancakes when you get home."

Thank God Cody hadn't been hurt physically, Knox thought as he listened to Allison talking to her son about all the friends and neighbors who had come out to help look for him.

Only time would tell if Cody suffered any emotional trauma. Thankfully children were supposed to be resilient and he hoped Cody would carry no scars from his ordeal. If necessary, they would see to it that Cody got some counseling.

His mother. Was she really here in Shadow Creek, and had she been in that basement with Earl and Cody? Or had Marlene Miller, the former owner of the Miller house, carried the same kind of handkerchiefs when she'd been alive? He dismissed the very idea, for the handkerchief had looked clean and new, not as if it had sat in a basement for over a year.

Thoughts of Livia continued to haunt him nearly two hours later when they gathered around the kitchen table for Allison's pancakes. Hopefully, some fingerprints could be pulled from the handkerchief and they would tell the tale.

Cody had been checked out by a doctor at the hospital who had pronounced him fine, and the three of them had returned to Allison's house.

The kitchen smelled of hot syrup and buttery pancakes and love. Knox watched as Allison reached over to touch Cody's arm, swept his hair off his forehead and then squeezed his shoulder, as if to assure herself that he was really here.

"I dreamed about this," Cody said as he wiped a dollop of syrup off his chin with the back of his hand. "I dreamed about pancakes and ham and cheese sandwiches and being here in this kitchen with all of us together."

"We dreamed about it, too." Allison handed him a napkin. "Well, not so much the food part, but we definitely dreamed about you being back here."

"The worst part was being scared and having nobody to talk to. I tried to talk to the guy who took me, but he never said a word to me. I've never gone so long without somebody talking to me," Cody said.

"You're probably going to wish your mother and I stop talking to you over the next couple of days," Knox said with a small laugh.

"No way," he replied.

Cody ate three pancakes and then rubbed his eyes tiredly.

"I'm not a baby or anything, but maybe would you keep the hall light on for the rest of the night?" he asked Allison.

"I've been sleeping on your bottom bunk while you've been gone," Knox said. "How about I do that for tonight and then I'll head home tomorrow?" He shot a quick glance at Allison, hoping he wasn't overstepping his boundaries, but she gave him a small smile.

"That would be great," Cody said.

"Now, how about you head upstairs for a quick bath while I clean up the kitchen?" Allison said.

"Can Knox come up and talk to me while I take my bath?" Cody asked.

"Sure," Knox replied. "And you can tell me the names of all the horses you have on your shelf. I know you told me once before, but I've forgotten some of them."

He followed Cody upstairs where he took a much-needed bath and then dressed in a clean pair of pajamas. By that time, Allison had joined them upstairs to tuck Cody into bed.

He watched from the doorway as she stood on the bottom rail and swept Cody's hair from his face, then kissed him on his forehead.

"I want you to have wonderful dreams. I want you to know that you're safe now and you have nothing to worry about. It was a bad person who took you, but there are a lot of good people in the world."

"I know. I love you, Mom."

"Oh, buddy, I love you, too." She kissed him once again and then pulled the sheet up around his neck. "I'll see you in the morning."

She got back on the floor and smiled at Knox. "Happy dreams to you, too."

He nodded, for a moment too much emotion in the

back of his throat to reply. When she left the room, Knox stripped to his boxer shorts and got into the lower bunk.

"I'm so glad I'm home," Cody said, the last word ending on a yawn. "Will you tell me a story before I go to sleep, Knox?"

Knox was in the middle of a story about the first time he'd ever ridden a horse when he knew Cody had fallen asleep. For the next fifteen minutes or so, he merely listened to the sound of his son's deep, even breathing.

Safe. Cody was finally safe and where he belonged, and Knox hoped that now he would be able to officially claim him, that the time was now right for Cody to know he had a father who loved him with all his heart and soul.

Now Knox had to figure out where he belonged. With this trauma over, the rest of his life suddenly loomed before him. One thing was clear in his head. He wasn't leaving Shadow Creek again. His son was there and the woman he loved was there.

He couldn't even pretend that he thought he had a future with Allison. With Cody home, she wouldn't need Knox anymore, and he believed it was the aching need of two grieving parents that had temporarily brought them together.

Certain that Cody's sleep was deep, he crept out of the bed to find Allison. He hadn't even had a chance to tell her about the handkerchief.

He found her in her bedroom, sitting on the edge of the bed and staring out the nearby window. "Allison," he said softly.

She turned and smiled at him. "Is he asleep?"

He nodded and walked over to the bed and sat down next to her. "I imagine he'll sleep until noon tomorrow. Hopefully he won't have any nightmares."

"I hope not, too." She released a sigh. "Thank God it's all over, although it was very strange, wasn't it?"

"Maybe not so strange," he replied and then told her about the lavender handkerchief found in the basement. "Before she was arrested, my mother was obsessed with fancy handkerchiefs. I know it was hers. She was down in that basement."

She looked at him in surprise and then slowly shook her head. "If it was your mother, then maybe she has some good in her, after all," she said. "I can't be sorry that she killed the man who stole Cody away from us. Who knows what he might have done with Cody before the exchange?"

"I'm just surprised she didn't wait until the actual exchange happened so she could kill Earl for the money he'd gotten from us. That's more like the mother I know."

"Don't look a gift horse in the mouth," she replied. "If she hadn't done what she did, there's a possibility we might have never gotten Cody back."

He nodded in agreement. "So I guess life returns to normal…whatever that is," he replied. Without the worry eating him up inside, without the fear tearing at his gut, his desire for her roared to the forefront. But that was not what he saw in her eyes at that moment, and he tamped down his want of her.

"I'd like to be with the two of you when Sheriff Jeffries interviews Cody, if that's okay," he said.

"I think before that happens, we need to tell Cody about you. It's a conversation that should have happened before. Maybe once breakfast is over in the morning?"

His heart swelled. "You know that's more than okay with me. And once that is over and after the sheriff talks to Cody, then I'll pack up my bags and get out of your hair." There was a small part of him that held its breath, hoping that she might say something that would indicate she wanted him there with her for always.

"What are your plans?"

That single question effectively killed any hope he had of a future with her. "I'm not sure. All I know is that my plans will be here in Shadow Creek. I'm not going back to the Rangers and I want to be here always and forever for my son."

He rose from the bed. "And now I think what both of us need is some good sleep. Good night, Allison."

"Good night, Knox."

He left the room and crawled back into the lower bunk. He should be deliriously happy. Cody was home safe, and tomorrow the boy would know that Knox was his father and that was all that mattered. And he was happy, except for the aching pain in his heart where Allison was concerned.

Chapter 16

Breakfast at ten thirty the next morning consisted of biscuits and gravy and plenty of laughter. Cody ate like he'd been starved for months and nobody mentioned the ordeal he'd been through.

Rather, the talk was about school and his friends and how he couldn't wait to get together with Josh and play. It was the normal chattering of a nine-year-old boy and Allison relished every word that fell out of his mouth.

It had taken her forever to go to sleep the night before. Where before it had been fear that had kept her tossing and turning, last night it had been gratitude. Thankfully, when she did finally fall asleep, it had been a rest with no nightmares.

"Now I'm full," Cody announced.

"I would think so," Knox said in a teasing voice. "You ate like a horse."

"I've got an idea. Why don't you go upstairs and make your bed while I clean up the kitchen? When you come back down here, Knox and I want to have a little talk with you," she said.

"Am I in trouble?" Cody asked.

"Heavens, no," Allison replied hurriedly. "It's going to be a good talk."

"Is it about a horse?" Cody asked eagerly.

"No, but it's about something as good as a horse. Now scoot. The faster you get your bed made, the faster you'll know what we're going to talk about."

"Come on, Cody. I'll go with you and between the two of us we can get that bed made in no time," Knox said.

As the two of them thundered up the stairs, Allison got busy clearing the table. It was time...past time for them to tell Cody the truth.

There was no question now in her mind that Knox would be the man Cody needed in his life, the father who would always be with him to guide and love him. She trusted Knox in a way she never had before.

There was also no doubt in her mind that Cody loved Knox, too. It showed in Cody's eyes when he looked at Knox, in the easy way he talked and laughed with him.

Yes, it was time for this talk to happen, for her son's sake and for Knox.

It didn't take long for the three of them to meet in the living room. Allison sat on the sofa next to Cody and Knox sat on the chair opposite them, positively vibrating with anticipation.

"Cody, do you remember when you asked me about your father and I told you he was off somewhere fighting crime?" she began.

"Yeah, I remember." Cody's blue eyes, so like Knox's, gazed at her curiously. "Have you talked to him? Does he know I got kidnapped?"

"Yes, he knew, and he did everything in his power to find you. He walked the streets and hunted all over the entire town to find you and bring you home," she said.

Cody leaned forward. "Is he here now? Can I see him?"

Allison smiled. "All you have to do is look across the room."

Cody stared at her for a long moment and then looked at Knox. "Is it you? Are you my dad, Knox?"

Never in a million years would Allison forget the expression on Knox's face as he answered. It was a mixture of love, of hope and a touch of soft vulnerability. "It's me, Cody. I'm your dad and I hope you aren't disappointed."

"Disappointed?" Cody jumped off the sofa and ran to Knox's open arms. "This is the most awesome day of my life and you are the most awesome dad."

Tears blurred her vision as Knox pulled Cody up on his lap and the two hugged. The world was finally right. Her son had the kind of father she wanted for him, the man he'd yearned for all his short life.

"I'm never going to leave you," Knox said as Cody clung to his neck. "I promise you, Cody, I'm always going to be here for you."

"This is way better than a horse," Cody said, and then they were all laughing and crying with tears of joy.

Surprisingly Cody had no questions. He just reveled in his newfound father. Unfortunately, the celebration was cut short by a call from the sheriff, telling them he was on his way over to talk to Cody.

"Are you okay to tell the sheriff everything that happened?" Knox asked Cody.

"Yeah, but I don't know much. I just got kidnapped and chained to a wall and then I ate bologna sandwiches. I only saw his face once and that was when he came down without his mask on. Then the next time he came down, he had on the mask and that other person killed him." Cody's eyes darkened. "That was kind of scary. I didn't know if I was going to get killed or not."

"I'm so sorry you had to go through that, but I'm so proud of how brave you are," Knox replied.

Cody puffed up his chest. "I guess I take after my parents," he said proudly.

"Oh, yeah? You know what I think the first official thing we should do as father and son is?" Knox asked.

"What?" Cody's eyes shone bright.

"Tickle Mom."

"Oh, no," Allison protested. She tried to get up from the sofa, but the two males were on her, Cody tickling her tummy and Knox holding on to one of her ankles and tickling her bare foot. She screamed and laughed and delighted them when she got the hiccups.

She was still hiccupping when Sheriff Jeffries arrived. She and Knox sat on the sofa with Cody between them. He held both of their hands as the sheriff eased down in the chair opposite them.

A united front, that's what the three of them represented as they faced Bud. Thankfully, the man had the good sense to be kind as he asked Cody question after question.

It took about an hour for the interrogation to be over and then Knox walked the sheriff out and Allison hugged her son close to her side. "I'm so very proud of you, Cody."

He looked up at her and a little line creased his forehead. "Mom, are you still gonna let me walk home from the bus stop? I didn't do anything wrong."

There was a part of her that wanted to scream no. She wanted to tell him that she didn't want him to go to school at all, that she never wanted him to leave her side again. But that was something she couldn't show him because she didn't want him to live in that fear.

"No, you didn't do anything wrong and, yes, of course you can still walk home from the bus stop," she agreed slowly. "A bad thing happened to you, but it's over and we shouldn't be afraid anymore."

"I'm not scared," Cody replied. "I've got a new dad and you promised me hot ham and cheese sandwiches for lunch and I don't want to be afraid of living my life."

Sometimes, Cody's wisdom and grown-up attitude amazed her and this was one of those times. She kissed him on the cheek and then stood. "Come on, it's about time for those sandwiches. and you can help me set the table."

They were in the kitchen when Knox joined them. "Anything new?" she asked.

"Nothing that can't wait," he replied, letting her know that he didn't want to speak in front of Cody about any information he'd gotten from the sheriff.

They finished lunch and the afternoon was filled with people coming and going. Dalton and Brett stopped by to gather up their equipment and say goodbye, and after they left Wendall and Jim stopped in to get their things.

"All's well that ends well," Wendall said as they walked the deputies to the front door.

"If you or Jim ever decide to run for sheriff, you'd have our support," Knox said.

"No way," Wendall laughed, and Jim echoed the sentiment. "Maybe you should run," Wendall added.

"Right now all I want to be is a father to my son," Knox replied.

At three thirty Cody asked if Josh could come over to play, and after a talk with the child's mother, Josh showed up and the two boys went up to Cody's room.

It was only then that she and Knox finally got an opportunity to talk alone. "There were no fingerprints on the handkerchief," he said as they sat at the kitchen table.

"So, even if it was your mother, there's no proof it was her."

"It was my mother," he replied flatly. "They found a burner cell phone on Earl and it basically told the whole story. Earl drove the van in my mother's escape from prison. He took her to the border, where she was supposed to pay him a large sum of money. She didn't pay him. Instead she shot him and left him for dead."

He paused and took a sip from his coffee cup and then continued. "Apparently, Earl kidnapped Cody in hopes of drawing my mother out. He thought she would care."

"But she killed Earl and saved Cody," Allison said.

Knox frowned. "No, she killed a loose end. Mother doesn't like loose ends. She tried to get rid of him once and it didn't work, so she came after him again. The coroner said his gunshot wound probably would have killed him anyway. Apparently, he'd gotten no medical help for it and it was badly infected. But the stab in the back did the trick. There's no doubt in my mind she killed Earl for herself, not for any love of Cody."

Allison didn't attempt to say anything in an effort to make him feel better. "Do you think she's still here in town?"

"Who knows? She's not my problem anymore." He got up from the chair and carried his cup to the sink. "And now it's time for me to get my things and get out of here. I guess we're back on for our usual visitation times?"

She nodded, not wanting him to go, but he'd said nothing to indicate that he wanted to stay. She got up from the table and walked with him to the bottom of the stairs.

"I'll grab my clothes and say goodbye to Cody. I'll be right back."

She watched him climb the stairs and her chest ached. He was still the protective teenager who had captured her heart, and he was still the man she wanted in her life forever.

When he came back down the stairs, he had the duffel of clothes that Thorne had brought to him. "I told Cody I'd pick him up after school on Thursday. I figured you'd want him here for the rest of tonight."

He walked to the front door, as if he suddenly couldn't wait to get away from her. "So, I'll see you Thursday afternoon."

And then he was gone, leaving only the faint scent of his cologne and an all-too-familiar heartache.

"Mom, we're home," Cody yelled as he opened the front door. Knox followed just behind him into the house.

Allison came down the stairs and greeted them with a wide smile. "I've been waiting for you. Come into the kitchen for cookies and milk before you take your bath and you can tell me all about your adventures."

"Can Dad have cookies, too?" Cody asked.

She nodded and smiled once again. "I already made the coffee." It was so nice to see her face with only happiness radiating outward and without the stress and fear that had marked her features for too long.

As always, she looked lovely in a casual, mint-green dress that kissed her curves as it fell to her ankles. And as always, Knox wanted her.

They all gathered around the kitchen table where Cody entertained his mother with stories about his time with Knox. "We ate at the café and everyone acted like I was a superstar or something," Cody said between bites of cookie. "People who I didn't even know stopped by our table to tell me they were glad I was okay."

"I told him not to let it all go to his head, that his superstar status would only last a minute," Knox said.

"That's okay, I just want to be a kid," Cody replied. "After we ate, we went to Jade's and rode. It was fun and Miss Jade said I could officially call her Aunt Jade now. Isn't that cool? I not only got a dad, but I also got an aunt."

"Don't forget Thorne. He's now Uncle Thorne," Knox said. "And there will be more aunts and uncles for you to meet and get to know."

Cody laughed with delight. "Our family is getting bigger and bigger, right, Mom?"

"That's right, Cody. Now get upstairs for your bath while I visit a few minutes longer with your dad."

Twenty minutes later, with Cody bathed and tucked into bed, Knox and Allison sat across from each other at the kitchen table. "He seems to be doing just fine," Knox said. *Cody is doing fine, but I'm not*, he thought to himself.

He wanted to be there every night to eat cookies and tuck his son into bed. And then he wanted to go to bed with Allison and make love to her and awaken in the morning with her, warm and sleepy in his arms.

He didn't just want her nights; he wanted her mornings and her days, too. He wanted to protect her and Cody, now more than ever.

With the definite possibility that his mother was still in the area, he had no idea if either of them could be in danger or not. He had no idea if Livia might figure out an angle where she could use Allison and Cody to her advantage.

He'd spoken with Bud about his concerns and had been grateful when the man had agreed to have his night patrol keep an eye on the house and do regular drive-bys.

He realized Allison was talking and he'd been in his own head and wasn't sure what she'd said. "I'm sorry, could you repeat that?"

"I was just saying that everything is back to normal and it feels wonderful. Cody appears to be just fine and I'm so grateful to have him home."

"I still want you to keep a close eye on him. I reminded him tonight that it is important for him to always be aware of his surroundings."

Her eyes darkened a bit. "Why? Do you think something else is going to happen?"

"No, nothing specific," he hurriedly replied. "It's just…she could still be out there, Ally, and nobody can guess what she might do next."

"I'm glad you had the talk with Cody, but I refuse to think about Livia right now. I've got my son back and things are going well at work. In fact, guess who came in to see me this morning?"

"Who?" He leaned back in the chair, loving the way her eyes sparkled with gold and green shards.

"The Billings brothers. They stopped in to tell me they were happy Cody had been saved and, while neither of them admitted anything, they told me they didn't expect me to have any more trouble on my job sites."

"How did Brad's nose look?"

She grinned. "Like you punched it. Anyway, I'm also taking applications for some new help. George told me that there have been several calls for potential new jobs and he thinks I need to hire a couple more men."

"I'd like to put in an application." His love for her quivered in his heart and trembled on his lips. Was it possible that finally, after all these years, it was time for them to get things right?

He had no idea what she really felt about him. He had no idea if she blamed him for Cody's kidnapping. But he knew he had to speak of what was in his heart. They would never get it right if he didn't take a chance.

"You want to work for the business?" she asked in surprise.

"That, too. But, what I'd really like to do is put in an application to have and to hold you for the rest of my life. We belong together, Allison. I'll never love another woman like I love you."

She stared at him. He wasn't sure what he'd expected, but he'd hoped she would joyously jump into his arms, tell him that she felt the same way about him.

"Are you saying this because you're afraid your mother might do something?" she finally asked.

"Absolutely not. You were right, Allison. I've allowed my anger and hatred of her to get in the way of my life. I'm not a little boy anymore and I have no need to please her. From here on out the only people I want to please are you, Cody and myself. I know what I want and it's you…it's always been you."

"You're hired," she said, her voice filled with joy. "Oh, Knox, you are so hired."

Happiness roared through him. He stood, grabbed her up into his arms and took her lips in a kiss that spoke of his fiery desire for her, of dreams they would share together with a love that was always meant to be.

When the kiss finally ended, he framed her face with his hands. "I was so afraid you blamed me for the kidnapping. It would have never happened if I hadn't come back here."

"I can't blame you for Earl and your mother, but I will admit your mother scares me—that's part of the reason why I didn't tell you about Cody."

"She'll never hurt us again, Allison. I'll do everything in my power to make sure of it. I love you, Ally, and I want to marry you."

"And I love you and I want to be your wife." Her eyes shimmered with tears of happiness. "I want to have you here each and every day. I don't ever want to let you go again."

"And from this day forward I will always run to you and not away from you," he promised.

Her hazel eyes glinted with her love for him and he wanted to drown in it, in her. "Tomorrow, you can drive over to Thorne's and get your things. Tonight I want to start our lives together. I want you in my bed and tomorrow morning we can tell Cody that he can be the ring bearer at our wedding."

"He's going to be over the moon," he replied. "Just like I feel at this very moment."

Minutes later, as he walked into the room that held the bed with the lavender bedspread and smelled of spicy apples and love, his heart was full.

This was a brand-new beginning for them, one without any more regrets or recriminations. They would raise their son together in love. He'd be Allison's lover, her protector, her husband, and he'd help her grow her business.

She joined him in the bedroom and he gathered her into his arms. "We'll get it right this time," he murmured against her ear. "Nobody is going to stand in our way of living and loving each other for the rest of our lives. And if anyone tries...I'll punch him or her in the nose."

She laughed and then they tumbled to the bed to begin their new journey together.

Epilogue

The ringing of hammering and the buzz of a saw filled the air. Cody stood next to Allison as a team of her men worked to build a dream tree house for him.

A dream. That's what she felt she'd been living for the past week. Knox's face being the first she saw in the morning and the last one she saw before sleep was beyond wonderful.

During the days, he'd been working with this crew of men and while he seemed content in his position, she had a feeling there were greater things ahead of him.

She believed he might secretly have his eye on a sheriff's badge, and she would fully support him if he decided to run against Bud Jeffries in the fall.

Shadow Creek deserved a lawman like Knox and she knew that most of the town would also support him. But, fall was months away and she was just enjoying living in the moment with the two males who held her heart.

She and Knox had spent long hours talking about their past, healing from any wounds and instead focusing on their future together. There had been no more information about Livia. She was still out there somewhere, with the authorities working hard to find her. But she wasn't much of a conversation piece anymore between Allison and Knox. They had far more important things to talk about than a sociopathic woman on the run.

"This is so totally awesome," Cody exclaimed as he danced around impatiently.

The tree house was almost done. The men were just putting on the finishing touches. Knox set the wooden rung ladder against the tree, tested the strength and then hammered it into place. He climbed up and disappeared into the wooden structure. A moment later, he appeared in the window, a huge grin on his face.

"Come on up, son," he said.

Cody scrambled up the stairs and soon after he appeared with Knox at the window. "Mom, you should come up here."

"Not me. That's strictly a man cave. But both of you stay where you are." She pulled her cell phone out of her pocket to take a picture. She was determined to capture every moment of happiness in their lives and had already taken more pictures in the last week than she had in the entire preceding year.

George and the other men began loading up their

tools as Knox came back down and joined her. "Can I bring some of my horses up here?" Cody asked. "And can I call Josh and have him come over to play? He's gonna freak when he sees this."

"That would be fine," she replied.

Cody climbed down and raced toward the back door. When he disappeared inside the house, Knox pulled her into his arms. "Happy?"

"Delirious," she replied.

"Cody is definitely happy, but I had a talk with him last night and I know what would make him even happier."

"A horse," she replied.

"No, something else."

She looked up at him curiously. "What?"

He leaned into her and nuzzled her ear and then whispered, "A brother or a sister."

Her heart glowed and danced at the thought of having a baby, with him here and present with her. "You know how much I like to make Cody happy," she said half-breathlessly.

His warm blue eyes held hers intently. "You're ready to have another baby?"

"Oh, Knox, I'd love to carry another one of your babies. I'd love for you to place your hand on my belly and feel him or her kick. You'll need to rub my back and make midnight runs to buy me butter toffee ice cream and cheeseburgers."

"You aren't scaring me," he said with a laugh.

"Then you can be with me in the delivery room

and…" Emotion choked her. "Like you should have been with Cody."

"Nothing from the past matters anymore, Ally. I'm with you now and always," he replied.

She gazed into his warm, emotion-filled eyes and knew that Fort Knox had been cracked. He kissed her then, a soft, gentle kiss that spoke of enduring love and hearts forever bound.

* * * * *

If you loved this novel,
don't miss the next thrilling romance in
the COLTONS OF SHADOW CREEK *miniseries:*
COLTON UNDERCOVER by USA TODAY
bestselling author Marie Ferrarella,
available in April 2017
from Harlequin Romantic Suspense!

And check out other suspenseful titles by
New York Times *bestselling author Carla Cassidy:*

OPERATION COWBOY DADDY
COWBOY AT ARMS
COWBOY UNDER FIRE
COWBOY OF INTEREST
A REAL COWBOY

Available now from Harlequin Romantic Suspense!

COMING NEXT MONTH FROM

H HARLEQUIN®
™

ROMANTIC suspense

Available April 4, 2017

#1939 COLTON UNDERCOVER
The Coltons of Shadow Creek • by Marie Ferrarella
Betrayed by her ex-lover, Leonor Colton, the daughter of a
notorious escaped serial killer, returns home to Shadow Creek
to lick her wounds. She catches the eye of Josh Howard, an
undercover FBI agent investigating her mother's jailbreak by
keeping tabs on her children. But a hit man may force Josh to
reveal himself—if Leonor doesn't end up a victim first!

#1940 THE TEXAN'S RETURN
by Karen Whiddon
Mac Morrison returns to his small hometown in Texas
determined to clear his ill father's name of murder and
reconnect with Hailey Green, his high school sweetheart. When
evidence begins to implicate him, will he be able to save the
woman he loves from a vicious killer *and* convince her they
belong together?

#1941 SECRET AGENT UNDER FIRE
Silver Valley P.D. • by Geri Krotow
The True Believers are still wreaking havoc in Silver Valley
when a string of fires are found to be linked to the cult. Fire
chief Keith Paruso is mesmerized by Trail Hiker secret agent
Abi Redland, but with an arsonist on the loose and Abi's own
secrets between them, their love might turn to ash before it can
even catch fire...

#1942 COVERT KISSES
Sons of Stillwater • by Jane Godman
Undercover cop Laurie Carter discovers two things when she
starts investigating Cameron Delaney: that he is *very* attractive
and that his girlfriend was murdered—by a serial killer! Cut off
from the FBI, Laurie must turn to Cameron—a man she's not
sure she can trust—to uncover the killer before he makes her
his next victim.

YOU CAN FIND MORE INFORMATION ON UPCOMING HARLEQUIN® TITLES,
FREE EXCERPTS AND MORE AT WWW.HARLEQUIN.COM.

HRSCNM0317

SPECIAL EXCERPT FROM

♦ **HARLEQUIN**®

ROMANTIC suspense

Undercover FBI agent Josh Howard is supposed to be investigating Leonor Colton's involvement in her mother's jailbreak, but a hitman may force him to reveal his identity to save her life!

Read on for a sneak preview of
COLTON UNDERCOVER, *the next book in the*
THE COLTONS OF SHADOW CREEK *continuity*
by USA TODAY *bestselling author Marie Ferrarella.*

"Back at the club, when we were dancing, you told me that I was too perfect." *If you only knew*, he couldn't help thinking. "But I'm not. I'm not perfect at all."

So far she hadn't seen anything to contradict her impression. "Let me guess, you use the wrong fork when you eat salad."

"I'm serious," Josh told her, pulling his vehicle into the parking lot.

"Okay, I'll bite. How are you not perfect?" Leonor asked, turning to look at him as she got out.

"Sometimes," Josh said as they walked into the B and B, "I find that my courage fails me."

She strongly doubted that, but maybe they weren't talking about the same thing, Leonor thought.

"You're going to have to give me more of an explanation than that," she told him.

Making their way through the lobby, they went straight to the elevator.

The car was waiting for them, opening its doors the second he pressed the up button.

He'd already said too much and he knew that the more he talked, the greater the likelihood that he would say something to give himself away. But knowing he had to say something, he kept it vague.

"Let's just say that I don't always follow through and do what I really want to do," Josh said vaguely.

That didn't sound like much of a flaw to her, Leonor thought.

After getting off the elevator, they walked to her suite. She used her key and opened her door, then turned toward him.

Her heart was hammering so hard in her throat, she found it difficult to talk.

"And just what is it that you really want to do—but don't?" she asked him in a voice that had mysteriously gone down to just above a whisper.

As it was, her voice sounded very close to husky—and he found it hopelessly seductive.

Standing just inside her suite, Leonor waited for him to answer while her heart continued to imitate the rhythm of a spontaneous drumroll that only grew louder by the moment.

Josh weighed his options for a moment. Damned if he did and damned if he didn't, he couldn't help thinking. And then he answered her.

"Kiss you," he told Leonor, saying the words softly, his breath caressing her face.

She felt her stomach muscles quickening.

"Maybe you should go ahead and do that," she told him. "I promise I won't stop you."

Don't miss
COLTON'S UNDERCOVER by Marie Ferrarella,
available April 2017 wherever
Harlequin® Romantic Suspense books
and ebooks are sold.

www.Harlequin.com

HRSEXP0317